MIKE TYRELL

Claire,

I hope you enjoy the Book!

God Bless

(TTL - page 21)

Detour Home

Detour Home

© 2022 Mike Tyrell

Print ISBN: 978-1-66785-824-1
eBook ISBN: 978-1-66785-825-8

Foreword

This novel is a fictional series of short stories sewn together to tell a bigger tale. It is loosely based upon actual events, although all names and characters, except for Kim, Mike and Angie the dog, are fictitious. The dialog, also fictional, is added to bring some life to the story.

My hope is that this story represents a meaningful truth to the reader. With that sentiment, I humbly present "Detour Home."

At St. Joseph's Indian School the motto says, *We Serve and Teach, We Receive and Learn*. Simply stated, the motto acknowledges life's reality that the more we give, the greater the rewards we receive.

This is a tale of a young married couple who moved to South Dakota and received rewards richer than they ever could have imagined. Loosely based on real events, here is that story…

CHAPTER 1
Heading West

Train to Chicago
June 9, 1986, 6:20 am

MIKE BOARDED QUICKLY. THE TRAIN *was set to leave Joliet, heading for the LaSalle Street Station in Chicago. He found a seat and sat down.*

Mike had a certain nervousness in his stomach this morning. He hadn't worked in downtown Chicago in nearly a year. Was he doing the right thing? He questioned his judgment.

As he stared out the window, he caught a glimpse of the morning sun on the horizon. With the sunlight brightening, the weather was sticky with a touch of wind. He looked around and noticed the people boarding the train, dressed mainly in business attire. There were newspapers in hand, everyone seemingly ready for the busy day.

Seriousness seemed to ooze out of every sleepy person that morning. To Mike, it appeared that each person had something to attend to. The morning paper looked to be a favorite way to stave off the grogginess or at least provided a barrier to hide behind.

"No smiles, no foolishness, no concern for their fellow man," Mike thought. "Everyone has a purpose. So why do I feel so unsure?"

For a moment, Mike's thoughts trailed off to rural South Dakota and his home for the past year. On this morning that place was a million miles away.

The nervous stomach came back into his consciousness. He wondered how long it would last. "Come on," he thought. "I guess it's back to the rat race. Me and everyone else."

Then his mind wandered…

Eleven Months Earlier
July 1985

Mike and Kim, with a U-Haul in tow, jumped onto the interstate heading out of Joliet. They left in the early morning to beat the heat and the traffic. Yet, they still found themselves in rush hour. It was stop-and-go on the interstate with the usual crazies driving excessively fast.

Mike looked over to see his wife – dressed in shorts, sporting white-rimmed sunglasses, shoes off and feet on the dash. She was eating sunflower seeds and staring straight ahead.

"Isn't it a bit early for seeds?" Mike inquired.

"Quit changing the radio stations," his wife shot back, continuing her gaze forward.

"I'm trying to find songs we both like. You didn't like that one? Anyway, rule is the driver controls the radio," Mike said curtly.

"Just leave it on one station. I'll ignore the songs I don't like. You keep changing the station every time I start to like what's on," Kim said shaking her head.

After fighting the traffic for the first hour, they continued on I-90 heading west, through northern Illinois. Aside from a few small tiffs while caught in rush hour, the couple drove out of Illinois and through Wisconsin without incident. There was a stop in La Crosse to get gas, buy a few treats and then get back on the interstate.

The radio blared pop tunes fading in and out. Kim and Mike had resigned themselves to the fact this would be a long drive. The air conditioner was blowing out cool air, but barely stayed ahead of the heat and humidity.

Out the window of their packed 1980 Nova, an occasional town sprang forth to break up the monotony. As far as the eye could see, crops and farmland stretched in all directions. The blue skyline was just that, blue, all the way across the horizon. No tall buildings except the occasional grain elevator standing alone. The farther they drove, the fewer cars they encountered.

As they drove through Minnesota, there were more cornfields. Mike drove and Kim slept, occasionally snoring. As expected, it was a long and very uneventful drive. There were more tunes, then some farm reports. Radio stations faded in and out.

Mike continued to surf the radio. He hummed and sang occasionally to the hit songs of the day. But he was now finding more farm reports than music.

"Too many reports about cows," Kim said as she suddenly awakened. "I told you to put those song tapes we made in the front seat. That way we could listen to them on the drive."

"Here's a Jimmy Buffet tape," Mike showed her, finding the one tape he had left under the front seat.

"I hate that one," Kim said, grabbing the tape and flinging it into the back seat.

Mike rolled his eyes. "Poor taste in music," he muttered under his breath.

This back-and-forth played out throughout the trip, with short conversations, then quiet, then occasional bantering about something. During the silence there was reflection, even anticipation of what was to come. At times Mike felt the slightest dread creep in when he thought about what he and Kim had gotten themselves into. He wondered if Kim felt the same way.

As the monotony of the driving took hold, Mike thought about the interview they'd had just four months earlier. He was amazed at how things had progressed.

It started with him and Kim looking for an adventure and included them researching volunteer jobs. After sending out a few letters of inquiry, a person by the name of Beth called. She was from St. Joseph's Indian School in South Dakota. Beth was traveling through Chicago and wanted to meet. There were houseparent positions available and she was meeting with a number of people.

They met Beth at a hotel near O'Hare airport. She was a middle-aged woman who introduced herself as a recruiter. She was short with medium-length graying hair. She appeared pleasant, with a coy smile.

Beth told them about the work that took place at the school. St. Joe's, as Beth referred to it, had been in existence for over 50 years.

Beth said, "The school's mission is to educate Native American youth who come from families affected by poverty and alcoholism. We work with students from first through eighth grade, coming from the reservations in South Dakota." She had been at the school for ten years.

Beth took a few minutes to explain the new houseparent concept that had been introduced the prior year. She spoke openly and with conviction, describing her personal experiences working at the school. Mike could tell, by her eyes and tone, that she believed in what she was saying.

Beth then asked, "Do you mind telling me about yourselves and your families growing up? Kim, you can go first."

"Well, I'm the middle child with two sisters. My father sold real estate for the railroad and my mom is a nurse. Because of my dad's job, my family moved around. We're Canadian so we lived in Hamilton, Ontario and then moved to the States. Here in the U.S., we've lived in Minneapolis, Des Moines,

Waukesha and Crystal Lake, a suburb of Chicago. We moved here when I was in grade school," Kim explained.

Kim told Beth that her dad, being a salesman, was good at talking with people. He was also an avid golfer who got angry quickly when his game went astray.

When Kim mentioned this about her dad, Mike wanted to tell Beth that Kim has her dad's temper because he'd seen it hundreds of times. But he thought it best not to be joking around during an interview.

Kim then talked about her mother. "It was sometimes tough to have a nurse as a mother. While growing up, my mom never thought I was sick enough to not go to school."

Kim added one funny story about her mom's parenting telling Beth, "My mom once caught me smoking as a freshman in high school. The consequence was that I had to smoke a cigarette in front of her while she smoked one herself."

After a pause, Kim thought better of her story, "I hope you don't think I'd do this with the kids."

Beth laughed, "I hope not."

Mike could tell that Kim's ability to warm up to people made an impression on Beth. He'd seen Kim's quick wit many times. He admired her self-confidence when it came to meeting others.

Mike was thankful Kim stayed clear of mentioning her rebellious side growing up. He knew she drove before she had a license, drank early in life and dated the worst kind of guys. This led to more than a few arguments with her parents.

What Kim did say was, "I had my ups and downs with my parents growing up. I think the greatest day for them was when I moved away to college."

"I can relate to that. Those teenage years sure are tough," Beth said with a smile.

Mike was next, "I was the sixth child in a family of ten children, born and raised in Joliet, Illinois. My family lived in a small house that didn't have air-conditioning, a garage, a basement, or a washer/dryer. I think growing up there allowed me to adjust to almost any living condition. My parents were not wealthy but they sacrificed to send all of us to Catholic School."

"My parents liked Mike because he was different from the guys I usually dated," Kim added with a laugh. "He goes to church and has a bunch of high school friends he's still close to."

Mike went on to explain that he and Kim were married last June. "We met five years earlier in college. We're thinking it might be interesting to volunteer for a year. Maybe we can do some good."

After meeting with Beth, Kim and Mike believed that being recently married disqualified them for the position of houseparent.

"We're looking for couples who have been married for at least a year," Beth said. "I'll be interviewing other candidates for these positions over the next several weeks."

On the drive home Mike told Kim, "Well, that's the last we'll hear from Beth. I secretly hoped she would have asked about our relationship. I was going to say, you're the life of the party but I make sure we get home safely. I save, you spend. I go to church and you tag along. And that living with you is always adventurous and never dull."

Kim replied, "If you'd said that, I would have added that our divorce is imminent."

Mike remembered their surprise when they received a phone call about a month after they met with Beth. She informed them that they had been selected for the job. After the call, Mike and Kim visited and were each shocked to find out the other was interested in taking the offer!

It took Kim and Mike a week to make a final decision. As they contemplated whether or not to accept the position, they chose not to tell family or friends what they were considering. They did not want to be influenced. After much discussion, they decided to take the job.

"What's a year?" Mike said, feeling like they had nothing to lose. "And we'll make a whopping, combined salary of $6,000 plus housing and food. Can't beat that!"

When they broke the news to family and friends, there were mixed reactions. Mike felt like coworkers, through non-verbals, probably thought he and Kim were crazy. On the other hand, family and friends were supportive, as Mike figured they would be.

"That's what families do," he told Kim. "Even if they don't understand, they'll support us."

CHAPTER TWO
South Dakota

THE CROSSING OF THE SOUTH Dakota border happened around mid-afternoon as the song "Borderline" played on the radio. After nine hours of driving, seeing the South Dakota sign was an exciting milestone.

"Cool. Our song *Borderline* comes on as we drive into South Dakota," said Mike. "Remember, after our wedding as we drove back from Wisconsin, the same song was playing as we crossed into Illinois? Must be good luck." He belted out the refrain.

Kim joined in the singing as she swayed with the music. As the song ended she said, "I don't remember that. Maybe you married someone else. Hope they liked your singing – if that's what that was," she laughed.

A few miles down the interstate, signs for Sioux Falls began to appear. "We have to stop for gas. Then we have two more hours to go," Mike said, having looked at the map many times prior to the trip.

After a fill-up and the purchase of two pops and strawberry licorice, the Nova was back on I-90.

"Westward ho! You can serenade me with that charming voice. That will keep me awake," Kim joked and Mike laughed.

The farther they traveled into South Dakota, the more they noticed the roadside signs for attractions like Wall Drug, the Corn Palace and Al's Oasis.

"What the hell is it with all these signs?" Kim said, only half-jokingly. Are we moving to some kind of statewide tourist trap? I swear this has to be the road sign capital of America!"

The halfway point was the town of Mitchell. Before it came into view, billboards encouraged drivers to visit an attraction known as the Corn Palace.

"What is *The World Famous Corn Palace*?" Kim asked reading another billboard. "That's the fifth sign I've seen and I can't figure out what it is."

"Whatever it is, I'm sure it's very corny," Mike quipped.

Then after a long silence from Kim, Mike asked, "Should we stop?"

"No, let's just get to Chamberlain. We'll stop here someday when we need a bag of corn to feed the cows," Kim said as she laughed.

Nearly 700 miles and twelve hours into their trip, they neared Chamberlain and their destination. They were both weary from the drive.

"How is it that the last two hours seemed to take forever?" Mike wondered aloud.

Then, almost out of nowhere, the car came over the crest of a large hill on the interstate and there it was. Below them in a huge valley, flowed the waters of the Missouri River. It was the most beautiful blue, stretching wide and filling the windshield. The view was stunning. The panorama included rolling hills and bluffs, backed by a deep blue sky that spanned the horizon.

Whether it was the fact they had reached their destination or the vastness of the river valley, the picture before them was breathtaking. Seeing the river meant they were at their journey's end. This would be their new home.

The Chamberlain exit came just before the river on I-90. Kim reached over and squeezed Mike's hand.

Their adventures were about to begin but first, they were starving. It was time to take a break and get their bearings. Tomorrow they would be at their new place of employment. Now, a meal was foremost on their minds. They exited the interstate onto Main Street and headed into Chamberlain.

Mike and Kim drove into a town boasting a population of 2,300 people. Being right on the banks of the Missouri River, Mike's research had uncovered that Chamberlain was a place where fishermen came in the spring, hunters in the fall and tourists in the summer.

The community's Main Street included a three-block downtown area. It reminded Mike and Kim of the old west, with storefronts of different shapes and sizes squeezed-in next to one another.

"I've seen this type of setting in the background of Rocky and Bullwinkle cartoons," Mike said to Kim as she laughed.

On Main Street, drivers in two different cars waved at them from their passing vehicles. Being from the Chicagoland area, they assumed these people must be angry with their driving. Kim gave Mike an inquisitive look.

"Are you speeding, or driving on the wrong side of the road, or what?" Kim asked exasperated.

After a third wave, they questioned if these people somehow knew them or mistook them for someone else. Finally, they began to think that they were just imagining that people were waving to them.

In the end, Mike's paranoia got the best of him as he said, "I wonder if maybe we are politely being 'flipped-off.' There has to be some reason for this bizarre behavior."

"Perhaps it's our out-of-state license plates?" Kim asked. "Why are these people waving at us? That's so weird."

They pulled up at a place called the River Café Grille. It looked to them like the local "greasy-spoon," a term they had learned in college. It was the kind of hangout where the food was good, but you could still see the last few meals that someone else had eaten – on the spoons, cups and plates.

As they entered the restaurant, Mike noticed that old red-and-white checked plastic tablecloths were in use. The decor was a 1950s style including wood paneling. There were no other patrons in the restaurant. A young family of four had left just as Kim and Mike came in.

Mike whispered to Kim, "There's nobody in here. If you were a clean-freak, this wouldn't be the place to stop."

As they slid into a booth, a door flew open. It had a loud creaking-banging sound as the waitress came out to greet them. The noise drew Mike and Kim's attention, and as the door was open, they could see the guts of the place. There, in the kitchen, stood the cook. He was a sweaty young guy wearing an old faded t-shirt with a cigarette in his mouth. Before the door closed, they saw him lift his shirt and wipe his brow.

Kim whispered, "Next time let's find a spot where we don't have to look directly into the kitchen."

The waitress came up to their table. She was young with short blond hair and a tan. Mike figured she was in high school. Her nametag said "Trisha."

"Welcome to River Grille. I'm Trish. Would you like something to drink?" Trish asked in a weary tone.

"Long day?" Kim asked.

"Not too bad. If I complained my mom wouldn't like it," Trish answered, her voice devoid of much pep.

Mike and Kim weren't sure what she meant. Kim couldn't help but ask some questions.

"You live in this town?" Kim asked. "That river out there looks beautiful!" Trish shrugged.

"With someone that looks like you, do you get on the river to ski or just to lay out?" Kim asked.

With the question, Trish perked up. Then a conversation between the two of them began. Throughout the meal, with no other patrons, Kim and Trish had an ongoing exchange. Of course, Kim asked many leading questions.

Mike and Kim found out Trish had recently graduated from Chamberlain High School. She was headed to college at the end of the summer and didn't have a steady boyfriend.

Mike had seen this before. Kim's questions and genuine interest allowed others to feel comfortable to the point where they would open up. As Mike figured, by meal's end Trish and Kim were like best friends.

At one point Kim joked with Trish. "Looks like the cook might make a good date."

"He's my brother," Trish said nonchalantly.

Kim looked mortified, with embarrassment turning her face red. Then Trish began to giggle.

"He's a slob. My parents can't always find help, so Phil fills in." She laughed at the sentence, repeating, "Phil fills in."

"Sorry," Kim said. "I shouldn't have said that. But I think I saw the family six-pack earlier."

"He's being a jerk today, so I'm going to tell him the customers are talking about him," Trish said.

"No, please don't. Well, at least I got my food already," Kim added with a smile as Trisha giggled again.

Toward the end of the meal, Kim asked, "Do know anything about St. Joseph's Indian School?"

"Yeah, I played sports against them when I was in middle school. The kids were always nice."

"Really? Do you know anyone who works there?" Mike asked.

Trish scribbled on her pad and ripped out the receipt. "A couple kids I know work the grounds, mow the lawn in the summer, things like that," she replied. "You can pay up at the register. No rush though!"

Trish then walked away, clearing tables of unused silverware as she went.

"I like her," Kim said.

"You like every waitress," Mike remarked.

"What's wrong with that?" Kim said, taking a last gulp of Coke. "How much cash do you have?"

As Mike settled the bill at the cash register, Kim said. "Trish, I'm Kim. We're moving here. We don't have a lot of cash on us, so next time we come in I'll make Mike give you a big tip." Trish smiled in response.

Leaving the restaurant, Mike and Kim went back to their car. They drove through town and parked at a local hotel. That moment exhaustion hit both of them. They grabbed a few items and checked in.

Their room was bathed in orange hues from the setting sun. Kim collapsed in the bed as Mike moved to the window. He paused for a second. Outside he now noticed the sun shimmering over the river. Above, streaks of purple were coming out from behind the low, billowing clouds.

Mike closed the shades. Kim had fallen asleep, face down on the pillow. He pulled off her shoes and slipped out of his as he lay next to her.

Kim's muffled voice came through the pillow, "It's after nine." She turned her head to face Mike. "How is it still light out? In Joliet it would be dark by now."

Mike rolled over to face her. "Welcome home," he whispered.

Train to Chicago
June 9, 1986, 6:30 am

Suddenly there was a jerk as the train moved forward out of the Joliet station. That slight jolt brought Mike back to reality. As he looked out the window, he wondered about the daily train trip. One hour and fifteen minutes, twice per day. It worried him.

Will it be worth it? he questioned. It doesn't compare to that five-minute ride to work back in South Dakota.

As downtown Joliet flew by, Mike's thoughts drifted again.

He wondered how fate had brought him and Kim to South Dakota. Mike, all of 24 years old, had worked in a brokerage firm. His job consisted of long hours trying to balance trades that brokers made for their customers. Although he liked the challenges of the work, he questioned whether he was really helping anyone. "All I'm doing is making the rich richer," he told Kim at different times when he was frustrated with work. He somehow believed that he had a calling to do something else. He just wasn't sure what that was.

Physically, Mike was in good shape, working out regularly. He had a predisposition to eating sweets, often inhaling as many breakroom donuts as possible. He blamed that on growing up in a large Catholic family. He always said he would be a fine specimen if he didn't have the donut curse.

Kim had worked in a health and diet store. She was in her early twenties, blonde, cute, and always critical of her looks. Her extroverted personality made her good at her job. Kim was comfortable with people of every sort. She was interested in others and that somehow made them feel very comfortable with her.

As a newly married couple, Mike's reserved disposition and Kim's outgoing personality sometimes clashed. Mike needed time to analyze, whereas Kim jumped first and asked questions later. When these elements were in balance it worked well. When out of balance, both could be quick to call their partner out.

Kim was not as excited as her husband was about doing volunteer work. She figured his idea would die out, so she played along. When it came to the relationship with her husband, she believed she could always get her way.

CHAPTER THREE

The Campus

July 1985

THEY WERE UP EARLY THE next morning. Mike went out for a short run along River Road. Running was part of his fitness routine and he thought today's run would give him a chance to check out where he and Kim would be living. He was awed by the bright sunlight, the town to the east and the banks across the Missouri River, to the west.

It was a cloudless and hot morning. The smell of summer was all around him. The heat was dry with a gentle warm wind blowing from across the river. Mike thought of his good fortune, amazed that he and Kim would be living in such a scenic town.

Kim and Mike left the motel and headed for St. Joseph's Indian School. They had little awareness of the school and what the work was truly about. On that first morning's drive, they were confident they could handle it.

The school was located at the north end of Chamberlain where the highway rises and curves away from the river, just before you drove out of town. As Mike turned the Nova into the entrance of the campus, the first thing he and Kim saw was a large white statue of St. Joseph holding baby Jesus. The statue was sitting up high, resting on a platform.

"Doesn't it look like St. Joseph is guarding the place?" Mike asked as he drove onto campus.

As they drove into the school's campus, under a canopy of trees, Kim and Mike noticed the beautifully cultivated grounds. Everything was neatly groomed and the various buildings looked well maintained.

"Are we in the right place?" Mike asked. "This is different than any grade school grounds I've ever seen."

"Our college campus was huge, but it would have been cool to go to a quaint place like this. Look at the river right over there." Kim said pointing to the west.

As they drove on, they passed a row of houses painted blue, gray and red. Mike assumed these were the student homes. They were two-story structures that Mike likened to a townhouse. Individual housing units were connected, sitting side-by-side, as duplexes. In total, Mike counted eight individual homes, each having a name on the outside.

There were other buildings as well. One looked to be some type of gymnasium with an indoor pool attached. Then they drove by a round building made of red brick that had a school sign in front. There were other structures that Mike figured were used for student activities. Most of these didn't have signs, so they were left to wonder.

Mike and Kim saw a few people they assumed were maintenance staff. One person was cutting grass and waved as they drove by. Two others were moving a large table into a building. Otherwise, they saw no one else around.

In the middle of the campus, there was a circular area surrounded by a small road. Inside the circle were at least a dozen cottonwood trees. The trees were huge, gently swaying in the ever-present South Dakota wind.

Surrounding the circle on two sides were buildings. One had a sign that read Benedictine Homes, describing an order of nuns who'd previously worked at the school. Mike correctly assumed there were multiple housing units in the large structure. In the corner of the circle was a church, with a white statue of Mary in Native dress. The likeness stood overhead, above the two doors at the front of the church.

Mike thought of the campus as some sort of "oasis," with the river providing a refreshing feel on that hot 100-degree day. Since there were no students and very few people, the campus was tranquil and peaceful.

Kim and Mike eventually found the superintendent's office. Kim knocked. Inside a paneled office, sitting at a desk was a gruff-looking man. He wore glasses, was slightly balding and wore a Packer's jersey. When he stood to greet them, Mike noticed he was short with a pleasant smile.

"Hi. I'm Wally the superintendent." The man held out his hand. Kim and Mike learned that Wally had been at the school for over twenty years.

"I worked in the dorms before the current cottages were built. I started as a kid, that's why I look so young," Wally joked.

In the discussion that followed, Kim and Mike found out this was only the second year of all the students living in homes instead of dorms. They had all been newly constructed over the past few years. Mike vaguely recalled Beth mentioning this.

"The home setup is an experiment, but seems to be working," Wally said as he caught himself, realizing it sounded like the program might not last.

"Actually, the home program is going very well" he continued. "It's still new but gives our students a better opportunity to bond with staff. Houseparents play a critical role in making the program work."

Mike changed the subject. "With all this Packer gear in your office, I'm sure you're real excited about the Bears this year."

"You know, bears were driven out of South Dakota decades ago. We're hoping all their fans went with them," Wally laughed.

Kim chimed in, "We had some Green Bay guys come and help us pack our car. They said they were out of work because the Bears in Green Bay forced them to 'Pack' and move out of town."

"Wally, I'll have you know that this is coming from someone who's never watched a game in her life," Mike said.

After the visit, Wally took Kim and Mike on a short tour of the campus. Eventually, he showed them a row of five white trailers, one in which they were assigned to live. Wally stopped at the door, gave them their keys, welcomed them one last time and left.

The trailer was located right along the riverbank. It provided Kim and Mike with a great view of the water. Upon entering, it was apparent to Mike that the trailer had not been used in a while. The heat inside was suffocating and there were spider webs all over.

"I saw mouse turds in the corner," Kim said. "I'm just going to ignore it."

"It's super-hot in here. The heat makes it hard to breathe. I'll go get the car from in front of that administration building. Then we can unpack the U-Haul," Mike said as he found the window air conditioner and turned it on full blast.

When he showed up with the car and trailer Kim met him outside. "I'm glad you're back. I was worried I'd see the mouse that left poop in the corner."

"I'll put down traps later, but you'll have to be the one to get rid of the dead mice," Mike laughed.

"Thank you, my protective husband," Kim retorted.

Mike and Kim each made two trips back and forth unloading the car and U-Haul. Each time they entered the trailer, they would stand in front of the window air conditioner to cool off. As much as they tried to be pleasant with one another, the heat put them both in an irritable mood.

"I wish you wouldn't hog the air conditioner," Kim said.

"It's going to take a while to cool this place off, so I'm just standing here for a second. Then I'll head back outside. If we alternate our trips, we won't have to stand here at the same time. Just let me bring in the rest of the stuff. You've been putting things right in front of the door and we're going to have to move it a second time," Mike said. He had nearly tripped on a box attempting to leave the trailer.

"You put stuff in the way too. Anyway, we're supposed to do this together. You know fifty-fifty," Kim said sarcastically.

"Yeah," Mike said rolling his eyes and shaking his head. He headed back outside into the heat.

The simple exercise of moving in exposed another thing Kim and Mike had naïvely ignored. They often did not work well together, having their own ideas on how to do things.

Later that evening, Mike and Kim went for a walk along the river. Things were cooling down from the day's high temperatures, but it was still warm with a slight wind blowing. As the sun slowly sank in the west over the banks of the Missouri River, they watched it reflect off the water.

At this time of day, the sun presented a majestic scene, as the rays flowed across a gently bouncing river. The sunlight outlined the longest horizon Mike had ever seen. Kim and Mike stood on the road facing the river with the back of the chapel behind them.

Looking over the edge of the road, Mike guessed it was about twenty yards down to the water. The reddish riprap that laid along the shoreline ran north and south as far as the eye could see. It appeared steep but not treacherous. Mike figured the rocks, of varying shapes and sizes, ensured adequate footing though probably slippery and uneven.

"I'm going to climb down to the river," Mike said.

"I'm going down there too," Kim said as they began to navigate the rocks aligning the bank.

"Watch your step. Some of the rocks are loose." Mike said as his footing slipped a couple of times.

"For an athlete, you aren't very coordinated," Kim mused.

"You're not so nimble yourself," Mike said laughing as Kim almost fell. She was now sitting on a big boulder just behind him, taking a break to steady herself.

After successfully climbing down to the shoreline, Mike now stood at the river's edge noticing the great width of the river.

"Wow!" said Mike pointing across the river. "It must be a mile to the bluffs over there. Great view!"

Mike then picked up a rock and threw it sidearm, bouncing once on the water. He was disappointed in only one skip.

"May God bless our adventures," Mike said.

Now Kim was at the water's edge, slightly behind Mike. She threw a rock that skipped twice.

Happy with her toss, Kim added, "Maybe we can do some good this year."

"Beat ya!" Mike responded by skipping another rock three times. "Let's try and do this with some passion. Maybe we can learn something."

"Look at the school of fish," Kim said throwing a handful of rocks just over Mike's head into the river.

Mike yelled, "Watch it!" as he ducked, then looked toward the river laughing.

"You must be teaching at that school. They all sunk right to the bottom," Mike joked.

Mike then noticed a dirty Mason jar tucked in the rocks near his foot. "What's that?" he asked pulling the jar out of the rocks. Inside he could see a sheet of paper. He unscrewed the top and stared at the paper.

"What's it say?" Kim asked.

"It says 'Trust the Lord.' It's handwritten."

Mike then respectfully put the note back in the bottle, secured the lid and set it afloat. Without saying anything, Kim and Mike both looked at the bottle gently bobbing on the water.

"Maybe that will bring good luck to the next person that finds it," Mike said.

Now the sun was behind the bluffs to the west. It was Kim and Mike's first sunset along the banks of the river. From the water level, Mike took a moment to absorb the quiet as dusk set in. He said a simple prayer to himself. Kim, standing directly beside him was quiet.

Kim then gently grabbed Mike's hand. "Come on. Help me up the rocks. The mosquitos are coming out."

CHAPTER FOUR

Venturing Out

KIM AND MIKE HAD A couple of weeks before orientation began, so they took several day trips. One trip was to Mitchell to return the trailer. It was also an opportunity to see the World's Only Corn Palace.

The Corn Palace was a large building, housing a basketball court and museum. Mike compared it to a small civic center. On the outside of the building there were murals made using different colored ears of corn. Mike heard the designs on the building change each year.

That year the Corn Palace theme was agricultural and featured harvest scenes. The square panels that spanned the entire building included pictures of tractors, old and new. Ears of corn in various shades of yellow, brown and russet were inlaid in the panels to make the murals come to life.

The whole setup seemed strange to the two big-city people. Kim and Mike actually giggled when they first saw it. Yet they were amazed that corn could be arranged on panels that looked as if an artist had painted images on a building.

Kim said, "Oh my God, I just heard someone call it a huge bird feeder."

"How did they get so many colors of corn?" Mike asked, surprised at the number of tourists taking pictures of the building.

"We have to tell everyone back home about our first South Dakota adventure, visiting the world-famous Corn Palace," Kim said jokingly.

Mitchell, having the closest McDonald's, was important to Mike's thinking. In Joliet, it felt like McDonald's existed every few blocks. Now as Chamberlain residents, he and Kim would have to drive sixty-five miles to have a Big Mac. With this revelation it began to sink in; they now lived in small-town, rural America.

Mike's realization about McDonald's demonstrated how far off the beaten path they were. "We're now using McDonald's as a reference point," he thought.

Sioux Falls was another destination they drove to in that first week. It was a two-hour trip down the interstate. However, it was a pick-me-up for Kim. It was the closest mall. On this trip, Kim got the opportunity to get her shopping fix in.

On the drive back from Sioux Falls Mike said, "I never would've imagined you'd be willing to live so far away from a mall and all its treasures."

During that week Kim and Mike also met a couple on campus by the name of Jesse and Jeannie. Jesse was born in Ireland. He had met Jeannie several years earlier when visiting the States. It was love at first sight and they eventually married.

Jesse stood 5'9" had a slight build, was balding and spoke with a slight Irish accent. Jeannie was small, slender with short hair. Both were dressed comfortably in tee shirts and shorts.

Jesse was an extrovert who loved a practical joke, while Jeannie was more reserved. Yet, she admired Jesse and loved his antics. They had a son, Jamie, who was two years old. Jamie was a pudgy active toddler with curly sandy hair.

Jeannie and Jesse were houseparents who enjoyed the students. They talked to Kim and Mike as if they already knew all the kids. Mike found much of this dialog about the students interesting. However, not actually knowing the students yet, he could not always relate.

Jesse and Jeannie had come to the school one year earlier. They described the job as easy, indicating the toughest part was working with other staff. They complained about all the "stupid rules" and warned Kim and Mike that they would understand this soon enough.

Mike recalled the first time they visited Jesse and Jeannie's trailer. It was located next to theirs. That night Kim had a white tee shirt on. As she entered the trailer, she picked up Jamie. Jamie then proceeded to start playing with a small, pointy object that was poking out of the front of her shirt.

Mike noticed what Jamie was attempting to play with, so he grabbed Jamie and nodded to Kim. He did this discretely hoping Jesse and Jeannie wouldn't see him. Kim then excused herself and left to use the bathroom.

When she came back Mike whispered, "Problem corrected?"

Overhearing the question, Jesse asked, "What're you two talking about?"

Being the ever-persistent guy he was, Jesse badgered Kim with the question for several minutes.

Finally, Kim answered. "What the hell. The underwire from my bra broke. It was sticking out and Jamie was playing with it. I had to take it out. Satisfied?"

Hearing this explanation, Jesse laughed hysterically. "Are you kidding me?" Jesse insisted on seeing what an underwire looked like so Kim showed him. He looked at the u-shape in total amazement. Jesse snatched the wire out of Kim's hands, took it over to a hook on the wall, and hung it up.

"I'll use it someday for something," Jesse mused.

From that point on Kim and Jesse were always teasing and arguing with one another. When this happened, Mike and Jeannie would just roll their eyes.

Jesse invited Kim and Mike to go with them to the Sturgis Motorcycle Rally later in the week. Sturgis, located in the Black Hills, had celebrated the Harley Davidson Motorcycle Rally since 1938. This year they were expecting over 40,000 bikers and Jesse wanted to see exactly what happened there.

Jesse explained to Mike, "I can't believe that many people will be there. Sturgis is a small town of barely 500 people. But I heard it can be wild."

Mike and Kim were a bit hesitant at the idea of attending a motorcycle rally but Jesse persisted. Eventually, they relented and said they'd go. What did they have to lose?

"It can't be that crazy," Mike told Kim in private. "This is South Dakota."

On a hot Saturday morning at the beginning of August, Jesse, Jeannie, Jamie, Kim and Mike headed west on I-90. They drove in Jesse's Suburban. Along the interstate there were streams of motorcycles with many more parked in rest areas. The one constant during the drive was the rumble of motorcycle engines.

Most of the riders traveled in packs and looked uncomfortable to Kim and Mike. Few bikers looked shaven or well-groomed. Smiles were not apparent as they concentrated on the road. Some riders had helmets, while most did not. Bikers wore sunglasses and had handkerchiefs or bandanas on their heads.

Mike noticed handlebars and seats in every conceivable position. There were bikes with two and three wheels and a few with sidecars. Motorcycles had the bikers' belongings packed on each side of the frame. Some bikes had one rider, some had two. Other rally goers had their bikes in tow on trailers.

As Jesse's Suburban followed the crowd into the Black Hills, with its pine trees and rolling elevations, the biker traffic intensified. There was a traffic jam about five miles outside of Sturgis. This brought the vehicle to a standstill on the interstate. As traffic crawled along one could see bikers everywhere and hear the distinct roar of their machines.

"It's unbelievable that so many people travel to this 'postage stamp' of a town," Jesse told Mike.

Jesse parked the vehicle on the outskirts of town. It was a dirt lot located near a wooded area nestled in among the pine trees. Then the two couples, with Jamie in a stroller, followed the foot traffic to the "Main Drag" as Mike referred to it.

On Main Street, Mike was amazed to see hundreds of bikes parked on both sides of the road, as well as down the middle of the street. The vast majority of rally goers were wearing leather and the color of the day was black. Sunburned people of all shapes and sizes were everywhere. With their white t-shirts and shorts, Jesse, Jeannie, Jamie, Kim and Mike joined the throng of people.

Large crowds lined up on both sides of the street, watching bikers as they roared past. Tattoo parlors, leather shops, bars and other stores framed in the crowd. There was a persistent smell of marijuana wafting about.

Accompanied by the occasional whoop of the crowd, a motorcycle would whiz down the road. Usually, the biker was toting a woman clinging to her man, with an over-stretched leather halter-top barely clung to her. Then came bikers with topless women aboard, abandoning the halter-top struggle altogether.

Finally the capstone: a woman hanging on for dear life to a bald, sun-glassed biker. She happened to be totally naked. Mike and Jesse nearly had whiplash when they first noticed this biker and woman. They were not the only ones.

"This definitely is not downtown Joliet," Mike yelled to Kim over the roar of bikes.

Rehashing the experience with Jesse later, Mike said, "To me, Sturgis is a subculture of people that intentionally or maybe accidentally stumbled onto the same location. The funny thing is that it sounds like the same stumbling happens every year."

Mike felt out of place while Kim gawked, or maybe it was the other way around. The show before them, motorcycles with bikers and scantily clothed women on board captivated both of them. Their passing by without so much as a faint acknowledgment that others were watching was all part of some big show Mike surmised. He truly did not quite know what to think.

The group eventually found a place to sit down to eat. They had burgers with a beer and watched all sorts of people stroll by. Mike thought Jamie's behavior was very good, but some passers-by gave them a look that said, "Why did you bring a toddler here?"

After a late lunch, they wandered around some more. Mike's eyes nearly pooped out of his head as he looked through a storefront window. There, he saw tattoos of all sorts being put on various body parts. Mike commented that it was "sickening" but still gawked. Jeannie agreed while Kim and Jesse seemed to think it was very cool.

Jesse and Kim were so enthralled that they wandered into one of the tattoo parlors. A few minutes later they emerged outside with big smiles; then they burst into laughter.

"Did you see where that guy was being tattooed?" Jesse asked.

Mike rolled his eyes and looked at Jeannie. "I'm not even going to venture a guess."

They left Sturgis in the early evening. Leaving sooner than planned was partly because they feared being there after dark. Throughout the day, as the beer flowed and the reefer smoke intensified, they noticed the crowd becoming wilder.

Back in Chamberlain after midnight, they joked about the day. Both couples agreed it was a different outing, one they normally would not have experienced. Nevertheless, they had fun and it served as a bonding experience. They appreciated that.

CHAPTER FIVE

White House in the Country

As the summer dragged on, Kim and Mike were anxious to begin their work. Their new jobs would begin with several days of orientation. As that date moved closer other staff arrived; some moving into the trailers adjacent to theirs. Mike and Kim met many people who came from a wide variety of backgrounds. They found everyone to be extremely friendly.

There was Gene from Ohio, a chicken farmer, as well as a couple from northern Minnesota who had worked in volunteer jobs in both the U.S. and Canada. Lloyd was an African American man from Detroit and Lacy and Ben were a Native American couple from South Dakota.

Kim and Mike also met Sally from Minneapolis, who had worked at St. Joe's for eight years. She started out working in the dorms before the homes were built. It was also during this timeframe that Kim met Nellie the Nurse. The two hit it off right away.

Everyone was very welcoming and had a unique story about why they came to the school. Mike noticed again how each person talked a lot about the kids they took care of or taught. He also recognized a collective use of humor that sheltered the realities surrounding the students' lives away from campus.

As a whole, Mike found the group held strongly to a belief that every soul deserved a chance, even when the odds of failure were great. It was a "one-day-at-a-time, one-kid-at-a-time, let's do our best today and not worry about what we cannot control" approach. Mike respected that and realized that each person they met, in his or her own way, loved the students.

A couple of days before orientation was set to begin, Kim came into the trailer saying she found a better place to live.

While out for coffee with Jeannie, she had learned of a house that was vacant and in need of renters. The house was two and a half miles out of town, just off the oil road. Best of all, the rent was only $100 a month. Mike was expectantly cautious. He knew Kim was an impulse buyer.

"Have you seen the place?" he asked.

"No, but it's out in the country. We can have horses, dogs, cats and a big garden. There's a lot of space for animals." Kim responded enthusiastically.

"Oh, so we're getting a horse now," said Mike exasperated. "You do know, we currently don't have to pay any rent?" Mike pictured an old, falling-down house that was unfit for man or beast.

"This is crazy and will never happen," Mike muttered to himself. "Just play along."

"Well, I set up a meeting with the landlord and I'm going whether you do or not," Kim said.

Late in the afternoon Mike and Kim drove north, up the steep hill for a mile, turned east on the blacktop for a half-mile, and south on a gravel road which, Mike noted, had little gravel and was mostly dirt. A few hundred yards down the path stood a house out in the open range.

It was an old, small one-story ranch structure, with white siding and a shingled roof. Behind it stood a large dilapidated red barn. The barn's paint was worn and the structure appeared to sway in the South Dakota breeze. Tall grasses and weeds grew in the fenced-in area surrounding the barn. All the vegetation stood waist-high.

Circling the small yard around the house was a dirt driveway. Behind the barn were fields of corn. The crumbling barn and all the tall grass were worrisome to Mike, but what he and Kim both noticed immediately was the open space. They were intrigued that there was nothing around except fields. This was quite a change from the Chicago suburbs.

Mike wondered if a move here was closer to the adventure he and Kim were expecting. Then he quickly came back to reality and thought, "No way."

The couple drove up to the house, got out of the car and waited for the landlord, as a gentle wind blew across the landscape. Several minutes later a man driving on a farm tractor pulled up. Once in the yard running adjacent to the house, he cranked the steering wheel so the tractor spiraled in a circle. He quickly jumped off leaving it turning slowly round and round, driverless.

Kim looked at Mike and excitedly asked the man as he walked toward them, "What's wrong with your tractor?"

He didn't flinch and explained, "The starter's burned out. Hope we're not going to be too long. I'll just let it spin."

The man introduced himself as Johnny. He was stocky, with thinning hair and a missing front tooth. He wore old dirty overalls and a white tee shirt.

Johnny said, "I own the farm at the corner on the oil road about a mile and a half back. The person who owns this property doesn't live here. I look after the place."

Mike, Kim and Johnny walked around to the front of the house as the tractor spiraled, unmanned. Kim continued to look back at the tractor and nearly tripped over a garbage can lid that was sitting in the yard.

"The water's trucked in. You just tripped over the lid to the water tank. It's buried. There's a pump in the house that moves the water from here into there," Johnny explained pointing from the tank lid to the house. "The cistern holds about 1,000 gallons of water. That lid is the way you access the tank."

Kim and Mike looked at one another. The idea of cistern water, as Johnny called it, was puzzling to them. Mike joked with him, "That 1,000 gallons will be gone after one of Kim's long showers."

"Wrong. With the small water heater this house has, that would be impossible!" Johnny laughed as did Mike and Kim, though warily.

The three went into the house using the one and only outside door. The entrance was located opposite the road, on the side of the house facing the barn. The first room was a small mudroom where a farmer might take off his dirty clothes after working in the field.

Moving from the mudroom, they entered a larger living room painted in a tan color. The floor was covered in cheap, brown carpet. On the north side of the room were two big windows that let outside light in. In the east corner of the room there was a round hole in the wall, where a chimney pipe should have been attached. The space in front of the hole was for some type of heater.

"Right now the house has no heat. You'll need to buy a fuel oil heater and place it there," Johnny said, pointing to the wall and acting as if they were going to rent the place.

Mike thought, "Isn't it cold here in the winter? Who'd rent a place in South Dakota that doesn't have heating?"

Adjacent to the living room and on the west side of the house were two modest bedrooms. They had small, framed windows with a nice view of the outside. There was also a smaller storage room next to the living room.

"Love those blue rooms," Kim said, commenting on the paint color.

Off the living room on the south end of the structure was an under-sized kitchen. An extension of the house, it had windows on the three outside walls. In between the two windows on the south wall, over the sink and metal cabinets, was open shelving made of plywood and two-by-fours. Everything in the kitchen was painted yellow, except the white cabinets, sink and countertop.

Off the north corner of the kitchen was a small pink bathroom. It had a bathtub, shower, toilet and sink. Everything looked very 1950 to Mike.

Before leaving the house Johnny went to a corner in the kitchen just in front of the bathroom. There he got down on his knees and lifted a large wooden square panel out of the floor. He then pointed downward to what he referred to as the basement.

Mike looked over the edge thinking it was more like a dungeon. He saw what he thought was a rickety, wooden homemade ladder made with two-by-fours.

"Is this how you climb down into the basement?" Mike asked.

"Sure is," said Johnny.

The basement had a dirt floor. The ceiling was only seven feet high. There were cinder block walls on four sides, with the basement covering about a quarter of the underside of the house. As they knelt and peered into the basement, Johnny pointed out the water heater and the water pump. "The water pump has been turned off for a while. You'll need to prime it when you move in. I think it still works," Johnny shrugged.

Mike found that he paid little attention when Johnny talked about the water pump. He was certain they weren't moving in.

As Johnny stood up he mentioned that the last tenants thought there was some type of animal living in the basement. With that comment, Kim took a step back and gasped.

"What do you mean?" she said anxiously, clearly worried.

"Oh, it's probably nothing. All you have to do is set a trap!"

Mike, being a city boy, quickly stood up. He didn't want to climb down into the filthy basement anyway, especially with some rodent down there.

He figured it was probably a skunk living under the house and he wanted no part of that.

Johnny left after a few more minutes of answering questions. He exited the house, caught up with his spinning tractor, and jumped on. He then yelled back to Kim and Mike, "Let me know if you plan on moving in."

As he drove away on the tractor, Johnny didn't seem to care how long they stayed in the house.

"Shouldn't he be concerned we might steal something?" Mike asked Kim. "He didn't even say anything about locking the door."

After Johnny departed Kim and Mike looked around for a time. They even went out to the old barn. As they walked toward it through the tall grass, they could hear the joints creaking in the wind. The red paint on the outside looked even more washed out than it did from the road.

There were no working doors to close up the barn, so when they walked in they spooked the birds up in the rafters. Kim ducked and screamed as barn swallows swooped just above her head.

Inside the barn, things were in disarray with broken boards and junk piled up. Mike could tell it hadn't been used in a while. He kicked an old bucket that was laying among some debris saying, "Kim, there's your feed bucket for the horses."

"Listen to that creaking," Mike said and stood still. "I wonder how long before this thing falls down."

All the while a familiar dance was taking shape. Mike, of course, thought the place was a dive and had no interest in moving in. He was practical.

"Why pay rent when you don't have to?" Mike had asked Kim on the drive up to the house.

Kim, on the other hand, had them moved in already. She could not wait for dogs, cats and horses in the barn. She, in Mike's opinion, was often impractical and impulsive.

In the end, as was usually the case, Kim prevailed.

They contacted Johnny that night and moved in the following day. Johnny required nothing except the next month's rent of $100. No rental agreement was signed.

Kim and Mike spent the morning moving. With no U-Haul, it took several trips back and forth from campus. In the hot August heat, it was a pain to have to relocate again. They finished moving everything before noon. Mike figured they could unpack over the next few days.

As they sat in the house on the floor, they realized there was no air conditioning. It was uncomfortable as both were sweating. Yet, neither complained.

Mike said to Kim, "There's no way we're moving again. This, our white house in the country, is the last move. Agree?"

Kim nodded her head, "Agree!"

One of Mike's first tasks was to get the cistern filled. He was given the name of a guy, Maximus who delivered water. He called Maximus who replied with a gruff voice, "I'll come up this afternoon."

Maximus was an old, hunched-over, tough-looking, gray-bearded man. He sported a long-sleeved work shirt with suspenders and a base-ball cap. Maximus was lean, standing about six feet and spoke in short, brusque sentences.

He drove a truck that carried a rusted-looking big round water tank on the back. He introduced himself and then proceeded to pull the garbage can lid off the cistern. He grabbed a hose from the tank on the back of the truck and then filled the cistern with water. Maximus made sure to over-fill the cistern.

"I run the water over the top," Maximus explained. "That way, any sediment in the tank will float to the top of the water, then run out into the yard." Once the water ran over the tank top, Maximus placed the lid back on the cistern.

Mike then asked Maximus a vital question, "How do you prime the pump?"

Maximus replied, "I'll show you."

Mike and Maximus went into the house. Once inside Mike climbed down into the basement. It was his first time down there. Then, Maximus knelt down over the top of the basement opening and explained to Mike how to prime the pump.

It didn't take long. After some sputtering and hissing, the pump loudly kicked on and the pipes filled with water. Then the pump automatically shut off. Kim and Mike now had running water.

"Thanks Maximus. I was worried the pump might not work," Mike said as he gave him $25 in cash. Both men walked to the door and shook hands.

After Maximus left Mike had a curious thought. He wondered if the water came directly out of the Missouri River and if they could drink it.

Later, Mike took a shower. Much to his satisfaction, the water was clean and clear.

That night Kim and Mike sat outside as dusk approached. There was a warm moderate breeze coming out of the west. Typical of what they'd come to know about South Dakota, this night's sunset was breathtaking. The sun in the west was a round red ball, slowly descending. The backdrop was a canvas of orange, red and pink hues. Wisps of clouds added accent.

In the nearby shelterbelt, they noticed several deer, rabbits and birds. The couple sat quietly, enjoying the beauty of the openness of the plains. It was all so peaceful.

In a discussion that evening, Kim and Mike both acknowledged a nervousness and excitement about starting their new jobs. They realized their first weeks in South Dakota had been more like a vacation than anything else. They were not sure what to expect from the job, with no prior experience to compare. Typical of their relationship, there was no long discussion about their feelings.

"At least we have each other," Mike said. "That's good enough for me!"

CHAPTER SIX

Orientation

IT WAS A MONDAY IN August. The temperature was hot and the air heavy with humidity. The closest radio station, about 50 miles away in Winner, South Dakota predicted temperatures to reach 104 degrees. Despite the sluggish weather, Kim and Mike were up and out the door by 7:00 a.m. It was the first day of orientation.

As they drove down the hill toward Chamberlain, the morning was bright and the river dark blue. The valley below was massive, divided by the Missouri River flowing south, under two bridges, as far as the eye could see. The bluffs on the west side of the river were entertaining the new day's sun and the view was stunning.

Kim and Mike headed to the River Café for breakfast. As they entered the restaurant, a few locals were having coffee and talking about the hot weather. Mike selected a booth with wooden benches in the corner that looked out the window.

"Best we avoid looking in the kitchen," Mike whispered to Kim with a smile.

As they sat down they heard the other patrons laughing and looking out the windows. Outside on Main Street, a car with Michigan license plates was heading in the wrong direction down the one-way street. Since there were no other cars on the road, the passengers were clueless, unaware of their error.

Mike could see everyone in the vehicle. Each seemed content looking at the various storefronts on both sides of the street.

"I wonder if everyone is waving to them," Mike whispered snidely to Kim.

"Happens all the time," said Trish as she approached the table startling the couple. "Hey Kim," she said. "How are you guys? People are always driving the wrong way on this street."

"We're doing great. We thought we'd come and see our favorite waitress. Do you work here all day and night?" Kim asked Trish, who was now smiling.

Kim and Trish quickly caught up on the summer happenings as Trish waited on several other tables. These two are just like old friends Mike thought.

Later, when Trish came back with Kim's coffee, Mike asked, "What is this weird thing where everyone waves at you? People you don't even know."

"I don't know," Trish said with a shrug. "Everybody just waves. Old people, like my grandma and grandpa, do it more than us younger people. Just to say 'Hey' I guess."

"Well, we're from near Chicago and back there, you might get shot if you waved to other cars," Mike said. "We noticed people waving the first time we came to town. We couldn't figure it out."

Trish was busy that morning with more customers so there was also a second waitress. Kim and Mike figured it was Trish's mom by the way they interacted. Both were busy working food orders, in and out of the kitchen, then settling up at the cash register.

Kim still found a way to converse with Trish. She and Mike found out Trish was heading to the state university in a few days. "Study hard. The boys will sure be glad a cute girl like you is going to their school," Kim said as they left the café.

As they walked to the car Mike said, "You gave a twenty-five dollar tip on top of a twelve dollar breakfast. Don't forget we don't make much money now."

"She needed it. She's going to college. Remember college, when we had no money? Don't be such a miser," Kim said seriously at first, then smiling at her husband.

Kim and Mike got in the car and planned to head straight to orientation. Instead of going directly out to the school, they decided to take a loop around Chamberlain. They headed over to River Road and drove along the water for over a mile. Noticing the waves, Mike could see the river was flowing more rapidly this morning.

As they drove along, Mike was happy knowing they'd solved the mystery of other drivers waving to them. Those waves were to say 'Hello,' not a sign of anger, Mike now knew. I guess that's part of living in a small town, he thought.

"People just wave, I get it!" Mike said as he and Kim waved back to a passing car, whose driver just happened to be waving at them.

Just then, over the river, Kim spotted what she thought was an eagle and pointed it out. Seeing an eagle for the first time was an awe-inspiring sight for the city people from Illinois. Mike pulled over and stopped the car for a few seconds as the couple watched in quiet.

Back on the road, they came to the south end of River Road. Once there, they headed back onto Main Street, driving the posted 20 miles per hour toward their new place of employment. Mike recognized his anxiety, but thinking about this new adventure brought excitement too. After another few minutes, there stood the statue of St. Joseph holding baby Jesus. The Nova took a left turn onto campus and unceremoniously, Kim and Mike's adventures began.

Orientation for all new staff began on the third floor of the school building, which used to be a boys' dorm, back when the school had dormitories. The room was rather large and had cinder block walls. Windows, sitting high at the top of the room were opened. The temperature was already hot and the building had no air conditioning. Much to Mike and Kim's dismay, the forecast was for temperatures to rise throughout the day.

Orientation began with a welcome from Wally. Mike was impressed that the new staff, a group of over twenty people, seemed ready to go. People of all shapes, sizes and ages stood up and introduced themselves. New staff at orientation included houseparents, teachers and support staff.

Throughout the morning different administrators presented overviews of the work taking place. In the presentations, new staff were given ideas about what to expect when working with the students. The meetings were not very energizing, to say the least. Most were done in a lecture format while the heat in the room rose. Both Mike and Kim struggled to pay attention. Mike nearly fell asleep.

Houseparents were assigned to staff the sixteen homes on campus. The duties of the position included living in the homes, working a shift of six days on-duty and three days off. The job required residential staff to act as parental figures in the homes. The morning's orientation provided some insights into the duties of this position.

Mike tallied up the number of new staff in attendance, quickly realizing this group represented a large percentage of the entire staff that worked directly with the students. By the numbers, Mike calculated there must be a lot of turnover at the school. When he and Kim visited with Beth, he didn't get that impression. This thought was fleeting though, as Mike tried to concentrate on the topics at hand.

The new staff came from different parts of the United States. The houseparent group included five married couples with the rest being single individuals. New employees were mainly Caucasian but there were three Native American individuals and one Hispanic woman.

A lunch of sandwiches, chips, fruit and cold drinks allowed more time to visit. Kim and Mike enjoyed getting to know the others. Kim connected with many of the people in very short order. Mike made some connections but to a lesser extent. He was not the best at learning names. When he and Kim compared notes later that evening, he found he was mostly confused as to who came from where.

After lunch, Kim and Mike sat through more presentations. All the while the air in the room grew thick and warm. They hung in there until 2:30 when the orientation session ended abruptly.

"Is anyone warm?" Wally asked. "Let's call it a day."

As they left the meeting, Mike had more questions than answers. On the way to the car, he and Kim wondered whether they would measure up to the job. Later that night, sitting outside at the white house in the country, Mike and Kim chatted about the day.

"A few times today I had a sinking feeling we're in over our heads," Mike admitted.

"It's good to know we're in the same boat with everyone else though," Kim added. "I don't think anyone's really worked with kids. It's hard to tell what to expect."

"Yeah, but we sure didn't learn a whole heck-of-a-lot today. I'm not sure I'm any more ready than I was yesterday," Mike said.

"Let's look at the bright side," Kim replied. "We felt very welcome today."

On the second day of orientation, new employees came together with the returning staff for what was termed All-Staff Orientation. The day began with Mass in Our Lady of the Sioux Chapel. The chapel was beautiful. What stood out to Mike was a tapestry titled *The Indian Christ* where the crucifix is normally hung in a Catholic church.

During Mass, the priest directed his homily to the tapestry noting it was based on a painting by a Native American artist named Oscar Howe. The priest pointed to the image that depicted Christ as a Native American hanging on the cross. What Mike found unique was that Jesus was not portrayed in a frontal view but from a side view. Mike found this perspective of the crucifixion interesting.

Mike appreciated the Liturgy. He also noticed that only about 35 staff members attended Mass, since this was not a mandatory event.

After Mass, the priest came over to the orientation meetings to welcome everyone. He talked about the organization's mission and said all the staff were an extension of this through the work they would be doing. His talk was brief and encouraging.

Then Wally took over the meeting. New policies were read aloud and some of the old ones were reiterated to everyone. For the most part, Kim and Mike were lost.

"Are these the rules Jesse mentioned?" Mike whispered to Kim.

As Mike looked over the crowd, he noted that most of the returning staff members were extremely bored. There were a lot of side conversations, side comments and eye-rolling when things were mentioned that veteran staff did not agree with.

Each new staff member was introduced to the larger group. Veteran employees then introduced themselves, including where they were from. Mike enjoyed that many had very funny introductions. Mike and Kim were also surprised that few of them came from South Dakota.

As the morning dragged on, Mike thought about the people he had met at orientation. Then it hit him. He and Kim had made a wrong assumption when they were hired. They thought the houseparent jobs were competitive and there were many applicants. Now, he understood that St. Joe's hired a lot of new people each year, some at the very last minute.

Mike recalled a story he heard a day earlier, as some of the supervisors were visiting at the end of lunch. Several years prior, those in charge of recruiting had actually gone down to the Chamberlain bus stop, in a desperate attempt to find enough staff. They had boarded the bus and asked if anyone was interested in working with Native American children.

As Mike thought of the story he continued piecing things together. He wondered if any of the current employees were the ones 'plucked-off' the bus. Maybe the veteran staff are thinking that Kim and I are desperate hires, he mused to himself.

The morning's orientation session finally finished before noon. The heat, the uncomfortable chairs and the lack of air-conditioning were making it hard to pay attention. By the end of the morning, Mike thought most everyone seemed restless.

Lunch that day consisted of a potluck. There was a lot of visiting and a sense of camaraderie among everyone present. As usual, Mike felt a little out of place, but Kim fit right in. She used her patented technique of asking questions, then being sincerely interested in what the other person said, and she seemed to have old friends in just minutes.

"Hey Gene," Kim said to someone she met earlier in the week. "You looked like you were sleeping through the meetings. That's a great example to set for the new staff."

"Kim," Gene said, happy she was talking to him, "houseparents don't get much sleep, so you have to take it while you can."

"Yes, but the snoring was louder than the presenter," Kim said as those around her laughed.

The temperature in the room rose again that afternoon. The intent of the meeting was for Wally to share information about more home rules. He presented this by continuing to read to the group from the handbook. The monotone presentation and the heat made Mike think that perhaps he and Kim were receiving their penance before they had confessed their sins.

When Wally again ended the meeting abruptly at 2:00 because of the heat, Mike said to Kim, "Our penance has been fulfilled. We have been redeemed. Thankfully."

Everyone cheered at the announcement that the meeting was over.

CHAPTER SEVEN
Change in Plans

THE THIRD AND LAST DAY of orientation included a short morning meeting. By now, no one was listening to the presentations. The session ended before noon and Mike and Kim went over to the Pinger Home. They had been asked by Sally, one of the home coordinators, to come over after the morning session ended.

Like all of the student homes on campus, each was named after someone who had worked at St. Joe's and was dedicated to its mission. In the case of the Pinger Home, it was named after Fr. George Pinger, SCJ. He was a Priest and a member of the Congregation of the Priests of the Sacred Heart. He had spent many years in South Dakota in the school's early days, dedicated to their mission to serve Native American families.

It was at the meeting with Sally that Kim and Mike found out their home placement had changed. Over the first two days of orientation, they heard that Scott and Barb were on their way back from Michigan. Scott and Barb were to be the full-time, or six-day houseparents, in the Pinger Home. They had worked in the home the previous year but had not arrived because of family issues. Now it turned out they were not coming at all.

Kim and Mike believed their role was to be alternate houseparent staff for two different homes. It would be a schedule of three days and nights in the first home, then three more days and nights in a second home. The final three days in the rotation were their days off. Kim and Mike figured this schedule would provide them with hands-on training, from two sets of veteran houseparents, who would work the six-day shift in the two homes.

Sally, now Kim and Mike's supervisor, wasted no time breaking the news. She sat down with them at the dining room table in the Pinger home. She was direct in her tone and manner.

"We're going to move you to be the full-time, six-day houseparents in the Pinger Home," Sally told a shocked Mike and Kim. "We are confident you can do a good job with the students."

"Are you sure? You know we're new to this," Mike said.

"I'm sure the kids will be great, as long as they know how to supervise themselves and run the home," Kim said awkwardly, trying to be humorous over her concern.

"We've been impressed with how you two interact with others. We think the kids will enjoy being in your home. We're going to add Gene and Andie as three-day staff. They've worked here for a while and can help you out," Sally said reassuringly.

Sally was 30-years old and had worked at the school for eight years. She began her work in the little girls' dorm right out of college.

To Mike, Sally was an imposing figure. She stood tall, with mid-length hair and had a no-nonsense look about her. Sally had a dry sense of humor that could come off as condescending. Mike thought this added to her seriousness.

As the conversation went on, Sally continued to assure Mike and Kim that they would do fine as the regular six-day houseparents. The more Sally talked, the more Mike wondered why Scott and Barb were not returning. He chose not to ask but considered that it had something to do with the students.

Mike and Kim also found out that Sally was not only their supervisor but would be working as a houseparent in the home right next door. That residence was called the Fisher Home.

At one point in the discussion, Sally left to answer a phone call. While she stepped away Kim and Mike spoke softly about the decision. Initially knowing that Sally would be next door, Kim and Mike figured she could help them out. However, the more they talked, the more they began to doubt that she would have a lot of time for training and supervision.

Mike told Kim, "I have a sinking feeling we're basically on our own when it comes to learning the job."

Mike and Kim had many questions for Sally when she finished the call, but there was no time for discussion. So they asked what they could, knowing their first priority was to have the home prepared for the students. Sally again reassured them that Gene and Andie would be very helpful.

"Gene will be over shortly," Sally told them. "He'll be a real asset working with you and getting the house ready."

As they waited for Gene, Mike wondered aloud to Kim, "Why weren't Gene and Andie given the six-day duties, since they know the students in the Pinger Home? They probably figured the kids would be too challenging and didn't want to deal with it. This way they get to work three days in the Pinger Home then take a break by working with students from another home."

"Let's not over-react," Kim, the one prone to over-reacting, said to Mike. "St. Joe's needs the help and that's why we signed on."

"You're right," Mike agreed taking a deep breath. "Relax, right?"

Mike and Kim, along with Gene, spent the afternoon preparing the Pinger Home for the students' return. Andie was working home prep in the other assigned three-day home that she and Gene supported. Even though the two-story Pinger Home was exceedingly warm without air conditioning, the group forged ahead with home preparations.

Home prep included making beds, cleaning common areas, adding homey touches and buying food and other staples from the small supermarket in town. The process took Gene, Kim and Mike the whole afternoon.

As they worked Mike became familiar with the home layout. It would be important in keeping track of twelve students. Outside there was a nice sized yard and a concrete slab that served as both a driveway and a basketball court. Cement steps led up to a small square porch and the home's front entrance. Mike thought he'd be able to stand on the porch and supervise students in the front yard.

Students entering through the front door of the home would come into a large room that served as a combination living and dining room, sometimes referred to as the great room. There was furniture on one side including a couch, chairs and a coffee table. On the other side of the room, just off the kitchen, were two long tables where everyone in the home would sit down and eat their meals.

The kitchen was large and had pressed wood cabinets placed along the outside wall. The cabinets were located both on top and below a large countertop. Appliances, such as a dishwasher and microwave were spaced out and fit into sections of the cabinets. The kitchen also had a large pantry and a freezer.

On the opposite side of the great room were two other good-sized areas. One was a TV room and the other was set up as a study for doing homework. The downstairs space also included a small office and extra staff bedroom. There was also a second entrance on the side of the home. Gene suggested that the students use that door when coming and going from school.

"Think of it as traffic flow," Gene said. "Plus it's functional. The students can hang up their coats and drop their winter gear at the back door. It's the closest door to the school and will make supervision a little easier if everyone is using the same entrance."

Near the front door of the great room was a long staircase. It led to an upstairs hallway that ran the length of the house. Coming off the hallway were six student bedrooms and one staff bedroom. The staff room was where Mike and Kim would sleep. At the end of the hall were two large bathrooms including showers, sinks and toilets. The boys in the home would be assigned to use those. One of the student rooms had a separate bathroom. The girls would all use that one to maintain privacy.

Through the prep process, Gene had lots of good suggestions for the home setup. After a few hours of working together, Kim and Mike were also able to get to know him personally.

Gene was in his early 40's, stocky, and balding with a black beard. He had a simple, practical way about him and Mike heard other staff tease him about being cheap. On this day he wore overalls with a white tee shirt. Sweat poured off him.

Kim and Mike already knew that Gene grew up on an Ohio chicken farm. Mike related more so, when Gene told him he was part of a big Catholic family of eleven.

Gene's experience was not only helpful but also practical. Being a veteran of six years he knew what needed to be done for home prep. Of course, after one afternoon of working together, Gene and Kim hit it off. By the end of the day, Mike found them making jokes about each other's bad traits.

At one point Gene teased, "Mike, you have to give me a break. Your wife is killing me with all these questions. And she's been making fun of my clothes. She told me my overalls weren't very attractive if I was looking for a date."

The following morning, Kim, Mike and Gene put the final touches on the home. By midmorning, they were ready for students.

Standing with Kim and Mike in the great room, Gene said, "Now the fun begins."

Kim and Mike had one last task to attend to. Along with Gene and Andie, they met with the school social worker. He gave a quick rundown of each of the students.

During the meeting, Kim and Mike learned a little about Andie's background. She was an enrolled member of the Rosebud Sioux Tribe, but grew up off the reservation. She was average height, lean, broad in the shoulder and had long braided black hair.

This was Andie's second year at the school. Mike guessed her to be in her mid-40s. She was dressed casually in jeans, had a quiet demeanor and spoke of having three grown sons.

In the meeting, Mike realized Andie had an understanding of the students and their backgrounds. During the discussion, she asked about the students' relatives, sometimes guessing whom they were related to. Mike figured this knowledge probably aided her in establishing relationships with the students.

With the end of the meeting, orientation was now officially over.

That afternoon Jesse invited Mike to the river to go canoeing. They went out for several hours exploring the shoreline, first on the east side, then the west side of the river. It was calm, with little to no current. The day was bright and the temperature again hot, over 90 degrees. It was very serene and peaceful to be on the water.

Mike was not a natural on the water, but he could swim well enough to save himself. Jesse on the other hand was a good swimmer. Life jackets were in the canoe, so neither was worried about being out on the main channel of the river. The two men paddled some, drifted some, and visited the whole time.

"I hope we can survive working in the Pinger Home," Mike said looking for some support.

"You'll be fine," Jesse replied. "What's the worst that can happen? All the kids run away because they don't like you and your wife? Anyway, let's forget about work for a while."

"Good idea," Mike said as the canoe floated peacefully along. "This sure is a nice break on a hot day."

Jesse said, "Jeannie and I hope to be here for a while. We've really come to enjoy the area and this river adds a lot of life to everything."

CHAPTER EIGHT

One Last Weekend

KIM AND MIKE HAD A nice start to the weekend. On Saturday they were up early and headed to the South Dakota State Fair. It was a 100-mile drive, partway on the interstate but mostly on a two-lane highway. It was on the highway that they were pulled over by a South Dakota Highway Patrolman.

Kim was driving. When the officer asked her to come back to his patrol car, Mike knew they were in for a ticket. After about ten minutes Kim came back to the car. She told Mike she just received a warning but no ticket.

Mike wondered, "How'd you pull that one off?"

"I played with my hair and fluttered my eyelashes," Kim joked. "You know, played the dumb blonde."

Laughing to himself and thinking Kim wasn't exactly role-playing, Mike quickly cut her off. "I'm not buying that. This isn't Chicago!" he said.

What happened was the officer had asked why they were in South Dakota. Since they had Illinois plates, he was surprised to learn they had taken employment in Chamberlain. He claimed he knew families that lived around Chamberlain, people that Kim and Mike naturally didn't know.

Kim said the officer was friendly enough. "He mentioned we need to get a South Dakota driver's license and plates for the car," she told Mike. "Plus, he recommended we go to tonight's concert at the state fair. Not bad for our first encounter with the law."

Kim and Mike spent the late morning and early afternoon at the fair. The fairgrounds in Huron, South Dakota, were not very big but the cost of admission was reasonable. There were carnival rides and games, many craft items, businesses hawking their wares and plenty of livestock.

The 4-H section was large, smelly, and interesting with young kids grooming and displaying their various livestock. There were cows, sheep, horses, pigs and some chickens. Mike even struck up a conversation with a rancher, asking why certain breeds and body types were more valuable than others. The rancher answered his questions pointing out differences.

A short while into the education session, Kim yawned and said, "Let's get going Mr. Farmer, we have cows to milk."

As Kim and Mike wandered around the fairgrounds, Mike realized two things. People in South Dakota were generally friendly and this was indeed a very small state. The state fair reminded him more of a county fair back in Illinois. Although, Mike would have had to admit that he'd never actually been to a county fair.

The afternoon sun was hot, so they decided to leave by early evening. On the way back to Chamberlain Mike dodged a few pheasants on the road. During the 90-minute ride they avoided being stopped again by the Highway Patrol.

As they neared Chamberlain Mike reminded Kim, "Notice how I didn't speed and got us here safely?"

"You drove like an old grandpa though," Kim laughed.

Later that night they went out to the Gold Rush Bar and Grille in Chamberlain. The Rush was a typical small-town bar. It smelled like stale beer and there was always cigarette smoke spilling out the front door. Most importantly to Kim and Mike, other St. Joe's staff were there.

The Rush was located on Main Street and even the outside of the bar looked rugged. It seemed the building had been added onto out of necessity, not out of design. It became a sort of biker bar during the Sturgis Motorcycle Rally and hosted locals during the rest of the year. In the summer and during hunting season, out-of-towners frequented the place.

That Saturday night, there was drinking and carousing, just like in any other small-town bar. Staff from the school joked, drank beer, played pool and even danced a bit to the jukebox music. It was apparent to Mike that everyone was anxious for the students to arrive. As Mike and Kim had seen before, even though they hadn't been with the school very long, the students were always a topic of discussion.

After the bar closed, Mike drove the Nova home. As they headed up the hill, then down the dirt road, Mike realized how dark and desolate it was. With no moon, the tall grass wafting in the wind on the side of the road gave an eerie feel to the drive.

Due to the heat, Mike drove with their windows down. When they pulled in and stopped the car, Mike heard something funny. There was loud hissing outside. He looked at Kim puzzled.

"Damn, that must be the water pump. Something sounds like it came loose," he told Kim. "That's what's causing the noise."

As Mike jumped out of the car and walked toward the house he suddenly stopped.

"Shit, it's a rattlesnake!" Mike yelled as he scrambled, nearly falling. As fast as he could, he jumped back into the car.

Fortunately for Mike, he had noticed the silhouette of a rattlesnake in the shadows while it was still beyond reaching him. It was up near the small cement walkway leading to the door of the house. The snake was agitated, hissing loudly, coiled and ready to strike.

Now Kim was screaming. "What are we going to do?" she yelled as Mike caught his breath.

"I know," Mike said as he started up the Nova and turned on the car lights.

Without saying anything, Mike put the car in drive. He angled the vehicle towards the snake, driving directly up to the house. As the snake tried to slither away, Mike ran it over. As quickly as that, the hissing stopped and all was quiet.

Mike slowly backed up as he and Kim now viewed, via headlights, a dead snake on the sidewalk.

Kim slapped the dashboard. "That was great! We city folks just killed our first rattlesnake, by way of our lethal Nova!"

"Yes, but we still have to get into the house," Mike said. "Ready to make a run for it?"

It took a few minutes for Kim and Mike to find their nerve and gather themselves. Eventually, they got out of the car and held hands. On the count of three, they ran towards the porch where they leaped over the snake carcass and rushed into the house. Once inside, it took a few minutes to calm down before calling it a day.

"I didn't know the house came with snakes," Mike said as he turned out the lights.

Kim and Mike took it easy on Sunday. They attended Mass with a few other coworkers, after which they went home and rested. They had purchased a window air conditioner for the bedroom and spent the day switching channels between CBS and PBS. Those two channels were all the reception they got out in the country.

That night as dusk fell, Mike went back to the Pinger Home. "Tomorrow's the big day," he said to himself. "Finally we get to meet the students."

After checking a few things, he left the home as the daylight dimmed. Mike drove to the west side of campus along the river. There he got out of the Nova to look at the river.

As the sunlight dropped below the horizon, the shadow of the bluffs on that side of the river made a spectacular silhouette. The setting sun, the shadows of grey and black on the water, with an orange, red and blue sky as a backdrop, gave the moment a surreal feel.

"Tomorrow we rock and roll," he yelled out over the water, feeling a sense of peace and excitement in his soul.

CHAPTER 9

Finally, Students...

Train to Chicago
June 9, 1986, 6:50 am

As the train bounced along, *Mike shook his head and closed his eyes. During the interview, Beth's stories of her experiences should have dispelled the notion that they were going to change the world. Both he and Kim had heard her words, but they still had no concept of how the work might impact their lives. In truth, they romanticized what working in a home with twelve Native American children would be like. Without any experience, they were indeed naïve in thinking it would be easy.*

On this bright, hot August Monday, Mike was up early for a run. The run was his way to ease the tension he was feeling. He ran on their gravel road with fields of corn on both sides. He couldn't help but notice the many grasshoppers bouncing all over the place.

Mike took a left on the oil road that he remembered others referring to as the "Farm to Market Road." The fact he knew and even remembered this made him chuckle.

"After a couple of weeks I'm now a South Dakotan. Yeah right!" he muttered to himself skeptically.

Mike turned south towards Chamberlain and ran down the hill. At some point he noticed thousands of mayflies along the road. This caused him to deliberately close his mouth leading to gasps for air further down the hill.

When Mike returned home he said, "Today's the day. Ready?"

"I think so," Kim responded with some apprehension. "It should be okay, I think. Why, what do you think?"

"I think we go to Pinger and see what happens. Like every beginning, there is always some uncertainty," Mike said, sounding more sure of himself than he was feeling.

Neither Kim nor Mike quite knew what to expect, therefore there was nervous tension. They also recognized this was the adventure they were here for, which generated excitement.

Vacillating between these two emotions, they both pondered what was to come. Like other situations in their marriage, they knew the tension was there but spoke little about their feelings.

Mike went over the plan in his head. There would be twelve students in their home, consisting of eight boys and four girls. The girls were all sisters and many of the boys were related. The meeting with the school's social worker had provided some information on each student's background.

Without a basis of working with youth, or knowing the Native population, or even understanding poverty, the social worker's reports seemed to be more of a movie script than real life. Mike and Kim wavered back and forth between feeling sorry for the students and not being able to relate to their circumstances.

At that meeting, Gene encouraged them by saying, "It helps to know the students' backgrounds, but keep it in perspective. You still have to work with them as individuals. They don't want you to feel sorry for them; they just want to be treated fairly. Sometimes too much background information can cause you to over-compensate. So it's best not to fall into that trap."

Andie added. "These kids don't want to be labeled. Labels are when you don't know someone. They want you to get to know them personally and to be treated as individuals. And if you are respectful and honest with them, they will eventually respect you."

Kim and Mike drove to the Pinger Home around 11:00 AM. Gene came in a few minutes later. He would be there to assist on that first day. Although they were ready, everyone took a minute to look around, as a means to temper some nervousness. Kim started to prepare barbeques for the students and their families.

The first group arrived shortly after noon. It was four brothers from White River. They drove up in an old dingy-green Chevy station wagon. Mike figured that the car was at least ten years old.

The car gave off a sharp noise with the tail end nearly dragging on the street. The exterior of the vehicle was rusted, the tires bald with no hubcaps. At orientation, some staff referred to this type of beat-up vehicle as a 'rez car.' Through the windows, Mike could see the station wagon was packed with people and clothing.

Once the vehicle stopped, people seemed to pour out. Each person had dark hair and olive skin. As Mike looked out from the Pinger Home, he viewed the scene as chaotic and likened it to a clown car. It seemed like more people than possible continued coming out of the car.

In the group were a young boy and girl, between three and five years old. Three girls appeared old enough for grade school. Mike remembered from the social worker's visit that these girls would be living in another home on campus.

Next Mike noticed a teenage boy. He got out of the driver's side of the station wagon. Quickly he walked around and assisted a very old-looking woman who climbed out from the passenger side of the car. Then came the four boys who would be living in the home.

Each boy grabbed a garbage bag from the back of the station wagon. Wayne, Kyle, Steve and Malachi had all been students at St. Joe's since first grade. Each boy had lived in the Pinger Home the year before.

Malachi, called Mally, was in the fifth grade and the smallest of the brothers. Short in stature, he spoke in a raspy voice, grew his braided hair long and wore jeans and a tee-shirt. He had a thin build.

Steve, the sixth-grader, was slightly taller and stockier, wore dirty jeans and a dark tee-shirt. His hair was short and his voice came off more like a whine. Mike could tell right away that Steve was treated as the baby of this group. His brothers were quick to scold him within the first few minutes of their arrival.

Kyle and Wayne were the oldest and both in the eighth grade. While taller than the two younger boys, Kyle was on the pudgy side. He wore jeans, a tee-shirt and had a mid-length haircut. The boy sweated profusely, particularly across his nose, on this hot August morning.

Wayne was the oldest of the four. Tall and thin, he had a bad complexion and his long hair covered his shoulders. Dressed in a tight tee-shirt and jeans, he came off as more reserved than his brothers did. Mike remembered that Wayne had fallen a year behind in school, which accounted for his more mature build.

Mike walked out to meet the group as they were coming in. "Welcome!" Mike said, happy that students finally had arrived. "Do you guys need help?"

No one said anything as everyone walked by and entered the home. As Kyle passed by, he gave what Mike referred to as a brush-off, with a look of "Who are you?"

Once in the home, there was a nervous pause for a few seconds as everyone stood together in a large group. Mike noticed the distinct Native American features. Everyone looked hot from being cooped up in the car for a while.

Kim broke the silence. "Hi, we're Kim and Mike. We'll be the house-parents this year. And you know Gene. He'll be working here too."

The short elderly woman in the group was Grandma Ancel. Her gray hair framed the frown on her face, one that was filled with lines and wrinkles. She wore a dress and walked with a limp aided by a cane. When she spoke Mike could see she was missing two front teeth and did not look to be in the best of health.

"Hi. These boys'll be living here again this year," Ancel slowly mumbled while pointing to the four boys.

After introductions, grandma sat and signed school paperwork for the boys. Levy, the boy who was driving, sat with Ancel as the rest of the boys milled around. Levy had a solid build and wore glasses on his round face. Levy helped fill out the paperwork as Mike noticed Ancel's sight was impaired.

Gene assisted in explaining where signatures were required on the forms. These were consent documents in case the boys needed medical assistance. Mike noticed none of the forms were read – just signed.

While Ancel signed the papers, Kim offered her coffee and then asked everyone if they wanted something to eat. The four boys tossed their bags in the corner before eating. Kyle took time to make sure the youngest girl and boy had something to eat. Everyone else sat at the table as the three older girls hung close to the grandmother. While eating, they mentioned several times that they wanted to leave. Mike guessed they were in a hurry to get to their home on campus.

Kim, putting her bubbly personality to work, was able to visit for a short while with Grandma Ancel. Mike guessed that the woman was in her seventies. She spoke softly, expressing concern about the boys' behavior over the summer.

With labored breathing Ancel said, "They need to be at this school. They didn't follow my directions at home."

Kim replied, "We'll take care of them. They'll be fine."

Kim also visited with Levy, who sometimes spoke for his grandma. He was the oldest boy living with the family. Closer up, Mike guessed he was 16 or 17 and wondered about his schooling. Off to the side, the two youngest kids bounced around the house after eating a small amount of food.

Mike was surprised the four brothers who would be living in Pinger said little or nothing at all to him and Kim. They did talk quietly with each other and joked about things back in White River. But that was the extent of their visiting, or non-visiting, as it were.

After twenty minutes, Ancel, Levy and the rest of the group got up to leave. The four boys said their goodbyes. Once they were gone, more awkward silence followed. The boys stood around, seemingly wondering what they were supposed to do next. Finally, Gene began to help the boys unpack.

The boys knew Gene from previous years, so he was able to engage them in conversation. He spoke of family members, such as Levy, who was a former student. Mike was glad Gene was there to get the boys to talk.

"Levy's good," Kyle reported. "He took grandma's car out a few times and didn't come back until morning – without the car. So I got the car and drove it back."

Mike stood there quietly thinking that Kyle was driving as an eighth-grader.

"Oh," Gene said, "you were driving. Could you see over the steering wheel?" he teased.

"Heck yeah!" said Kyle. "I'm a good driver."

As the boys dumped out their bags of clothes, Steve picked out a plastic bone from his pile.

"Mally, I got your dog's toy," he laughed nervously.

"Sheeze, why'd you bring that?" Mally asked irritably. "I told you not to mess with that. Now Bobo won't have his toy."

"You always get into everyone's stuff," Kyle added. "You're such a baby and always tattling."

"Why you always picking on me?" Steve retorted weakly.

"You cry all the time," Kyle said throwing a mean look at Steve.

Gene intervened, "Okay, okay. Let's go through your stuff and get started on laundry."

Kim and Mike had heard a few stories about the boy's situation in talking with different staff. Much of this was confirmed when visiting with the social worker. They were part of the Picollet and Wild clans, as they were referred to at the school.

The story was that Grandma Ancel had four grown children. Between them they had twenty-three kids. Alcohol abuse and problems with the law caused the parents to be in and out of their children's lives. Fifteen of the children lived with Grandma Ancel and seven attended St. Joe's.

The next student to arrive was Elijah from Oglála. His mom, uncle, and two younger sisters accompanied him.

Elijah was tall for his age and athletic-looking. He wore shorts, a basketball jersey and entered the home smiling. He seemed relaxed.

Elijah's mom introduced herself. "I'm Vinnie and this is my son Eli. I was a student here a long time ago. I lived in the girls' dorm, 'back in the day.'"

Vinnie had a round face, was short in stature, slender, with thick black mid-length hair. She then introduced her two daughters and Elijah's uncle who she referred to as Moore. Moore was tall, rather large with a big belly and sported a cowboy hat and boots. Mike said hello and shook his hand.

Vinnie had an animated personality and mentioned the names of a few students and employees she knew when she was a student at St. Joe's. Naturally, Mike and Kim didn't recognize any of them. Her demeanor suggested that she must have had a good experience at the school since she laughed pleasantly when remembering the names of people.

As they ate, Elijah's family sat and visited at the dining room table. They mentioned they had a four-hour drive back to Oglála, so they wanted to get back on the road. Vinnie gave Elijah a big hug before leaving.

"You be good Eli," Vinnie said, then added, "Mike and Kim, take care of my boy."

When his family had gone, Kim asked. "Do you prefer being called Elijah or Eli?"

"Everyone calls me Eli," he said quietly, again showing off a big smile.

"Easy enough to remember. Eli it is," Kim replied kindly with a smile and wink. "How many years have you been a student here?" she asked.

"I've been going here since third grade," Eli replied.

The four sisters arrived next, in the mid-afternoon. They were dropped off in a van that belonged to their tribe. Sage, Kellie, Vera and Sadie each had only one small suitcase or bag for a semester's worth of clothes. Mike met them at the van and made sure they had all their belongings.

The social worker had told Kim and Mike that their mom had secured a ride for them because she didn't have reliable transportation. This was the girls' first time being at the school. Mike understood their anxious looks when the van pulled up outside the home.

"Hi girls. Welcome to Pinger. Come on in," Mike said as he met the girls at the van. "Follow me."

As they entered the home, Sage was in the lead. She had a shy smile and was barely taller than her sister Kellie who was a year younger. Mike could see her nervousness and thought she probably felt overwhelmed. She was slender, neatly groomed with short black hair. She wore jeans and a short-sleeve shirt with a collar.

Kellie was next. Unlike her older sister, she had long curly hair and a broader build. Kellie wore a frown and looked around warily, trying to figure out her new surroundings. She had on loose, faded jeans and a tee-shirt with the words 'Watch Out' on the front.

"Sheeze, this is a big house," Mike heard Kellie whisper to Sage.

Vera and Sadie trailed the two older girls. Both were much smaller than their older sisters. They each wore shorts and a tee shirt. They were twins, though not identical. Vera was the taller of the two, with shorter hair and a slender build. She had that "I might start to cry" look, and seemed the most nervous of all the girls.

Mike identified Sadie as the baby of the group. Physically the smallest, she had the longest hair. Sadie spoke in a high-pitched voice that carried easily throughout the home. She seemed comfortable expecting the others to look out for her.

Now, with their bags in hand and standing nervously in the great room, the girls looked at Mike and Kim. By their expressions, Mike could tell they wanted to know what to do next. The boys who were now settled in and watching television in the tv room took little notice of the girls' arrival.

"Hi, I'm Kim and this is Mike. That's Gene over there. How was your trip? Why don't you put your things over there?" Kim said pointing to the corner of the room. "Do you want something to eat?" she then offered.

The girls just looked at one another not sure what to say. Finally, Kellie responded, "Okay, thanks."

"By the way," Kim said, "Can you introduce yourselves?"

Once introductions were accomplished, the four girls grabbed food and sat together at the end of the dining room table. Shyly they whispered among themselves. They weren't impolite, just embarrassed and unsure. There was no way for the girls to avoid the difficult nature of this type of initial meeting with strangers. Mike and Kim came to understand that these were kids who had never been taught the skills of how to converse with people they didn't know.

Benny arrived at 4:00. Just like the first four boys to arrive, he also was from White River. His aunt, whom he lived with, dropped him off.

Benny sported baggy jeans and a sleeveless tee-shirt. His hair was long and looked un-kept in a ponytail. He was initially quiet when he came in and appeared tired out. Then when he saw the other four boys in the TV room, he quickly walked over.

Loudly Benny blurted out, "Hey guys! I'll be back in White River before you know it!"

Mike was not sure exactly what Benny meant.

His aunt visited briefly, ate and then headed on her way. Before leaving she told Kim, "Benny had a bad summer. He was caught a few times huffing spray paint."

Welson Cottonwood showed up a little later. He was the final eighth-grader to arrive. His family drove up in a nicer-looking Chevy, but the car didn't have a muffler so was extremely loud. In the car with Welson were his aunt, his grandma and two younger siblings that Mike guessed to be about five or six years old.

Welson was tall, slender and had a well-groomed look. His hair was short and neatly cut. He was dressed in nice pants and a collared shirt.

Welson introduced himself, shaking Mike's hand and saying, "All my friends call me Cott."

Mike was impressed with Welson's self-confidence. He was the only student to introduce himself and shake his hand.

"Cott, that's a great name and easy to remember. Welcome!" Mike replied.

Cott's grandma and aunt ate quickly while the two younger kids played with him. The family stayed for only a short while, then left. They were headed back to the Cheyenne River Reservation, a long three-hour drive.

A short time later, Mike visited with Cott as they went through his clothing. He didn't have many clothes in his bag.

"I had to leave some of my stuff back at home," Cott told Mike in a sullen tone. "We didn't have room in the car."

Mike wondered if there was more to the story than what Cott was saying. So he said as non-judgmentally as possible, "No problem. We can get you more clothes if you need them."

The last student to arrive was Wačháŋǧa or Sweet Grass, known as Sweets. He was only a first-grader.

Mike watched Sweets as he tumbled out of the car and into the home. He immediately made himself comfortable, almost acting as if he had lived in Pinger before. Sweets was accompanied by his grandmother who trailed behind him.

When Sweets got inside he inquired loudly, "Whatcha got to eat?"

Walking to the kitchen with grubby hands, he proceeded to grab a plate and make himself right at home. He reached in and took a handful of chips, then a bun as he attempted to put sloppy joe mix on top. In his haste food began to fall off the plate.

Kim quickly told Sweets, "Oh dear, let me help you."

As Sweets sat down to eat, with his grandma watching patiently, Mike asked, "Do you have any bags?"

Sweets replied, "Yeah, they're in the car. Can someone get them?"

Gene quickly jumped in saying, "No, Sweets, you go out and bring your own bags in."

Sweets looked at Gene, mumbled under his breath, stood up went out to the car. His grandma accompanied him outside. A minute later Sweets came back followed by his grandma who was carrying his two bags.

Sweets then finished eating as Kim visited with his grandma. She was an elderly woman who stooped over a little when she stood up and peered over her glasses as she spoke. She expressed concern about Sweets, mainly worrying about him getting enough to eat.

Mike found grandma's concerns interesting, as Sweets stood 4 feet and 6 inches tall, and was overweight. To accommodate for the size of his middle, Sweets wore a pair of jeans that were cut off at the bottom. He used a rope for a belt to keep his pants up. He also wore a loose-fitting tee shirt.

Sweets' grandma asked to see his room and wanted to put his things away. Kim assured her that Sweets was capable of putting his clothes away. After more visiting, his grandmother kissed him on the head and reluctantly left. Sweet Grass by then had left the table and was sitting in front of the TV. He barely acknowledged her leaving.

Throughout the rest of the day and early evening, Gene assisted Kim and Mike with student check-in. His experience with the families and the check-in process was extremely helpful. Mike was not sure they could have gotten through the day without Gene.

The process of check-in included luggage inspection. Student bags were opened and the contents spilled out. Any banned items were to be taken away, although none were found. Clothing was then labeled with markers. Notes were made if students needed any clothing items. With some students, laundering was needed so there was often a backlog of laundry. Mike's job was to keep that part of the process moving.

Students were given room assignments and asked to put their things away. Each student room consisted of two beds and two dressers, one for each child. Roommate assignments were made ahead of time. No student objections were noted so Mike felt happy about this.

Next, Gene helped conduct a quick "home meeting" where the rules were explained. The students said little and there were no questions. Kim,

Mike and Gene introduced themselves as part of the meeting. The students were then asked to introduce themselves and what grade they were in.

All the students introduced themselves differently. The four sisters were quiet and barely audible. Benny acted like he'd forgotten his name. Sweets tried to be funny, but no one laughed.

Cott said, "My last name is Cottonwood, but call me Cott. Don't forget the name. Someday I'll be famous!"

The final part of the check-in process was for students to go to the infirmary to be medically evaluated. That included a quick look at the eye chart, measurements of weight and height, and a general health check-up. The process also included a head examination. Students' hair and scalp were inspected to see if they had any nits or lice.

The good news was that all the students in the home seemed to be in good physical health. The bad news was that three of the girls and three of the boys had lice. Although this was certainly not what Mike and Kim wanted to hear, they really did not understand what they were in for!

Once back at the home, Kim began the process of working with the students who had lice. First, a special shampoo was applied. This was supposed to kill off all the live critters and eggs. Then the combing took place.

Mike and Kim agreed that combing would fall to Kim. It consisted of placing towels around the student's shoulders, wetting the child's head and then combing out the eggs near the scalp with a metal comb. The comb had teeth that were close together, so the combing had to be done in small sections.

Since Gene was available, he jumped in to assist Kim.

"This is the best part of the job," Gene said sarcastically.

Kim retorted, "Gene, I thought the best part was working with you. This must be a close second though."

It often took twenty minutes or more, per student, to complete the combing process. Sometimes the effort paid off the first time, but often the child had to be treated and combed several times. This was especially true if the student's hair was long and thick, which it was for most of them. Plus, the more traditional families believed that an individual's hair was sacred and those boys and girls let their hair grow.

Meanwhile, Mike helped to keep the laundry moving. It was important that clothing was clean, organized and not mixed up with another student's items. Mike did his best to make a list of clothing needs for the boys while Kim handled the list for the girls.

After dinner Gene took Mike and Kim aside.

"Here's an idea. Why don't you take the kids up to the rest area on the interstate? It's a great view of the river and very scenic. Plus it'll be a good first activity and shouldn't take very long," Gene suggested.

"Isn't that right off the interstate?" Kim asked. "We really enjoyed the view when we first came to town.

"Yes," Gene responded. "You can see for miles up there. The kids will like it."

"Are you sure that's a good idea?" Mike questioned. "We barely know the kids' names."

"It'll be fine," Gene said reassuringly.

Mike and Kim then announced to the students they were going up to the rest area to get some fresh air. The group piled into the fourteen-passenger van. Mike made the ten-minute drive from campus to the I-90 rest area. It provided a great view of the river valley, one that spanned miles.

Once arriving, everyone piled out of the vehicle. Kim gave the students instructions not to stray out of sight. Students were told the group would gather in twenty minutes. All the students nodded in agreement to the instructions, as the older students headed in several directions.

"Sadie and Vera stay with me," Kim said.

"Why can't we go with Kellie and Sage?" Sadie asked as she pouted.

After a few minutes, Sadie and Vera were more pleasant, each now holding Kim's hands. Kim used the opportunity to ask them all kinds of questions. Kellie and Sage did not stray very far away either. They were close enough that Kim could see them.

All the boys took off except for Sweets who Mike instructed, "Stick with me."

"Why can't I go with the guys?" Sweets whined as he huffed and puffed.

After the allotted twenty minutes, Mike called for the boys. Eli and Cott came right away. After another twenty minutes, the other boys showed up. They came out of a tree line on the west side of the rest area. This area sloped directly over the Missouri River.

Mike initially said to himself, "I should question the guys. But since it's the first day, no harm, no foul. They're just being kids."

Changing his mind, Mike asked, "Where were you guys? You were supposed to stay close and be back after twenty minutes."

Benny was quick to answer, "We were just playing in the trees. We didn't hear you call us."

With Benny's comment, the other boys were silent. Mike did notice a smirk on Kyle's face. He also thought Wayne and Steve seemed nervous. This was all a passing thought though, as Mike chalked it up to the boys being questioned by a guy they had just met less than eight hours earlier.

"Of course, they're nervous," Mike reasoned as he walked with the boys.

Mike and Kim gathered the group by the van. As they stood nearby Mike said, "Nice job everyone. This was our first successful outing together."

"Thanks Kim and Mike," Kyle said with a big grin. The others all nodded in agreement.

As the sun was setting in the west, the Pinger Home students loaded into the van. At that time of evening, the sun was a red ball in the sky. Mike and Kim smiled at one another, acknowledging they had succeeded in the navigation of their first off-campus trip. Everyone in the van was quiet as they drove to the school.

Back in the Pinger Home, it was shower time. This process involved a couple of students heading upstairs to shower in different parts of the home. Once showered, each student came downstairs to the main floor, watched television and had a snack. Another student would then go up and shower.

At the end of the evening, everyone gathered for a prayer. When called for prayer time, the girls and Sweets came out of the television room immediately. Some of the boys, on the other hand, acted as if they did not hear the request and kept on watching television. Mike called the boys a second time and there was still no movement.

Finally, Mike went into the TV room and raised his voice. "Guys, let's go. It's prayer time and you were already called twice." This time the boys came quickly.

With everyone finally assembled, Kim asked the students, "How was your day?" No one replied.

After an awkward silence, Kim added. "Well, I hope you all had a good day. We plan to have a good year ahead of us here in Pinger.

Mike added, "Each night we'll take a moment to say a prayer of thanks and pray for anything important to us. Does anyone want to pray for someone or anything tonight?"

Again, there was silence.

Mike then led the group in the Our Father. He was the only one reciting the prayer.

After prayer the students headed up to bed. It took a while for everyone to settle in that first night. Mike stayed upstairs, walking up and down the hallway to make sure everyone was in bed and stayed there. This took close to an hour. During that time Kim wrote in the Daily Home Logbook.

Kim's log entry was short and sweet:

Had a good day! We hope this is the start to a great school year!

CHAPTER TEN

The Routine

THE FIRST MORNING OF SCHOOL was rushed and disorganized. Each student was roused at 7:00 a.m. Students were to make their beds, pick up their rooms and be ready for breakfast in fifteen minutes. The meal that morning was a simple one – cereal, toast and juice.

Mike had to wake up half the students a second time because they were sleepy. Since the students didn't have any type of schedule over the summer, most were accustomed to sleeping in and everyone moved slowly.

When Mike came in a third time to wake Kyle, Kyle was angry. "Why are you bothering me? I'm tired," he said as he pulled the sheets over his head.

Mike didn't like Kyle's tone so he tried to ignore the comment but still rouse him out of bed.

"Let's get moving. Now," Mike said in a more stern voice.

Reluctantly, Kyle sat up and got out of bed. He then stared at Mike with an angry scowl as Mike left the room.

After a quick breakfast students were to work on their assigned "charge." If they finished early, they could watch television. The Pinger Home would follow this same routine for the entire year.

A charge was a work assignment that students were to complete. The assigned jobs were usually set up to keep the house functional and clean, and they rotated weekly. The idea was to give the students ownership of the home. Assignments included cleaning and vacuuming the TV room; cleaning the downstairs common bathroom; washing, drying and folding the towels; and setting up the kitchen for meals as well as assisting with cleanup afterward.

Mike and Kim tried to make sure charges were done properly. Gene was also present that first morning. The rule was that each child had to have their charge checked, by an adult, before it was considered finished.

The first student to complain was Benny.

"Why do we have to do this work? Isn't that your job?" he said to Mike.

Mike responded, "You need to take some pride in your home."

Benny retorted, "My home is in White River. This ain't my home."

"Get it done and quit complaining," Mike said ending the conversation.

Sweets grumbled as he mopped the floor. "Sheeze, this is too hard for a first-grader."

Gene responded, "If you want to live here, you have to pitch in."

"Oh, all right," Sweets sighed.

At 8:00 a.m. students from all the homes walked across campus to school. For the Pinger Home students, it was a quarter-mile walk. At least one houseparent was to walk with the students to make sure they arrived safely.

Once at the school, houseparents took a few minutes to hand off supervision of their kids to the teaching staff. The handoff, or changeover, included giving a short update on how the student had fared the prior evening and in the morning before school. Most times, these visits were short. If there were problems, it could take longer.

With up to six teachers to visit, houseparents became experts at making communications precise and to the point. Houseparents had an additional motivation. Once they were no longer responsible for the students, they went off duty. The teachers had an incentive to be brief at the end of the day, as they were trying to finish paperwork so they could head home. Thus, the changeover process became clear-cut and efficient over time.

Kim said to Sweets' first-grade teacher that morning, "Well, we got him here, but no promises."

The teacher smiled and said, "I'll take it from here."

Kim and Mike were glad they had made it through that first hectic morning. On their way back to Pinger they saw Sally and stopped briefly to chat.

Kim said, "Well, Sally, we made it. Not sure it was an award winner, but the kids are at school."

"I'm sure it went fine," Sally replied.

Kim headed over to the donated items department to look for clothing for the students, while Mike headed back to the home. Upon arriving at the Pinger Home he noticed how cluttered everything looked and how poorly the charges were done. While heading upstairs, Mike detected that two of the students had wet their beds. Neither student had done anything but make the bed and cover up the wet sheets.

"Oh no, this isn't good," Mike said to Gene, who had stayed back at the home.

"This can be a constant problem if we don't figure something out," Gene replied.

Meanwhile, Kim was looking for clothing. Downstairs in the old dorm building, two rather elderly ladies, Ruth and Mary, oversaw donated items. These women were referred to as the "sewing ladies." In their early days working for the organization, they were charged with mending the students' clothing. Mike and Kim had heard that both women loved to visit, but were considered territorial in the way they dealt with the hand-me-downs.

Donated items came to the school through this department. The majority of donations were clothes, but on occasion toys also showed up. Ruth and Mary's job was to receive, then wash and prepare the clothing for the students. They also sorted through the toys determining which were salvageable.

Once the garments were ready to be distributed, the "sewing ladies" would place the articles into large bins, separated by size and gender. Houseparent staff would rummage through the bins looking for appropriate clothing items for their students. Shoes were set on the outside wall of the room and separated by size. Toys were kept in a separate room that was locked. Getting into the room required permission from either Ruth or Mary.

Donated clothing was sorted into two broad categories. "Regular daily wear" included articles like jeans and tee shirts. "Dress up items" like church outfits and dress shoes were included in the second category. These were items worn by the students to Mass on Sundays. Toys were kept for special occasions like birthdays and Christmas.

Kim told Mike she heard that finessing Ruth and Mary was an important skill. Through the campus grapevine, Kim learned that Ruth and Mary treated the donated items as if they were their own. Since they controlled what staff had access to, they often hid some of the better items, supposedly for a rainy day. They felt they had to do this because, in their opinion, the houseparents often took too many items.

The houseparents felt differently, expecting to see all the clothing items that were available for their students. Since everything was donated and secondhand, they believed clothing should be used as soon as possible and not rationed. Houseparents naturally saw it as important to get the best possible clothing for the kids in their home.

Developing a working relationship with the sewing ladies was part of the intangible skillset important to every houseparent. Yet, like many other parts of the houseparenting position, it was what Mike referred to as an 'unwritten rule.'

Sally had told Kim and Mike. "They don't mention it at orientation because it's just part of doing the job, but you better figure out how to work with the sewing ladies. That is, if you want your students to get the best items."

Since Kim was good at figuring out people, she was confident she'd be able to secure decent clothing items for the Pinger Home kids. On that first morning, Kim felt successful in her trip, acquiring clothing items the students needed. Future negotiating 'for the good stuff' will be a regular thing she thought.

"You have lots of good items here," Kim was quick to tell Ruth and Mary, before departing their area. "I'm sure I'll be back many times throughout the year. I look forward to seeing you often."

Kim returned to the home after she visited with the sewing ladies. She had a load of clothing items for those students who were missing things. She told Mike her foray into the donated items department was a success.

As Kim and Mike reflected on the last twenty-four hours, they both admitted to feeling worn out – partly because they slept so poorly. With no air conditioning in the home, it was hot. The bed in their room was as hard as a rock and uncomfortable. Plus they worried about students getting up and possibly running away, so this factored into their sleep deprivation.

Mike exhaustedly said to Kim, "It feels like we slept with one eye open last night. I hope this gets better."

"Me too," Kim agreed, also fatigued.

Kim and Mike spent the next hour straightening up the Pinger Home. Mike started laundry to wash the sheets for the two bed-wetters. Kim tackled the kitchen.

Mike and Kim headed home mid-morning. They used this time for relaxation and napping, returning to campus in the early afternoon. Kim ran to the store and grabbed food for dinner while Mike dried the laundry.

At 3:00 Mike went to the school, collected the students and then walked them home while Kim prepared dinner. After school, Vera and Sadie seemed happy. The other students appeared indifferent to the events of their first day of school. It seemed odd to Mike that while Kim was cheery and welcoming, the students were distant and uninterested.

After school activities consisted of a snack, spending time outside, television watching and dinner preparation. Just like in Mike and Kim's little white house, the home had two television channels, PBS and CBS. Occasionally the home could get the NBC station out of Pierre, but only on cloudy days. The kids enjoyed watching cartoons in the morning as well as after school. Nighttime TV was limited because there was an expectation of getting homework completed.

Mike went outside with some of the boys. While Cott, Kyle, Benny and Wayne played basketball, Mike threw the football around with Eli.

"You throw a good spiral," Mike said.

"Thanks," said Eli. "I like to play quarterback."

"To be good athletically takes a lot of hard work and discipline. Who knows, maybe you can play at Notre Dame someday," Mike replied.

Dinner consisted of roast beef, potatoes and carrots. Steve and Kyle, who had lived in the home the year before, chose to complain.

"These potatoes are mushy," said Kyle.

"Yeah," added Steve. "Scott and Barb always made the best meals for us."

"Okay guys, quit complaining," Mike said.

Mike was not sure how to take their criticism of Kim. Being new to the job, he chose to downplay the complaining this time since it was Pinger Home's first real meal. By his way of thinking, he could not understand why kids, some of whom had little to eat all summer long, would complain about any kind of food.

Kim took the comments in stride.

"Steve and Kyle, perhaps you could get the recipe from Scott or Barb." She said this knowing they had no way of getting in contact with either of them.

After dinner, the meal charges were completed and homework time began. However, on the first day of school there weren't any assignments. Kim used the time to check the heads of the six students who had lice. Of course, checking heads took time. Of the six with lice, two of the sisters and one of the boys still had visible live eggs.

Kim once again assumed the duty of combing out the students, although she was beginning to regret that she'd agreed to this. It was a tedious task that took a good hour to finish. She began to realize that the hope of one treatment, resulting in no more bugs, was an incorrect assumption.

In the meantime, Mike decided a table football game would be fun. The rules were simple. Players slid a three-sided paper football across the dining room table. If any point of the paper was over the edge of the table, the participant was credited with a touchdown. If it fell off, it was the other person's turn.

Scoring a touchdown allowed the chance for an extra point by way of a field goal. This was "kicked" with one's fingers. The kick was considered one point if the paper went through the makeshift goalpost the opponent made with his fingers.

Except for Steve, all of the boys participated. The four sisters weren't interested. Mike played too, devising a simple playoff system. Everyone was paired off. Undefeated teams were placed in the winner's bracket.

Many of the rounds were fun with most of the boys acting as good sports. Sweets had not played before so Mally tried to explain the game to him.

"Sweets, you slide the ball like this," Mally said demonstrating for him.

"I'm going to win," boasted Sweets as he slid the triangle super-fast and straight off the table.

The group played until only two players remained, Mike and Eli.

"I'm going to beat you," Mike chided employing the banter he used in most sporting competitions. Mike made other comments during the game like, "I'm going to be the champ."

As the two squared off Eli took an early lead, as he sported his usual smile. Then Mike had a last-minute comeback. Eli became flustered and angry. When Mike kicked the game-winning extra point, Eli stood up and threw the paper football at Mike. He then ran upstairs to his room.

"You suck," Eli said as he departed.

Mike didn't know how to react to Eli getting mad. Kim excused herself from head combing and went up to visit with him. After five minutes she returned. Eli came downstairs a bit later. He walked up to Mike and with his head down said, "I'm sorry."

Mike replied, "It's my fault, I was taunting you." He was grateful to Kim for resolving the situation.

Later that evening there were showers, snacks and prayer time followed by the students heading upstairs to bed. Mike again monitored the hallway for an hour. Some of the students were talking, a bit wound up from the day. As usual, it was also quite warm upstairs.

After a while, it quieted and Mike headed downstairs. He then went to the kitchen to get a drink. Filling a cup with water, he turned around and there stood Sweets.

"I'm going to watch TV," he said.

Mike was surprised to see him. Without saying a word, he quickly escorted Sweets back upstairs to bed.

When they got to Sweets and Mally's room, Mally reminded his room-mate throatily, "I told you. This isn't a hotel."

Mike took Mally's comment as one little victory. "At least somebody gets it," he mumbled as he left the room.

After some more monitoring of the hallway, Mike went back downstairs. When he got to the bottom of the stairs this time, he heard two voices. Sally from next door had come over to check on them.

Speaking to Kim, Mike heard Sally ask, "How did things go today?"

"Hey, Sally," Mike interjected, "another day is in the books."

Mike completed the log that night at the dining room table while he listened to Kim and Sally visit. His lengthy log entry ended with this thought:

Had a good day in Pinger. Hoping to get a better handle on running the home though.

CHAPTER ELEVEN

Twelve Personalities

THE FIRST SHIFT OF WORK started on Monday and ended six days later on Sunday morning. Each day flew by quickly as Kim and Mike tried to get their bearings. It was also a time in which the students were trying to adjust to living in the Pinger Home. Part of the process was trying to figure out Mike and Kim's expectations.

The grapevine was how news and gossip spread across campus. Mike and Kim heard of several deaths of family members of students from other homes. There was a suicide of a seventeen-year-old mother. Even without much detail, it sounded awful to Mike and Kim, who hadn't had a lot of real-life experience with suicide.

Then there was an accident that took place on a nearby reservation. It involved a fourteen-year-old who stole a car. He and two friends went joy-riding. They were intoxicated or high. The driver died in a rollover. The two friends in the back seat were ejected from the vehicle but survived.

Kim and Mike felt bad about these tragic deaths. It did not take long to realize many of the students experienced trauma regularly because of so many unexpected and heartbreaking losses among family and friends. These casualties happened to young and old alike.

To Mike, it felt like these tragedies were under-reported in the press. If he didn't hear about them on campus, he wouldn't hear about them anywhere else. The lack of published and televised information gave Mike the impression that Native American news mattered to a lesser extent, because other accidents in the state were covered regularly.

In terms of other campus news, Kim and Mike learned that two boys had killed a rattlesnake. Their home had been playing on the football field at the north end of campus. The houseparents were distracted by other things when it happened. The boys took the rattles off the snake and were caught showing them to other students the next day.

Hearing this led houseparents to worry that other students might try to kill rattlesnakes. The venom of a rattlesnake could be lethal. Word came down from the administration to talk to the students and tell them to stay away from any rattlesnakes.

"It sure seems like common sense to avoid rattlers. But with our recent experience, we'd better talk to the students. Plus I'll keep the car on idle," Mike suggested to Kim with a wink.

Getting to know students from other homes across campus, Kim and Mike observed the beautiful features all the students possessed. Olive-brown skin, sleek noses, dark brown eyes and deep black hair gave a distinct look to many of the students. As was Kim's nature, she often told the four Pinger Home girls they were beautiful.

Students had a certain way of speaking that was distinct to people living on the reservation. Their speech was accompanied by certain slang.

The student often would say "sheeze" in a slow rollout of the "ze". The term was generally used when the students were asked to do something they did not want to do or were not expecting. Mike would describe it as an "I can't believe this" response.

When Mike first heard the word "sheeze" he wanted to tell the students not to swear. He thought it sounded like they were about to say "shit," but the "t" was never actually articulated. After a while, Mike realized that "sheeze" was more of an expression than a swear word. Like any slang, it was sometimes used to joke around or to emphasize something important.

Another example was the way some of the students would question things. It didn't come in the form of "what?" It came as "huh?" or more of a guttural sound, sometimes sounding like "nuh?" Mike would recall Kim's conversations with the students sounding more like grunting than talking.

"Huh" could be part of a question or inquisitive gesture. Mike remembered hearing the students saying this, especially when Kim was giving them a hard time. They were usually trying to figure out if she was teasing them or telling the truth. He recalled Kim having a discussion with Kyle in the first week when he was trying to learn more about where Mike and Kim came from.

Kyle asked, "What did Mike do in Chicago?"

Kim responded, "He once played for the Chicago Bears."

"When? Really!" Kyle commented skeptically with a puzzled look on his face.

"Really. He got cut from the team so we decided to come to South Dakota to work with you," Kim added.

Kyle looked at her trying to figure out the truth. Finally he said, "Nuh-huh, that's not true. Sheeze."

In the meeting with the social worker that first week, Andie spoke of something she referred to as Thiyóšpaye. She said it was a Lakota term for extended family. It stressed the importance of family and belonging in the culture.

Andie said, "You want to allow the Pinger students to feel part of a thiyóšpaye, like members of an extended family. That should be a goal for everyone to feel like they belong."

In Andi's description of thiyóšpaye she noted, "The idea of a family unit entails a larger number of individuals than you might include. That is a reason why a student might refer to his or her first cousin as a brother, or why some of the students might say they have so many uncles."

Mike and Kim liked the concept of a thiyóšpaye and incorporated that thinking into how they wanted the students to view the Pinger home. At least they hoped that everyone would feel a sense of belonging and attachment.

One of Kim and Mike's goals on the first six-day shift was to set up a routine so the Pinger Home ran smoothly. The morning charges showed marginal improvement each day. Mike hoped that trend would continue. However, some of the students seemed content to do their charges slowly, even poorly.

Mike confided in Kim, "Some of the kids act like they never had to do charges before. That's fine except when it comes from the boys who lived in Pinger last year."

There was low-level disobedience that Mike understood as testing. Sometimes students pretended not to hear a request being made. They acted like bedtimes were too early or that they'd never had prayer time before. Kim handled this better than Mike. Both had learned in orientation that testing by the students, toward two people they'd only known for a short time, was natural and to be expected.

Mike was concerned about Steve and Sweets' bed-wetting. Being unfamiliar with the issue, he figured a quick talk with the boys would resolve the problem. Kim, who wet the bed growing up had a different perspective.

"Mike, it's important that we be sensitive," Kim said. "If we show some patience with the boys, it can help the problem, plus keep them from feeling embarrassed."

Later, Kim led a discussion with Steve and Sweets. "I'm not passing judgment. I also wet the bed growing up. So, let's try not to drink liquids after 7:00."

Sweets, embarrassed, said, "All right, I'll try," followed with a sigh.

Steve was a bit apprehensive but agreed. "Okay. It'll be hard, but I'll try."

That evening's snack was brownies. Some students had milk or water with their brownies. Of course, both Steve and Sweets forgot their pledge and got drinks.

"Guys, I thought we talked about this," Mike whispered, trying to be sensitive. "Remember, no drinks after seven o'clock."

Both boys then wet their beds the next two nights in a row. In the morning, they would get up, make their beds and head to school. Mike ended up stripping their beds after all the students left. He would wash and dry the bed linens during the day, making the students' beds before they arrived home from school.

The students' individual personalities were beginning to show. Although the four sisters still clung together, one could see how they began to establish themselves in various peer groups in different activities and other areas of the campus.

Mike noticed how the girls gravitated towards Kim when they wanted to visit. She had insights the girls seemed to like to hear. Plus, Kim knew fashion. She knew hair and she knew little tidbits that could help each girl look good and feel confident. The girls liked that.

Sage posed a question that first week that the girls would ask at different times throughout the whole year. She asked Kim, "How does this look?" as she showed off new jeans Kim had gotten from the sewing ladies.

Sage liked to hear Kim's perspective on a variety of things, especially her fashion tips. She was a cute girl who, by being the oldest, was the default leader of the sisters. She was more reserved than Kellie but had street smarts. Sage would listen intently to Kim on topics of interest to her.

Kim sometimes embarrassed Sage with her comments. "Sage, what's it like to be smart and beautiful?"

Kellie was not as mature physically as her older sister but had a tougher persona. She was not afraid to mix it up with the boys. She had an "I can hang with the boys and I'm proud of it" disposition. She was not afraid to clash with other students, verbally or physically, girl or boy. This was especially true if she thought they had wronged her or her sisters.

Kellie would tell Kim, "If those boys bother me, they'd better watch out. I'm not afraid of them."

"Boys like girls who take charge, so be careful. They're all going to be after you. But you have to curb the physical stuff and not resort to fighting," Kim said as Kellie nodded.

Vera and Sadie's relationship was interesting. They hung together but were different in looks so weren't recognized as twins usually are. Vera came off sweet and motherly. She had a warmth about her. She grew to be very comfortable with Kim, treating her as a mother figure.

"Kim, can I help you with anything?" was a question Vera often asked.

Sadie was the more immature of the two. She enjoyed this role. Sometimes her sisters challenged Sadie when she wanted them to do her bidding. More often though, they just took care of her without any acknowledgment of what they were doing.

The girls lived just off of a reservation, three hours away from Chamberlain. Mike and Kim didn't receive a lot of history about the girls but learned they lived with their mom in an impoverished situation. The girls would sometimes hint at running out of food while at home. Each of them spoke fondly of their mom who had problems with alcohol. Even with some difficulties in their upbringing, the girls were pleasant and respectful.

As far as the boys, Eli hit it off quickest with Mike. Since he'd been at the school for a few years, he knew the system and how to fit in. He liked sports, especially basketball, which was king on the reservation. His pleasant personality and persistent smile allowed him to get along with everyone. Over time, Eli would grow to be a Notre Dame fan as a result of Mike's enthusiasm for the university.

Mike enjoyed it when Eli would ask, "Who does Notre Dame play this week?"

At one point Mike told Eli, "I grew up a Notre Dame fan. I've been to a couple of games there."

"Was it fun?" Eli asked.

"Yeah, it's a cool place. You know, I should tell you how you can recognize a true Notre Dame fan. But it's a secret," Mike added.

"Let me in! I won't tell," Eli responded in a whisper.

"Real Notre Dame fans, when they talk about the team, always end the conversation with 'Go Irish,' no matter what. If a person doesn't say that, then they aren't really a fan," Mike said.

"Ok then. I won't tell anyone. Go Irish!" Eli said quietly with his usual smile.

Mally, Steve, Kyle and Wayne were not all brothers in the usual sense. They were either brothers or first cousins. In the "Indian way" they all considered themselves brothers and acted that way. Mike appreciated Andie alerting him and Kim to this understanding.

As individuals, the four boys did their own thing and had different interests. Because of this, they did not always come off as members of the same family unit. They could be supportive but tended to tease each other, sometimes to the point of being cruel. They had all been at St. Joe's since first grade.

Mally had a curiosity about many things and asked many questions, in his raspy voice. He liked animals and said he had a dog by the name of Bobo. Mally was agreeable and his kind-hearted patience allowed him to be a good roommate for Sweets.

Mike remembered one of the first things Mally asked him, "Why do you have so much hair on your arms and legs? Are you a wolf-man?"

Mike replied, "No, but my uncle was. That new movie *Teenwolf* is about him."

"Nuh-huh, sheeze!" Mally replied in his gruff voice, not sure what to believe.

Steve was treated like the baby of the group and acted like it. His siblings teased him mostly for his bed-wetting and tattling. He had low self-esteem and made excuses when he got into trouble.

Mike complained to Kim, "Steve's low self-esteem never gets in the way of his whining."

Kyle initially came off as rebellious due to his negative, questioning attitude. Over the first few weeks he expressed negative opinions about many things in the home. Early on, Kim saw through this and pegged him as a softie. Kyle was a bit pudgy and sensitive when his brothers would taunt him about his belly.

Kyle grumbled about the way Kim and Mike attempted to run the home. One of his early complaints was about the dinner menu. Kyle was quick to mention that the food was better in the past with other houseparents. He complained intentionally to get under Kim and Mike's skin and knew how to do this very well.

Kyle would critique Kim just to get her reaction. He would say things like, "You don't know how to cook very well." Or, "You and Mike have too many rules." Or, "Other houseparents are a lot nicer than you."

Wayne was quiet, reserved and unsure of himself. He didn't communicate well at all. Wayne had a wary smile and a bad complexion, due to acne. At one point, after several six-day shifts, Mike realized he had not had one conversation with Wayne.

Back in White River, the conditions these boys lived in were poor. It was a case of too many kids confined to a small trailer. From what Mike understood, the kids lived in one trailer, located in a row of run-down trailers. For fun, they played in a nearby burned-out building. The kids were mostly unsupervised while at home, with the older ones caring for the younger kids. Because their mothers and fathers were often gone, in jail or drinking, it fell to their Grandma Ancel to try to manage the chaos.

Benny was also from White River, so he knew the four brothers. He hung out with the boys in the summers. He would say odd things to get attention, trying to make staff think he was weird. It was his way to push people away and he worked hard to do that. Benny was quick to say he didn't want to be at the school.

Kim and Mike learned, not only from his aunt but from his social worker too, that Benny liked to huff substances such as spray paint and gasoline. He had done a lot of huffing over the last two summers. Benny had been at St. Joe's since third grade.

Mike was shocked when he overheard Benny tell other students, "Silver and black spray paint are my favorites."

Cott was from the small community of Cherry Creek. Mike appreciated his good sense of humor. He came off as confident but was socially awkward. Yet Mike and Kim agreed that his playfulness allowed him to connect with others.

Cott was what Mike described as a 'put-together.' He was concerned about his looks so he took extra time to make sure his hair was combed and clothing matched. Being tall for his age aided in him looking more mature. Deep down though, he was just a kid. This was his first year at the school, so over the initial weeks, he tried to use humor to make inroads with others.

"Kim," Cott would say often, "Let me tell you something funny that happened to me once." Or in response to something amusing, Cott would add, "You think that's funny, I got one for you."

Finally, there was Sweets. He was short, hefty and loud by nature. This caused him to come off as abrasive. He would shuffle along, usually breathing hard. He had been pampered by his grandma and had no filter when he wanted something.

Sweets' personality caused him to be teased. Because of his weight, the other kids often called him "fat boy" and mocked him about his name. He came from Pine Ridge.

One particularly interesting incident during the first week of school gave Kim an idea of what it was going to be like to work with Sweets. It was after school and he was outside playing basketball. He was not very coordinated partly because of his short, pudgy stature.

Kim happened to be looking out the home window as Sweets turned around while dribbling. Unexpectedly, his pants fell to his ankles. Underneath, Sweets was missing an essential piece of clothing, his underwear. There he stood fully exposed, yet he continued to dribble the basketball.

Mally, who was outside, yelled at Kim through the window, "Kim. Kim. You better get Sweets!"

Kim immediately went outside. "Sweet Grass, pull your pants up and come inside."

Sweets smiled, looked down and said, "Sorry Kim, guess I forgot something."

On Friday evenings, the students were allowed to pick out a movie to watch. *Footloose* was selected that week. It was the first of many times the home watched that film. It became a favorite. Mike would always remember the "ew, gross" coming from the students during the scene where the kid picks his nose. Everyone in the home would eventually know all the words to all the songs in the movie.

The school had an inventory of movies that could be shown in the homes. Mike recalled that many of these selections were of older movies and cartoons. They came on videodiscs that were inserted into an RCA disc player. These discs were the size of LPs and were never as popular as the videotapes of the day.

Mike remembered the RCA disc player not being very reliable. Frequently the disc would get stuck and freeze the picture on the TV screen. Mike was charged with getting the movie un-stuck, as he did not want students messing with the disc players.

Dealing with the videodisc was 'an art' that Mike learned over time. You had to be gentle when inserting the disc but sometimes the machine might need a harder tap to restart a frozen movie. Whether it was a hard or soft tap was where the "artistry" came into play. Having this skill was necessary if the home wanted to watch movies.

Sally stopped over regularly after the students were in bed. The stop-overs started as a time for Sally to support Kim and Mike. Eventually, they migrated to a time for Kim and Sally to visit and catch up on the gossip.

Kim and Mike worked their very first shift until Sunday morning when their relief staff, Gene and Andie came on. There was a quick changeover meeting, then the couple left for home. Mike could feel that he and Kim were exhausted.

Over the first six days, Mike's revelation about houseparenting was confirmed. He realized that although they slept overnight in the homes, they never quite slept soundly. The over-riding worry that students might need something or the possibility of runaways, exacerbated the couple's sleep deprivation.

Mike and Kim also had a personal worry. They wanted the Pinger Home to be viewed as running well under their direction. Working in a campus setting that sometimes felt more like a fishbowl, led them to want to prove their competence.

At changeover that morning, Mike recapped their first shift as houseparents. He thought it went ok, but did mention that the older boys were sometimes insubordinate. He suggested this added stress to the home. He also verbalized his feelings that their behavior was undermining attempts to have a positive and supportive home environment for the students.

"Perseverance Mike. Perseverance," was Gene's response. "More shifts to come."

On the drive to their white house in the country, Mike told Kim, "I'm glad we made it through our first shift. Overall, I think it went ok."

"And I'm glad we made it to our three days off," Kim said. "I'm tired."

Before leaving, Mike wrote the last entry in the log for that shift.

Quick week, but I think/hope we are getting the hang of this. The students have been okay, but there seems to be some undermining taking place.

CHAPTER TWELVE

No Water

AROUND MIDDAY, ON THEIR DAY off, Mike went out to rent movies at the local convenience store in Chamberlain. During previous visits there, Mike was amazed by what you could get at the store. There was the gas of course, plus movies, food, alcohol and cigarettes. There were also fishing and hunting items including guns and ammo kept on a sidewall.

Mike told Kim, "Just add gambling and you'll be able to find every vice in one stop."

Mike picked up a couple of movies and snacks before heading home. Once home, Kim mentioned that the water was not working. She thought the pump was running.

Mike went outside and checked the cistern. He pulled the lid open only to find the tank empty. Kneeling down and using a flashlight, he noticed two small holes in the bottom of the cistern.

"Damn," he yelled to Kim. "The cistern has holes in it."

Mike then realized the water pump was running and he needed to turn it off. He went into the house, lifted the flooring and shimmied down the old ladder onto a dirt floor crawl space. As he bent down to turn off the pump, he noticed two eyes glaring at him. He nearly leaped out of the hole.

Mike quickly composed himself, turned off the pump and quietly said, "Kim, Kim come here!"

Of course, Kim didn't hear him so he slowly climbed up the ladder. Once on the main floor, he sprinted and got her.

"There's a varmint in the basement," he said. "I hope it's not a skunk."

Kim screamed, "What?"

Together, walking quietly, they went over to the hole in the floor. They knelt down and slowly peered over the edge. "I don't see anything," Kim said, punching Mike in the arm.

"Just wait here," Mike said as he went and got a flashlight.

After grabbing a flashlight, he and Kim again peered over the edge of the open flooring. As Mike moved the light around, it suddenly came upon two eyes. Kim screamed and Mike nearly dropped the flashlight.

Regaining his composure, Mike worked the flashlight to the point where he had a better angle. There in the corner was a rabbit. It appeared docile and was breathing but not moving.

"Whew!" Mike said. "Thank God it's not a skunk!"

Without water, Mike and Kim went down to the school that evening and showered in the pool's locker room in Rec Center. They also filled a couple of milk jugs with drinking water.

Later that night Kim and Mike sat outside in the quiet, rural landscape. The night's sunset was again breathtaking. There were assorted reds, blues and even some brown covering the horizon. In the center, a dark reddish orange sun slowly descended. Although they had reason to complain about things like no running water, the peace at that moment dominated all other thoughts and emotions.

The following morning, Mike called Maximus about the water situation. He came over shortly thereafter. When he arrived, Maximus took a flashlight and looked at the bottom of the tank. From top to bottom it was about eight feet down. He then pointed to the small holes that needed patching.

Maximus suggested, "How about we climb in and fix the holes?"

Mike thought that would be great until he eventually figured out Maximus was kidding.

Knowing it was his water tank to fix, Mike asked, "Is this even fixable and if so, what do I do?"

Maximus said gruffly, "No. It can't be fixed." Then he laughed wheezing a bit. "Yes, it can be fixed. It just needs to be sealed."

After getting instructions from Maximus, Mike went to town and bought sealant. Arriving home, he asked Kim to assist as he proceeded to climb into the cistern. Since the opening at the top of the tank top wasn't very wide, Mike realized he could only fit through by extending his arms over his head.

So to get into the cistern, Mike first sat down and put his legs into the opening. Next, he turned onto his stomach. From there he shimmied down up to his armpits, eventually dropping down to the floor. As he lowered himself in, he held his arms straight up so he'd fit in the opening.

Once in, Mike yelled to Kim, "Just stand by the tank. That way you can grab anything I might need."

Mike's first task was drying the floor with a towel. Next, Kim handed him down the sealant. He promptly opened it and began brushing it on the floor. However, it was an epoxy sealer. As Mike worked at the bottom of the tank, the fumes began to get bad.

He called up to Kim, "Hey, I better get out of here."

Mike then realized he had not thought through getting out of the tank. With the narrow opening, it was impossible to climb out without assistance. Plus, the distance he had to drop down was farther than he thought.

"Ah, Kim," Mike said, "we have a problem here."

Kim, recognizing the dicey situation, quickly reacted. She ran into the house where she found a small footstool. She grabbed it and ran back outside.

Mike yelled up from his confined space, "Hurry up Kim, the fumes are getting worse."

"Use this," Kim said as she handed him the stool.

Mike quickly placed the twelve-inch footstool at the bottom of the cistern and stood on it. Next, he reached his arms straight up. Kim then grabbed his hands and attempted to yank him to safety.

After much flailing, Kim was able to pull Mike up just high enough. He then shimmied himself to a point where his head was out of the tank. With his armpits straddling the hole in the tank, Kim tugged on Mike's shirt, then his belt. Mike finally got all the way out of the tank. As he did, he and Kim fell to the ground laughing.

"We're so dumb!" Mike said.

"You're awfully lucky that I'm becoming a strong South Dakota woman," Kim said as she caught her breath.

At that moment, Maximus drove up. He saw Kim and Mike laying on the ground.

"How's it going?" he asked with a smirk on his face.

Now embarrassed, Kim and Mike stood up.

"Just patching the holes," Mike replied trying to act as normal as possible.

Maximus helped Mike fetch the stool out of the cistern. Mike noticed Maximus had a puzzled look but was glad he did not ask why it was in there.

Maximus then said. "You could've used a sealant other than epoxy. And I should have suggested you use an extension on the brush. Save you from having to climb in there. Anyway, I'll bring you water tomorrow."

"Good to know," Mike muttered embarrassed.

With no running water, Kim and Mike went to visit Jesse and Jeannie that evening. They too were on their days off, relaxing in their trailer. The talk immediately turned to the St. Joe's students.

Jeannie asked, "How were your six days in the Pinger Home?"

Kim said, "I think it went pretty well."

Mike was more honest. "There seems to be underlying tension and continual undermining, especially coming from the boys. I wonder if we're doing things wrong?"

"You're being tested," Jesse told them. "The Native population has been treated unfairly since the continent was settled. Look at the reservations. People come in with promises of land, jobs and programs, but then it gets tough and they leave or take things. The U.S. government has done this forever; made promises and then reneged. Our kids are part of this cycle."

"You can add to that poverty and the breakdown of the family," Jesse continued. "Look how many of your kids don't have both or either parent living with them. Why should they trust you – two white people?"

Mike remembered the passion and conviction in Jesse's voice. He wondered if his being an Irishman somehow influenced his perspective in terms of the government's treatment of Native Americans.

The next day, their third day off, went by quickly. Maximus had delivered water, so they finally had running water once more. Of course, it smelled like epoxy for a while.

"Now, at least we can shower," Mike told Kim. "Let's hope the smell goes away."

That night they watched the television series *Wings*. This was becoming a favorite on their days off. It came on daily at 10:30 on the CBS station. They also began to think about their second shift that would begin tomorrow.

CHAPTER THIRTEEN

Testing Period

WHEN MIKE AND KIM RETURNED to Pinger after their days off, Sally came over to see them. She arrived before the students returned home from school with a serious look on her face.

"We're tracking down a rumor that maybe some of your students were out on the railroad bridge," Sally told them. "That's the bridge south of the interstate. You can walk to it from the rest area. I know you went to the rest area during your last shift. Though I wasn't sure why?"

Mike swallowed hard. "Yes, we went up with the kids," he said looking toward Kim.

"It sounds like a student overheard Steve and Kyle bickering and Steve said he was going to tell about the railroad bridge. The student who overheard told other students and then finally a teacher in the school heard about it," Sally said.

"You can walk to the railroad bridge from the rest area?" Kim asked as she questioned whether this was possible. "We didn't know that."

"Kyle and Steve weren't very forthcoming when the principal spoke to them. I'm going to visit with the whole home when they get back from school today. I called Gene and he'll be here. I'm going to get to the bottom of this," Sally said assuredly.

After Sally left Mike pondered what this meant. "If true, I'm sure we're in big trouble. I do recall the boys were gone for a while but no way they had time to go to that bridge."

Mike walked the students back after school but didn't say anything about the bridge incident. As everyone entered the home at the back door, there was the normal bustle as students took care of school bags and transitioned to being in the home. As everyone came in Kim instructed them to put their things away so we could have a quick home meeting. There were a few "why" questions but everyone complied.

Sally arrived a short time later and asked all of the students to sit around the dining room table. She announced, "There's a rumor that some of you were on the railroad tracks, on the bridge, the night the home went to the rest area. Anybody know anything about that?"

The room was quiet as the students looked at Sally, one another, and then at Kim and Mike. Mike noticed Benny had a smirk on his face.

Then Sally said seriously, "Okay, so no one was on the bridge. Now, I want everyone to put your head down on your arms on the table. I don't want anyone peaking."

Mike and Kim looked on as all twelve Pinger Home students put their heads down on their arms. The room was quiet.

"I'm asking you to rethink your answers and would like to know if any of you were on the bridge the other night. Raise your hand if you were. I need you to be honest and tell the truth."

Sweets' hand shot up immediately. Mike rolled his eyes knowing that he was with Sweets the whole time.

Mike was initially relieved thinking it was a good sign that no one except Sweets had raised their hand. His thinking was short-lived as he quickly realized he was trying to make himself feel better. As he thought about it, his instincts told him there was more to the story.

As the silence persisted, Mike was intrigued by Sally's next question.

"Okay, I appreciate the two of you being honest. Who else was on the bridge?" Sally asked.

Thinking that others had confessed, Kyle, Mally and Steve now raised their hands.

"Anyone else?" Sally asked as Benny and Wayne now verified their involvement.

"You can all sit up now and lift your heads. Those who did not raise their hands can leave the table," Sally said.

Mike sighed as he looked at Kim.

Telling Sweet he was dismissed, Sally and Mike met with the five other boys individually over the next hour. This took place in the home's office.

In each meeting, the boys were asked what happened. Mike noticed that every boy, at first, dropped his head and looked at the floor when questioned. He wondered why Sally did not tell the boys to sit up straight, look her in the eye, act respectfully and pay attention. But he was smart enough not to ask.

Wayne sat through his session and said little, other than "yes" or "no." He admitted right away that he was on the bridge. He was clearly very nervous and uncomfortable. Mike noticed his hands shaking and felt sorry for him.

Benny was up next. After lowering his head at first, his lackluster attitude then came out. He acted like he didn't care.

"I did it," Benny confessed right away. "Are you going to kick me out?"

Mike honestly thought Benny's admission was done in the hope of being sent home.

"No Benny, you're not being kicked out. But this is serious," Sally said.

Kyle was questioned next by Sally and Mike. He initially tried to act tough but within a minute, dropped his head and quickly confessed.

As the discussion ended, Kyle sighed and said, "I'm sorry, we should have known better."

Steve whined as he made excuses and blamed everyone else. "I told them not to go but they made me go anyway. Kyle said if I told anyone, they'd blame the whole thing on me."

Mally didn't seem nervous and quickly admitted they were on the bridge. He added, "Sheeze, that bridge was high and you could see a long way. It was kind of cool. Maybe we could go there again sometime. Nah?"

With Mally's comments, Sally looked at Mike and tried to maintain her composure.

After sorting it out, Mike and Sally determined what had happened. Beyond the rest area, the railroad tracks sit below the tree line and run a few hundred yards to the point where the railroad bridge starts. The old bridge platform, sitting 80 feet above the water, spans the river for over a mile.

Leaving the rest area, Wayne, Kyle, Benny, Steve and Mally walked toward the trees and noticed railroad tracks. The boys decided to walk down to the tracks. This decision led them onto the bridge where they began throwing rocks and other debris into the river.

At one point Benny challenged Kyle to walk near the side of the bridge. When Kyle got close to the edge, he tripped on an untied shoelace. Wayne ran over and grabbed Kyle as both boys nearly toppled off the side together. Somehow, they stayed on the tracks. Benny, Mally and Steve then hustled towards the boys to assist, pulling them to safety.

At some point, the boys heard Mike calling and walked back to solid ground where the rest of the group was. They knew they were late getting back and were surprised no one asked them more questions. The boys swore never to tell their new houseparents, knowing they'd get into trouble. Kyle also threatened Steve, fearing he might be the first to confess.

After the individual meetings, Mike, Kim, Gene and Sally met quickly in the corner of the living room, away from the students.

"You'll have to give the boys early bed and some kind of restriction," Sally said. "But I'm worried about the supervision and why you went to the rest area in the first place."

Gene then stopped Sally and said, "It was my idea for them to take the students up there. I shouldn't have suggested it, or at least have gone with them."

Sally was immediately angry with Gene. "It wasn't a very good idea to send out brand new staff, with the students, on the first day. What were you thinking?"

Gene seemed put out by her question. "Things were going fine that day and I thought it would be a nice break. Besides, it turned out to be a good learning experience for everyone."

Sally and Gene argued quietly, back and forth for a few minutes. Then Sally abruptly left. She was angry.

"I'm going back to my home," Sally said leaving out the front door.

Gene then turned to Kim and Mike, "Don't worry about it. It's my fault. Just remember, you need to make sure you know where everyone is at all times."

Although Sally never brought up the incident again, Mike and Kim had learned a valuable lesson. The incident reinforced the importance of good supervision, as well as providing insights into their young charges.

Two days later, fish was on the menu for dinner. As everyone sat around the dining table and food was passed, all of the students avoided taking the fish. At the same time, they ate the other food that was served and drank their milk.

Then came a comment from Kyle. "Why did you cook this? It smells funny. I've never had this before."

Benny threw out another hurtful comment, "Gene and Andie are both better cooks than you. They know how to make fry bread and everything."

Kyle added, "Yeah Kim, I wish you could cook better. At least Gene and Andie know what we like."

Benny chimed in again. "You're houseparents. You're supposed to make what we like, not what you like."

Kim was not happy and showed her displeasure by saying to Kyle and Benny. "Guess who's cooking dinner tomorrow?"

Kyle responded, "That's fine, we'll just make hotdogs."

Kim retorted, "Sorry, but you have to follow the set menu and the menu says tater-tot casserole for dinner."

Kyle was now muttering under his breath. Many of the students had their heads down as well. It became very quiet at the dinner table.

If Kim and Mike had had more experience, they would have recognized that the honeymoon, if indeed there had ever been one, was officially over.

There was a rule that if you didn't eat your dinner, you didn't get a snack. This rule added to the dissent later in the evening. With no snacks, the students complained they were hungry.

Steve whined, "We're being starved. We have a right to have something to eat."

Mike tried to be patient and not overreact. Finally in his frustration, he yelled at Steve. Mike told the other students they should have known better when they chose not to eat their dinner. This led to a round of under-the-breath comments from the group.

The next day, Kyle and Benny attempted to cook dinner. Kim planned to sit back and provide little assistance. She watched as they came into the home after school and went into the kitchen. As she had assumed, they had no clue where to even start.

In the end, Kim helped Kyle and Benny prepare the meal. As it was served, Kyle and Benny seemed very nervous. Mike figured they were worried about what their peers might say. But with help from Kim, everything turned out fine. Luckily for Kyle and Benny, their peers said nothing unfavorable about the meal.

Around campus, there was more gossip coming through the grapevine. An eighth-grader snuck out in the middle of the night and borrowed that home's vehicle. Earlier in the evening the child had been disciplined. Unhappy with the situation, she drove herself home – 100 miles away.

The houseparents on duty didn't realize the student was gone. Just before waking the other children up in the morning, they got a call from the student's grandma. She wanted the houseparents to know the girl was at home sleeping.

The two houseparents on duty were embarrassed. It was unfortunate that the thirteen-year-old was able to get into the key room, and disconcerting that the room just happened to be located next to where the houseparents slept. The fact that they were unaware the student was missing was even more humiliating. This led to an ongoing discussion among the houseparent staff across campus about supervision.

"Would we know if a student had run away in the middle of the night?" Mike wondered, asking Kim. "We obviously didn't know our boys were on the railroad bridge."

Throughout the six-day shift, the defiance continued. This led to a home environment that was unpleasant, moving toward toxic. Each night between showers, snacks, home prayer and bedtime, it seemed as if a different student or students would act out. It usually involved questioning Kim and Mike's authority or challenging the routine. This caused the need for more discipline, which then led to more disobedience.

Mike and Kim planned to ignore most of the acting out. It was not easy though. For example, Mike would ask Kyle to complete a particular task and he'd do it at the slowest pace possible. This type of disrespect annoyed Mike. There was also some back talk, most of it coming from the boys. Another irritant to both Kim and Mike was the students muttering under their breath, about something they didn't like.

Some of the boys continued to insinuate that other staff would do a better job as their houseparents. They would tell Kim and Mike that Scott and Barb were the best. One day, even Cott and Sweets talked about Scott and Barb in this way.

Mike reminded them, "I know they were great, but you didn't go to school here last year."

Since the students mentioned Scott and Barb so many times, Mike was curious about them.

Mike asked Sally, "The kids talk positively about Scott and Barb. What was it like for them last year?"

Sally answered, "It wasn't that smooth. They ended up leaving a month before the school year ended. They said it was because of family issues and planned to return this year. It was rocky though. Other houseparents guessed that the students ran them off. I honestly thought they would return as we had contact with them throughout the summer, which is why they were initially listed to work in the Pinger Home."

"Interesting," Mike said. "By the way Kyle talked about them, I wondered..."

Kim was better than Mike at dealing with student testing. Mike saw it as disrespectful and began to confront the students suggesting they show more respect. Mike's experience with discipline while growing up was to be yelled at. Sometimes, out of frustration, he took this approach with the students. He found out quickly that raising his voice did not work.

Mike noticed early on that the students would drop their heads and eyes when they were in trouble. This was different than the "look at me when I'm speaking to you" type of discipline that was part of his upbringing. He asked Andie about it at a changeover meeting.

Andie explained, "The students drop their heads and eyes as a sign of respect. It's part of our culture. As far as the Pinger students, they may not have respect for you personally right now but they respect authority. You have to build that trust before they will show you respect."

Mike felt like he was punishing students all the time and this was negatively impacting his attempt to develop relationships. Kim's relationship with the students was better, partly because of her quick wit. However, she too was frustrated at times. For several six-day shifts, the question of who was in charge, the student or the houseparent, influenced the home environment.

Mike and Kim resorted to the consequence of early bed often during their first few shifts. Overuse caused it to be less effective over time. Those who had early bed would just go up to their rooms and play around. This caused Mike the added hassle of constantly having to run upstairs to patrol the hallway.

When he was not upstairs supervising, the students would run between rooms and hide. Then they would try to get back into their room before Mike would catch them. Mike told Kim it was like a game of cat and mouse.

Kim and Mike tried to be consistent with discipline and expectations. This sometimes seemed to add to the student rebellion. When confronted the students often responded with "Sheeze, you're mean people," or "We wish you didn't work here."

First Mike, then Kim, began to feel like they were losing the battle. Each night when Sally would come over and visit, she let them vent. She tried to give them tips on the best way to work with the kids. Mostly though, she listened. Sally believed that perseverance would "win the day."

She told them, "In my experience, students test new staff under the guise of defiance and disrespect. If you hang in there and come to work each day, the students will eventually trust you. Might even grow to love you."

She continued, "It's not easy. There's no way to speed up the process of building trust. Securing positive relationships takes time."

Mike and Kim did not see Jesse and Jeannie as much as they had before the students' arrival on campus. The houseparent routine kept everyone busy. When they did see each other for any length of time, Mike sometimes left with what he called an inferiority complex.

Mike always got the impression that Jesse and Jeannie were in control of their home and the work was easy. Having structure while enjoying the students just seemed natural to them, yet difficult for him and Kim. Mike was especially appreciative that Jesse and Jeannie were able to listen, more than give advice.

It was the same with Gene and Andie, who were also supportive. They were well aware that there were no shortcuts to gaining the students' trust. They also knew some new people made it and others didn't. They hoped Kim and Mike could persevere.

Mike felt a little better when they had developed a new plan for the bed-wetters. He planned to wake the two boys up in the middle of the night to use the bathroom. Mike would set the alarm when he and Kim went to bed at midnight. Then he would wake the boys up at 2:30.

Mike was appreciative that Steve and Sweets were now taking more ownership and doing their laundry. Mike still had to check the beds each morning because the boys occasionally found it easier to make their beds when they were wet. Mike better understood that when this happened, it was mainly to avoid embarrassment. Now, if Mike did find wet sheets and discretely pointed it out to the boys, they were quick to take care of it.

There was one other incident that took place during those first shifts and Mike would remember that it brought Kim to tears. It was on a Friday morning and happened after he took the students to school. Kim noticed her scalp was itchy, then she found a bug.

This young woman who prided herself in her beautiful, long blonde hair had discovered that she had lice. Once Kim recognized she had a bug, she screamed and ran over to see Sally next door. Mike followed her.

"Sally, Sally, please check my head. Please, oh please don't let there be live bugs in my hair." Kim pleaded aloud.

Sally sat Kim down, checked her head and said, "Sorry to tell you this, but you have lice."

Kim began to cry. "Will I have to shave my head?"

"No," Sally said sympathetically. "We'll get this figured out."

Sally cleared her schedule. Painstakingly over several hours, she combed the nits out of Kim's thick blonde hair. It took a couple of days, but Kim won "the battle of the bugs!"

Mike recalled a changeover meeting that took place after a particularly challenging six-day period. Returning from taking the students to school, Mike and Kim met with Gene and Andie. Over that shift, Gene had come in a few times to assist.

Gene said, "Tough shift, huh?" It was a question, but he also knew the answer.

Mike and Kim had no reply. Once the meeting ended, they grabbed their stuff and left. Mike remembered feeling exhausted. He wondered aloud to Kim, "Did we make a mistake coming to South Dakota?"

The closing entry in the home log the night before said it all.

"The kids were generally defiant and disrespectful. We had six students with early bed tonight. The students do not like us right now. Very difficult shift!"

CHAPTER FOURTEEN
Hide and Seek

As Mike and Kim headed home Mike realized he wasn't sure what day it was. He had come to understand that working for six days then being off for three did not sync up with the rest of the world. He noted that on a few mornings he and Kim would wake up in the Pinger Home trying to figure out what day it was.

Mike felt that being out of sync with the days of the week added to a sense of isolation from life outside the school. On that first day off, Kim and Mike tried to reset their internal clocks to a seven-day "real-world" schedule. This was not as simple as it sounded because their days off always began on a different day of the week.

Kim and Mike were exhausted. They took it easy on that first day off, napping in the afternoon. That night Nellie the nurse called Kim. She was going to Sioux Falls shopping the next day. She wondered if Kim wanted to tag along.

Nellie worked in the school's infirmary. She was one of those people who loved the spotlight. Nellie was quick with a joke and could easily take her antics to an adult-rated theme. She and Kim had befriended one another, hitting it off quickly.

Mike would tell others. "Kim and Nellie are two outgoing personalities who tell bad jokes. Worse yet, they feed off one another. It's like they are members of each other's fan club."

That next morning Kim and Nellie headed to Sioux Falls. Along the way, they stopped in Mitchell for coffee. As they left town Kim began to have stomach cramps. Something was not agreeing with her.

Believing she could make it to Sioux Falls and not knowing Nellie all that well, Kim held tight. Finally, twenty miles outside of Sioux Falls, Kim couldn't take it anymore.

She begged Nellie, "I'm not going to make it. I have to find a bathroom!"

"Really?" Nellie asked, seeing Kim looking rather uncomfortable

Nellie was puzzled since Kim had not said anything previously. Once she assessed the situation, her nurse's training kicked in. Nellie spotted the next exit and drove onto the off-ramp at a high rate of speed, tires squealing. One mile down the road she found a convenience store.

Nellie wasted no time. She drove into the parking lot towards the store, stopping right on the sidewalk. The car was now right up beside the restroom door. As Kim tried to get out of the car, she realized Nellie had pulled up so close that she could not fully open the car door. Nellie quickly reversed, nearly hitting a parked car. She then re-parked the car, giving Kim more room to exit.

Kim ran in, did her business and then got back into the car. Neither Nellie nor Kim spoke of the incident the rest of the day.

Kim told Mike the story later. "Nellie's driving sure saved the day." She said. "Now, our friendship is officially sealed in deep doo-doo."

After Kim's trip to Sioux Falls and the sealing of her new friendship, the rest of their time-off was uneventful. Kim and Mike watched more of their favorite TV show *Wings*. Mike enjoyed it but wondered if he was losing his mind because he liked such a simple-minded program.

Dread had also crept into their lives. That dread was knowing they had to go back to work in the Pinger Home. The oft-repeated question, "Are we in over our heads?" crept into Mike's thoughts as the next shift came closer.

Mike sensed that Kim was also feeling anxious. They both tried hard to keep their work concerns out of conversations, especially on their days off. Past practice for their marriage was that "quiet avoidance" was much better than "stated worry."

In mid-September, they were back at work on a Friday afternoon. The upcoming weekend was the school's annual Wačhípi or Powwow. Kim and Mike had heard different things about the event. They were told it was a time of celebration and the kids' dancing was fun to watch. They were also warned that supervision could be difficult, and it was a long day.

Students' families were invited to the event, which presented the opportunity for students to see their loved ones. Mike and Kim were alerted to the fact that sometimes parents would tell the students they were coming but failed to show up. This could be tough on the child. Even with these concerns, Kim and Mike were looking forward to their first Wačhípi.

Back to work, Mike and Kim met the kids as they arrived home from school. Sally had walked both her students and the Pinger children home that day. The students' welcome was slightly friendlier than it had been on the first day back on other shifts. Kim asked who was planning to dance the next day. Only two of the students, Mally and Sweets, said they were dancing.

Because the girls indicated they were not going to participate, Mike figured that they hadn't been exposed to the traditional dancing that took place at a powwow. The older boys were also not interested, partly because it was not perceived to be cool. Of the two that were dancing, Mally borrowed regalia from the Native American Studies teacher at the school. Sweet Grass's grandma was planning to bring his regalia on Saturday.

On that Friday night, there was an air of excitement around campus. Mike and Kim decided they needed to redirect some of the excess energy. Kim devised a game of indoor hide-and-seek.

In setting up the game Kim told the students, "You can hide anywhere in the home. The lights will be turned off and the blinds closed. The person who is 'it' will have a flashlight. If you're 'it' your job is to find those who are hiding."

As the house lights were turned off the energy level in the home rose. The game started. Mike was "it" first.

The students spread out all over the house and found great hiding places. They hid in dryers, under the lowest shelves in the pantry and in other clever places.

Mike finished his count and went looking, but could only find a few of the students. At one point, he found Mally when he accidentally tripped over him. He had neatly tucked himself under a sofa and happened to have one foot hanging out.

After a couple of rounds with different students being "it," there were laughter and smiles all around. The evening ended with the home watching *Footloose* once again and eating ice cream. It was the first night where everyone had fun, followed the rules and got to bed on time.

Kim wrote in the log that night.

We actually had a nice night tonight.

CHAPTER FIFTEEN

Let's Powwow

THE WAČHÍPI WAS SET TO begin at noon on the football field, on campus. Earlier that morning the students waited in anticipation. Eli, Cott and Sweets had family planning to check them out. This meant that these students would attend but under the supervision of a parent or guardian.

Eli and Sweets' families came and checked them out in the morning before the powwow began. Cott's aunt did not show up, so he walked with Kim, Mike and the rest of the Pinger Home students over to the grounds, before noon.

The football field, located on the north edge of the campus was designated as the official powwow grounds. A large crowd was in attendance including the students, student families, staff and a few benefactors of the school.

As is tradition, the grounds were set up in a circle with drum groups sitting at different points around the circular dance area. Bystanders and guests sat further out outside the perimeter in chairs and bleachers.

Drum groups consisted of Native American singers sitting in a circle around a drum. Of the four groups in attendance, Mike noticed that each group had a different number of singers. All the members of the group sang as they rhythmically beat on the instrument with an Ičábu (drumsticks), singing in Lakȟóta. The beat of the drum was loud and could be heard across the entire campus, throughout the day.

Pinger Home sat together on the side of the powwow ground, in an area that overlooked not only the grounds but the river. From that vantage point, Mike could see the bluish-gray water. On this day, its waves were dancing with the help of the ever-present South Dakota wind.

The powwow started with the Grand Entry just after noon. An eagle staff was carried onto the grounds by the staff bearer. The eagle staff is a sacred item made of a long wooden pole that usually has a crook on top. This staff had eagle feathers attached to it. Wearing regalia, the staff bearer danced to the beat of the drum, leading the honor guard and the other dancers.

The United States flag was carried into the arena behind the eagle staff by a Native American military veteran. Individual tribal flags were carried in next. The dancers, in brightly colored regalia, followed in line. The drummers set the beat with their songs. Participants circled the arena, dancing traditional steps as the drumming continued. Finally, the drumming and singing ended. Everything stopped, as a prayer was offered in both Lakota and English.

After the prayer and a few introductions, the Grand Entry concluded as the dancers left the arena. The flags were set in a place of prominence at the head of the circle. Then the powwow started in earnest, led by the voice of the announcer.

Throughout the day, there were individual competitive dances. Students wore different types of regalia based on their specific dance category. Mike heard titles like fancy, traditional and grass dancing. All the competitive groupings were separated by gender.

There were other events in which all the participants danced at the same time. The announcer referred to these as intertribal dances, the round dance, or the potato dance. These were not competitive. From what Mike could tell, these events were more social in nature.

During the Wačhípi, the announcer worked the microphone, organizing various categories of dancers. He let the dancers and drum groups know when certain segments were coming up. Mike appreciated the arena announcer's great sense of humor, as he told many jokes and stories, filling time as dancers entered and exited the arena.

Mike was curious about the powwow and dances so he asked a few students what was going on. He was surprised and disappointed to find out that most of the Pinger Home students had little knowledge of the dances. He was further disheartened that the students had more interest in playing on the playground and socializing, than in watching and participating in the actual event.

Mike recalled elements of the day being near perfect. The South Dakota sky was deep blue dotted with white billowy clouds and for a change, the temperature was pleasant. Additional sights and sounds such as the movement of the dancers in their bright regalia, a light wind out of the west, the beat of the drums, with the backdrop of the Missouri River, etched a beautiful memory into his mind.

"Wow, this is almost surreal," Mike told Kim. "What a great way to celebrate past traditions in the modern day."

During one of the competitions, a dancer accidentally dropped an eagle feather to the ground. Everything stopped abruptly. The powwow grounds grew quiet and an undeniable reverence took over. An elder approached the feather and prayed over it before picking it up.

Mike asked Wayne what was going on and he declared, "It's an eagle feather!" without further explanation.

Mike would later find out that an eagle feather is sacred and the Native American people show respect any time one of these feathers touches the ground. Although he was unaware of the tradition, Mike appreciated the reverence of that moment.

Mally danced many times throughout the day. He had simple regalia consisting of a long-sleeved dark blue shirt. Light and dark blue ribbons and yarn were attached in a circular pattern around the front and the back of the shirt. He also wore a do-rag on his head, shorts with a breechcloth and gym shoes which he wore in place of moccasins. As he danced, he spun in a large circular pattern, moving clockwise around the arena.

Kim told Mally after watching him dance, "You look great when you're out there dancing. You were working hard to maintain the beat."

"I don't know why, but when I dance it makes me a proud Lakȟóta," Mally said in reply. "I feel good. Like I'm a million miles away."

Sweet Grass had regalia for a traditional dancer that included feathers with a headband, a red ribbon shirt, breastplate, shorts and moccasins. Sweets danced a few times in the afternoon. However, as the day wore on, he got tired and seemed uninterested in finishing the competitive dancing.

Sweets was with his grandma who, as expected, doted on him. She worried that he might overexert himself. Sweets and his grandma sat close enough to the Pinger Home that Mike could see the attention. Although excessive, he was happy that Sweets had his grandma there to watch him dance.

"Grandma, I'm tired of dancing," Mike overheard Sweets say, as sweat poured down his nose.

"Come sit in the shade," his grandma replied patting the ground beside her. "I'll get you something to drink."

Over the course of the day, some of the students got into trouble. Mike caught Wayne sharing a stash of chewing tobacco, referred to as 'chew,' with some boys Mike didn't recognize. This took place near the playground while Mike walked around doing supervision. All the boys had chew in their mouths, which was a school violation.

"Wayne, you have to stick with me the rest of the day," Mike said.

"Ugh," Wayne grunted dejectedly. "Why me?"

The first session of dancing ended around 5:00. All the students and staff went over to Our Lady of the Sioux Chapel for Mass. Following Mass, there was a feed consisting of buffalo stew, fry bread and a cookie for dessert. The Pinger Home ate together and then went out to the second session of the powwow.

As dusk set in, Kim caught Sage making out with a boy from another home. She and the boy were back behind the parked cars. When Kim found the two students she made them separate, sending the boy back to his houseparents.

"Sage," Kim said, "you have to stay with me for the rest of the powwow. I'm disappointed in your behavior."

Sage had tears in her eyes. "I'm sorry," she said woefully.

Kyle was defiant all day. Told to report in every hour, he chose not to. Mike was able to spot him often enough that supervision was not a real problem. Kyle then grumbled when told it was time to go to Mass. Later, he could not understand why the home had to sit together during the meal. His attitude and complaints challenged Mike and Kim to the point where Mike was losing patience.

"Kyle," Mike said while watching the second session. "I'm tired of your complaining. Is there anything that makes you happy?"

"If you quit telling me what to do, then I'd be happy," Kyle responded with a scowl on his face.

Cott had a difficult day also. His aunt never arrived so he spent most of the time with Kim. His hurt was apparent, but he tried to tough it out. One did not have to be a child psychologist to understand that Cott felt let down. Mike respected how he tried to mask it with his self-derogatory humor.

"Kim, you're the lucky one. You got to spend time with me today. Lots of people wish they could," Mike heard Cott tell Kim.

"It made my day for sure," Kim reassured Cott with a smile.

The Pinger Home left the powwow after 9:00 p.m. as most of the other homes had already departed. It was now dark and had become chilly as the South Dakota sun had set. The powwow was now taking place under the football field lights.

When everyone arrived back at the Pinger Home, Mike and Kim said the students could stay up a while longer. Everyone crowded into the TV room to watch television. An hour later, Mike reminded the group that they would have to head up to bed shortly.

Mike heard Kyle then yell, "You're always making us go to bed early. I thought you said we could stay up for a while?"

Mike then confronted Kyle directly, in a loud voice. "Kyle, you've been whining all day. Why can't you just be quiet and keep your mouth shut?"

Kyle turned away towards the other boys and smirked, ignoring Mike. "Sheeze," was his response.

Mike then said angrily, "You go upstairs right now, Kyle. Get to bed!"

Kyle then stood up and shouted, "Fuck you *Wašíču*! You're like Custer, you hate Indians."

Kyle then shoved Mike as he stormed off tromping loudly up the stairs to his room.

Pointing at Mike, Benny shouted. "Custer. That's you!"

The other students didn't say a word as wide eyes appeared all across the TV room. Mike was angry and the students knew this. Everyone watched to see what was going to happen next. Perhaps sensing he should have not said anything, even Benny looked uneasy.

As Mike left the TV room, he moved towards the steps. Kim told him, "Stop. Let's give Kyle a few minutes."

Kim and Mike now retreated into the kitchen, hoping that would calm things down. After a short time, Kim headed up to visit with Kyle. She reported to Mike that he was in bed, quietly crying.

Kim had said to Kyle in a quiet motherly way, "Everything will be okay."

Thirty minutes later, Mike directed the rest of the students to head up to bed. As Mike stood near the bottom of the steps, each student passed by him, not saying a word.

Mally was the last student in line. As he walked by, he paused and then said in his husky voice, "Remember, Custer lost."

Mike didn't say anything realizing that Mally said this, not out of disrespect, but to add humor and perspective to a delicate situation.

In the log that night Mike wrote.

The powwow was interesting, but we feel like we are losing control of the home.

CHAPTER SIXTEEN
Losing Ground

SUNDAY IN THE PINGER HOME was a lazy day. The students woke up late and moved slowly.

Mike and Kim visited privately and were torn about the previous day. The powwow was great, but different incidents put a damper on things. Mike felt bad about the confrontation with Kyle.

Mike told Kim, "I'm sure I didn't help the situation. But that constant complaining is grating on me."

"I know, but he's still a kid," Kim responded.

Mike figured the home could use some exercise so he took the group on a hike. They went to a place referred to as the Chalk Hills, located at the northern end of the campus. Everyone trekked around the bluffs and inlets just off the river and enjoyed the nice weather. Mike was happy to have a slower-paced day after the excitement of the powwow.

Those students who had gotten in trouble on Saturday received their consequences on Sunday evening.

While visiting with Wayne in the office, Mike and Kim surmised that he had chewed tobacco all summer while at home. Wayne indicated he initially tried to quit but had secretly been chewing for the past month. He did this mainly while in bed. Wayne admitted to bringing chew in with him when he arrived in August.

Mike and Kim tried to piece together all circumstances revolving around Wayne's chewing. During the discussion, Wayne mainly sat in silence with his head down. Mike and Kim used yes and no questions to figure it out. All the time Wayne's hands and legs shook nervously.

"Poor guy," Kim told Mike after the meeting. "That shaking."

"I felt bad too, but I'm not sure we even know half the story," Mike admitted.

Wayne got two days of restriction that included limited activities and staying in the sight of an adult at all times. In addition, he was given early bed for the next three days and had to do the dinner charges for Mally.

Sage was placed on restriction for two days. She was given Sweets' morning kitchen charges and early bed for both days. For the first time, Sage was not happy with Kim and Mike. As the meeting ended, she got teary-eyed and stormed up to her room.

On the way upstairs Sage yelled, "This isn't fair. You're just being mean to me."

"That's a surprise," Kim said to Mike after Sage left the room.

Kyle was given four days of supervision, restriction and early bed. His negative behavior and being disrespectful was not the main problem though. The fact that he shoved Mike was considered a greater offense, thus he received more consequences.

Mike said sternly, "You cannot go outside or go on a pass to another home for the next four days. Got it?"

With his head down Kyle grumbled angrily under his breath, "This isn't fair."

Then Mike saw a tear roll down his face and fall to the floor. Mike now felt sorry for Kyle.

Monday morning finally came, ending the long weekend. After taking the kids to school, both Mike and Kim felt a bit of relief. They needed time to gather themselves. After doing some quick organizing in Pinger, they were able to head home and take a much-needed nap.

After school and into the evening, there was that same tension between the students and Mike and Kim. Because he was on restriction, Kyle sulked as he sat in sight of the houseparents. This caused Benny to act like he was outraged in support of Kyle.

Benny showed his indignation by complaining that Kyle was being treated unfairly. He whined and nagged Kim until she told him to head outside or his consequence would be early bed. Upon hearing Kim's threat, Benny quickly relented but continued to complain under his breath.

"Everything is so unfair. I wish I didn't live here." Benny stated.

At dinner that night, an interesting pattern began to emerge. Since August, the seating arrangement for meals had gravitated to Mike sitting at one end of the long dinner table with Kim sitting at the other. Since Kim cooked nearly every meal, she sat on the side closest to the kitchen. The students then filled in, sitting randomly between Kim and Mike, on either side of the table.

That night, the seating arrangement became more set. Now the four girls sat on Kim's end of the table along with Kyle and Benny. Eli and Mally sat closest to Mike. Wayne, Steve and Cott sat in the middle, as did Sweets. Sweet Grass tended to be the odd-man-out as he bounced around to any group that was nice to him.

Mike realized the dinner seating set-up was now formed around alliances, based upon which houseparent each particular student felt most comfortable with. There was an occasional variation, but for the most part, this seating pattern was now set.

Later that night, the three early bed students were in no hurry to head upstairs. Sage took her time, talking to her sisters. She eventually was the first to head to her room, but it took more prompting than usual.

Kyle asked to stay downstairs for an extra few minutes as he tried to watch TV from the table in the dining room. He knew he was not supposed to do this while on restriction. He then wandered in and out of the kitchen, acting as if he was looking for a second snack. He was stalling, with Wayne following his lead.

Benny, whose true personality was starting to emerge, egged on Kyle and Wayne. Mike saw Benny as a pot-stirrer, who riled everyone up behind the scenes. He had a smart-alecky response for everything. Benny thought he was pulling a fast one on Kim and Mike but it was easy to figure out what he was up to.

Mike reminded Kyle and Wayne, "Guys, time to head up to bed. Let's get moving. This is the second time I've told you."

Quietly Benny whispered to Wayne and Kyle, "Just pretend like you don't hear them. That'll make Mike mad."

To Mike's dismay, the boys did not move. They looked around, talked under their breath to one another and acted like they did not know they had early bed. Finally, Kim got them to head up by threatening more days of early bed.

The slow pace of the two boys caused Mike's patience to grow thin. For some reason, he found Wayne's behavior less challenging, while his relationship with Kyle was turning contentious. Kim too was running out of patience, and earlier in the evening threatened Kyle with a week's worth of restriction, if he did not head up to bed when told to do so.

Wayne and Kyle did finally head up to bed. A little while later, when Mike went upstairs to check on the boys, he found Wayne in Kyle's room. Neither boy was in bed.

"Wayne you have ten seconds. One, two…" Mike threatened loudly.

This caused the boys to scurry. Right away Kyle jumped into bed and Wayne ran to his room, diving into his bed.

Once upstairs, Sage was not a problem that night. She seemed to grow more amenable, understanding that her discipline measures were the result of her own actions. Mike and Kim appreciated Sage beginning to take more accountability and accepting the consequences.

"At least Sage seems better and less annoyed with her consequences," Kim told Mike as a means to lessen his frustration with the boys.

Unbeknownst to Kim and Mike, Sage had matches in her room. She had brought them from home in August and they were never confiscated during the bag check. She had hidden them in some of her clothing.

While upstairs for early bed that night, Sage had taken the matches out. She had learned that she could use the ash on the matches to highlight her eyelashes. This acted as a substitute for mascara and she put it directly on her lashes.

During one of his trips upstairs, Mike thought he smelled something like smoke. He was unable to trace the source so thought he must have been mistaken. On this night, Sage got away with the beauty treatment.

The next few days had the same defiant vibe. Students were testing the limits and challenging authority. It was enough to make the atmosphere in the home unpleasant and tense.

The need to get some control in the Pinger Home led Kim and Mike to "over-discipline." The student responded by continuing to test the limits. All of this was perpetuating a vicious circle. It was not all of the students all the time, but enough of the students that it made Mike feel like it was never-ending.

The plan of waking the bed-wetters was not working either. This added to Mike's frustration. Over time the success rate was poor. Each boy continued to wet the bed periodically. Since there was no pattern to it, Mike was faced with what seemed to be one wet bed every morning.

Mike told Kim and Sally, "This is ineffective and not working. I'm exhausted from a lack of sleep. There has to be another way."

Through this period of continued tension, there was still some levity for Mike and Kim. One night after the students went to bed, Jesse came over. Kim and Sally were visiting, snacking and discussing the day's gossip. Mike took a minute away from writing the log to visit with Jesse.

Jesse asked if the water was working, saying there was no water in his home. Sally, closest to the kitchen went over and turned on the faucet. "Whoosh" came a stream of water from the handheld sprayer. As it soaked Sally, Jesse laughed hysterically and ran out of the house.

Little did anyone know, Jesse had taped the handle of the sprayer down, so anyone who turned on the tap would be soaked. Sally was not too happy but Kim and Mike roared with laughter.

"I'm going to kill that guy," Sally said.

"You may want to get out of your wet clothes first," Mike laughed.

Later that night as Mike woke up the bed-wetters, Kim asked that he grab her purse from downstairs. As he headed downstairs, he decided to get a drink. "Whoosh" came the water, soaking him.

"Dammit!" Mike said.

After Jesse left, Mike forgot to remove the tape on the handheld spray head.

One Wednesday night in late September, Mike finished the log with the following:

We are losing ground. Most of the students are just plain disrespectful. I wish they had more appreciation for being here at St. Joe's.

CHAPTER SEVENTEEN

Leaving

Train to Chicago
June 9, 1986, 6:55 am

THE TRAIN SLOWED, THEN STOPPED at Mokena. Mike was jostled back to the present. He watched passengers quickly board and find seats. He noticed it seemed so natural how everyone scurried onto the train.

The stop was quick. Then with another jolt, the ride began again.

Then he thought back. "Why did we stay?" he asked himself.

Mike remembered a mid-October day as being pivotal. The changeover meeting that morning consisted of the normal exchange of information between Mike, Kim, Gene and Andie. During the discussion, Mike noted that problems with the students persisted.

Mike and Kim used the meeting to air their frustrations. Gene and Andie listened, then offered suggestions. Gene, in his folksy way, stated that it would get better, encouraging them as usual. Andie added the kids want to feel like they belong and challenged Mike and Kim to get to know each child individually.

"You know, they do want you to like them, but they have to trust you first," Andie suggested.

After the changeover meeting, Mike and Kim got into their car. The parked Nova happened to be facing east, with I-90 just a few miles away.

Mike turned to Kim, "Should we just take off and head back to Joliet?" It was a moment of quiet excitement as the couple pondered the thought of leaving.

"Maybe," Kim said.

"We can call from on the road and tell them we had a family emergency," Mike said.

The pause and contemplation dragged on and they were both quiet. The moment was halted abruptly with a loud thud that jolted Kim and Mike back to reality. Jesse had just sent a basketball ricocheting off the car window. There he stood a few feet from the car laughing.

Kim rolled down her window and Jesse said, "Make sure you keep your husband's balls in the yard where they belong."

The onset of fall was in the air that morning. It was cool, windy and overcast. Mike and Kim headed up to their house. Later Mike took the time to go for a run. He noticed the fields being harvested. As he ran down the oil road he was surprised to see so many pheasants flying right over his head.

On his run, Mike saw several vehicles, mostly pickups and Suburbans, leaving town and heading out to the country. He'd heard about this time of year. These were pheasant hunters.

Mike wondered if he was somehow in danger, running out in the country during pheasant season. Then he laughed, recognizing himself as a city guy who'd never shot a gun.

"If I was hunting, everybody should be worried. Even some guy out for a run!" Mike chuckled.

In the afternoon it started to rain, coming down in a light, cold mist. It rained harder as the day went on. That evening Mike and Kim went out for dinner with Jesse and Jeannie. They enjoyed a few beers, playing pool and darts. A few other staff also joined them at Chandler's Grille, a restaurant and bar located across the river. Jesse was his usual self, carrying on and giving Kim a hard time.

There was a lot of discussion that night. Of course, the conversation eventually turned back to the students and campus gossip. Mike remembered this happening back in August but now it was different. This time he and Kim knew the students and staff. They too were becoming "insiders" with the common bond being the students. Without fully recognizing it, they were beginning to feel more at home.

The rain continued as Mike drove Kim back home. After turning off the paved road towards home, they encountered a low spot where the gravel was thin. The portion of the road ran about ten yards and now consisted of extremely slick mud. Since there had only been minimal rain after they moved in, this part of the road had never been a problem.

As they approached the slippery spot on the road, the car fishtailed and started to move sideways. Mike and Kim had heard people refer to this type of mud as "South Dakota gumbo." Now they knew firsthand what that meant. It was not good for driving.

Initially, Mike thought it was funny that they were fishtailing through the mud. It was much like an icy road. His amusement ended however, when the car stopped moving as the tires spun.

"Shit!" said Mike. "We're stuck!"

As they sat there trying to devise a plan, Mike finally said, "Kim, slide over behind the wheel. I'll get out and push." Mike left the car and walked to the back. Positioning himself near the rear bumper, he yelled, "Go!" as Kim hit the gas and spun the tires.

Mike began to push, eventually making some progress. Of course, the mud was also spraying him like crazy. Once Kim got traction, she picked up just enough speed to make it to the part of the road that had more gravel. There the car began to move forward slowly.

Mike then jogged up to the driver's side window, full of mud from head to toe. As the car continued to move along, Kim rolled down her window and laughed.

"Mike, sorry but the car's clean! You need to figure out your own ride home big guy." Kim said as she rolled up the window, accelerated and left him there.

Mike remembered that soggy quarter-mile walk to the house. He was covered with mud, cold, and wearing his nice new penny loafers as the rain continued to fall. He felt he had reason to be angry but when he arrived home, Kim greeted him with a smile and hot cocoa.

"Let's go see if we can catch another episode of *Wings*," Kim said.

The next day Kim and Mike met Jesse and Jeannie in Mitchell. They had planned this the night before, and Mike looked forward to eating at McDonald's to get his fast-food fix. After the couples ate, everyone walked down Main Street with Jamie in his stroller. As they looked around at the various shops, they once again ended up at the World's Only Corn Palace.

"It amazes me how many people like to take pictures of this place," Mike said to Jesse.

Later in the day, they all headed back to Chamberlain. Kim and Mike were in their Nova, following Jesse and Jeannie in their Suburban. Twenty miles east of Mitchell on I-90, with both vehicles traveling over 75 miles an hour, a pheasant flew out of the ditch. It came across from left to right and smacked into Jesse's vehicle. The force of the collision knocked off the driver's side mirror. The detached mirror then smashed into the side window.

"Holy shit, did you see that?" Mike asked Kim excitedly.

"I hope they're okay," Kim said.

Jesse, who was driving, swerved but then moved over to pull off at the next exit. Fortunately, the exit was right there. Kim and Mike followed.

Once stopped on the off-ramp, Mike and Kim ran up to their friends. Jesse now had his door open, examining the driver-side window, which was shattered. The left side of his head was bleeding.

Jesse told Kim and Mike, "I don't think the cuts are too bad and luckily the Suburban is drivable. The good news is that I got my limit of pheasants today," he added jokingly.

"Wow, we're glad you're okay. Way to keep your vehicle on the road," Mike said admiringly.

Kim chimed in with a laugh. "Jesse, this is the first time a pheasant went searching for a Suburban and driver. How does it feel to be hunted?"

Mike and Kim followed Jesse and Jeannie back to Chamberlain. They now had Jamie, in his car seat, in the back of the Nova. Once back in Chamberlain the group unloaded. Jesse quickly addressed his wounds and headed to the local dealership. He had to get his prized Suburban fixed.

Mike still had not figured out how to heat their little white house in the country. He had been putting it off because he had no clue what to do.

Realizing temperatures were getting colder, he finally made some inquiries and got the phone number of a man in town who supposedly knew about heating systems.

"Hi, this is Mike. I'm trying to reach Frank. I have a heating problem and was told he might be able to help me out," Mike said, after dialing the number he had been given.

"I'm sorry, you must have the wrong number," the man on the phone responded. "Can I ask what kind of problems you are having?"

"I don't want to waste your time," Mike responded, as he was ready to hang up.

"It's not a waste of time. My name's Bill and I've fixed a few heaters in my day. So what's the problem?" the man on the other end of the phone asked.

Mike thought, "What the heck, why not?" since his mechanical aptitude was close to zero.

"Well, my wife and I live in this little white house and we need a heater. The house doesn't have one. There's a fuel oil tank out back and a spot inside where an exhaust pipe could hook into the chimney. That's the extent of my knowledge of heaters," Mike said, surprised he was so forthcoming to a stranger.

To Mike's surprise, Bill responded, "How about I come over to your place to see if I can help you out?"

Mike, not knowing what to think said, "Sure, that would be great."

When Kim heard that Mike had called the wrong number and the person who was not supposed to be called was coming over, she couldn't believe it.

Mike, knowing his lack of handyman skills trumped his wife's concerns said, "I'm just happy that someone's coming out to look at the situation. Besides, if we don't get a heater, we'll freeze!"

Kim said, "Well, what if he's a serial killer?"

Mike assured her, "I'm sure he's not a serial killer. If he is, I'll throw him in the basement with the varmint."

Kim retorted, "Well, with our luck his car won't have brakes and he'll leave it running, doing loops around the house."

Bill stopped by the next day. He was a pleasant elderly fellow who lived in nearby Pukwana, a small town east of Chamberlain. He looked at the setup and suggested Mike try to find a used fuel-oil heater. Bill claimed he knew of one being sold at an auction later in the week. Bill gave Mike information on the person holding the auction, suggesting he go over and visit the owner.

"Maybe you can work something out and not even have to go to the auction," Bill mentioned.

After Bill left, Mike contacted the owner of the fuel oil heater and arranged a visit. By early evening, the white house in the country had a heater. Now all that was needed was to hook it up.

The following morning, Mike called the man who delivered fuel oil. Mike asked if he could come by and look at the heater. Later, the oilman came over and filled the tank. He then hooked up a valve that connected the heater to the fuel oil tank. While he did this, Mike connected the exhaust pipe. Lastly, the oilman showed Mike how the furnace worked.

The oilman said, "The heater looks old, but should be okay for the winter."

After the pilot light was lit, it stayed burning. As long as he could see a flame, Mike was satisfied. Now he and Kim would be warm throughout the winter, in their little white house in the country.

CHAPTER EIGHTEEN

Sleeping In

MIKE AND KIM STARTED THEIR next shift on a Saturday. After a quick change-over with Gene and Andie, they were back with the students. The students had to do super-charges on Saturdays. This meant that extra cleaning was to take place before other weekend activities.

After super-charges were completed and lunch was consumed, the Pinger Home walked to town. The weather was perfect on this bright, sunny October day. Traditionally, many homes walked to the business district of town on Saturdays. It presented an opportunity to get off campus and enjoy some exercise and a change of scenery.

There were two ways students could get money to spend on Saturdays. A parent or guardian could send them money or students could earn it by doing extra work. The work, called job-corp, allowed students to earn a few dollars. Each home had a system set up to account for individual students' money.

There were a few distractions in town. The movie theater might have a matinee. From what Mike could tell, movie releases ran two months behind the same release in bigger cities. Plus, there were always shopping opportunities at the local Variety Store, sometimes referred to as a "five-and-dime." Students might be able to get a pop or buy a small toy.

In all the stores, supervision of the students was covered by houseparents. Supervision was a bigger issue when a student went into a store and did not have money with them.

Mike noticed how the store personnel reacted the first time that he took the students to the Variety Store. Several clerks would position themselves so they could strategically watch the students. Their goal was simply to prevent stealing.

The students knew they were being watched when in this store. Mike recognized they didn't like it but he thought little of their concern. If asked, he would have sided with the store workers, knowing they were trying to prevent theft.

After this Saturday's trip, Eli asked Mike, almost in tears, "Why are they always watching us?" Mike was surprised that Eli, who usually was smiling, was so emotional.

Later Kellie said, "It's not very nice that they watch us. We should go in there and pound them."

"Yeah," Sage said. "It's embarrassing and rude."

Over time, Mike heard similar comments and wondered why this was such a big deal to the kids. For his part, he didn't think anyone was being hurt.

The rest of that Saturday, including playing at the rec center and eating dinner, was laid back and non-eventful. That night the home watched two movies. The first was a cartoon. The second movie was, of course, *Footloose*. That night Mike and Kim allowed the kids to stay up a bit later as an incentive for it being such a good day.

Sunday started with Mass and was followed by brunch. It was Cott's birthday and happened to be the first Pinger Home birthday that Mike and Kim celebrated. Cott's meal request was pancakes, eggs and bacon.

After brunch, Kim led everyone in singing Happy Birthday. Then Cott was given a few presents. One of the gifts was a nice leather coat that Kim found in the donated items department. When Cott opened the gift, he put it on immediately.

"Thank you Kim," Cott said with a big smile. "This is cool."

Mike then chimed in, "Why do you think Kim was the one who got that for you?"

"Just look at you and your clothes," Kim retorted, as everyone laughed.

The home then went to the pool in the Rec Center and swam. Afterward there was dinner, television, eating Cott's birthday cake and prayer-time. The whole day seemed to go smoothly, up to and including bedtime.

Later that night, Mike reflected on the less structured times during the weekend and how this seemed good for everyone. He thought about Kim talking with the girls, covering a range of topics, many things deemed feminine. The girls naturally gravitated to her, and good conversations developed. He could see they respected and listened to her opinion.

Mike, on the other hand, played a little basketball with the boys at the Rec Center. There was good-natured ribbing as the boys drifted in and out of different games. Mike was happy that all the boys seemed to get along.

Cott and Eli had the best basketball skills so Mike guarded them most often. At one point, Cott called Mike an "old man." This was when Mike was showing off his patented one-handed approach to shooting free throws. All the boys laughed at this.

As the game was ending, Mike demonstrated his juggling abilities. He revealed his talent using three basketballs.

As Mike juggled Kyle, usually the one to complain, seemed impressed. "Mike, I think I know what you did before you came here. You were in the circus, weren't you?"

Overall, Mike rated it as a good weekend. Some of the negativity seemed to have subsided and a nice routine had developed. By the end of the weekend, everyone was tired, but in a good mood.

Though tired, Kim and Mike stayed up late and visited on Sunday night. They both felt this weekend went better than past ones. Later that night Mike got up with the bed-wetters.

Upon returning to bed, Mike muttered to a sleepy Kim. "I hope this is working because I'm exhausted."

It was at 8:03 on Monday morning when Mike, then Kim, were startled by a loud knock at their bedroom door. They both rose quickly and Mike answered the door. It was Sally.

With a half-smirk on her face she said, "Is Pinger Home taking the day off?"

"Oh shit," Kim said, instantly angry with Mike. "Why didn't you wake me up?"

Now a mad scramble ensued. Mike ran to each room and called for the students to get up.

Out of breath, Mike exclaimed, "You have five minutes to get ready!"

Kim raced downstairs to prepare breakfast. She filled twelve bowls of cereal and placed them on the table along with milk and spoons.

Mike continued to prompt the students while upstairs, going from room to room, telling them to hurry. Most of the students got it. Sweets was a bit slow, to no one's surprise.

"Why did you wake us up? I'm tired. I just want to go back to sleep," Sweets whined.

Mally told him, "Hurry up, we're going to be late," in a tone of support yet urgency.

The next fifteen minutes were chaotic. All the students hustled and got downstairs promptly. Most ate a quick bowl of cereal.

Cott said, "We'll be fine until lunch. Don't worry about us," as Kyle and Wayne agreed.

Mike and Kim had no time to object to the boys deciding not to eat. Mike then realized they were helping. It was a small gesture but appreciated.

"Hey, thanks guys. I'm grateful you're working with us on this," Mike told the three older boys.

After the quick breakfast, everyone put on shoes and grabbed jackets while Mike and Kim made sure everyone had all their school items. In the frenzy, the group even helped Sweet Grass when he was slow in getting his things together. In record time, everyone was ready.

Their usual five-minute walk to school turned into a jog. Even hurrying, the Pinger Home was still twenty minutes late. As they arrived, Mike, Kim and the students were welcomed with many smiles from the school staff. Through the campus grapevine, everyone already knew the home had overslept.

On this morning the changeover between Kim, Mike and the teachers was nonexistent because the teachers had already started their classes. Kim and Mike were feeling very embarrassed, but the students handled it well. Each one went directly to their classrooms without saying a word.

On the way back to Pinger, Kim and Mike ran into Jesse.

He questioned, "How'd you sleep last night?" followed by a loud laugh.

Once back at Pinger, Sally was there waiting.

Kim asked, "Are we going to get fired?"

"No, but this is honestly a first. Most houseparents hurry to get their kids to school after the weekend. In your case, I'm glad you wanted to spend more time with them." Sally replied trying to be serious, but unable to hide the smirk.

Chagrined, Mike lowered his head.

That morning no beds were made, no dishes were done and nothing was picked up. Mike and Kim observed that the home was a total disaster. They tried to do some straightening up, but Sally told them that the students could clean up after school.

"Who knows, this might have been a good group exercise," Sally said. "And make sure you get away from campus for a few hours. You need the break."

Later that morning, while at the white house in the country, Mike got a call from a former Illinois co-worker. His name was Arthur and Mike had worked with him in his previous job.

"I heard a crazy story that you guys are in the Dakotas doing missionary work. If that's true, how long are you in for?" Arthur asked.

"We made a commitment through the school year," Mike replied, thinking there was no way to explain to Arthur how they'd slept in earlier that morning.

"I'm taking a job in Chicago and was thinking how well we worked together in the past. There might be an opportunity to do that again," Arthur said. "Get back to me after the first of the year, and we'll talk. You never know."

"I'm definitely interested," Mike said.

When Mike and Kim returned to campus that afternoon, they tried to get things organized before the students returned. When the students came home, Mike was stunned that there was little mention of the morning. The kids even took direction with limited fuss, getting their rooms and the rest of the house in order.

Kim said to Mike somewhat perplexed, "Maybe we should sleep in more often."

At dinner Kim asked, "Did anybody at school say anything?"

Vera responded. "The girls in my class thought it was cool that our home got to come late." Everyone around the table nodded and smiled at that comment. Then the conversation moved on to other things.

Kim wrote in the journal that night.

Not a bad weekend, but only we would sleep in on a school day. Good bonding experience though!

CHAPTER NINETEEN

Halloween

MIKE AND KIM HAD HEARD how much fun Halloween was on campus. In mid-October, Wally said in a staff meeting that the Halloween Committee had met and set up a plan for the students. Mike was excited to hear the plan.

"On the Saturday before Halloween, we're going to tell the students we're taking them to a haunted house in Pukwana. Each home will come over and load up in vans, believing a haunted house is their destination. On the way, the vans will be commandeered and students driven back to campus. Once back on campus we'll have our haunted house in the tunnels below the chapel. Only students in grades five through eight can participate," Wally told the staff.

Mike and Kim were aware that a series of tunnels ran underneath the campus. In past years the tunnels allowed students to move from the dorms to the school on extremely cold days. Now, tunnels were used for infrastructure, such as piping and phone lines, which were routed underground.

The tunnels running under the chapel were creepy, dark and damp. They were made of concrete and brick walls. The lighting was not always consistent as some lightbulbs burned out, adding to the eerie feeling. There were places where the passageways were easy to walk through. At other points, they narrowed and a person would have to slide through sideways.

The tunnels made a great backdrop for a haunted house. One veteran staff person told Mike that it was an annual Halloween tradition. Those same staff always seemed to have funny stories when reminiscing about past activities.

On that Saturday before Halloween, the plan came together. Students were told the haunted house would be off-campus this year and they were going later that evening. Individual homes brought students to the pick-up area at their scheduled time. Students then entered assigned vans.

As the vans left, the drivers drove each vehicle across the road, just off-campus. As the vans moved along, the drivers mentioned that they heard the haunted house was very scary this year. Suddenly, two masked men jumped out from the side of the road and stopped the vehicle.

"Get out of the van," the two masked men told the driver. "We're taking over."

At that point, the captors took the vehicle and drove back to campus. In some cases, the plan worked too well. Some of the students got very scared and there were a few screams before the kids figured out what was going on. In a couple of cases, a child even tried to escape the van.

Once back on campus, students followed staff members who guided them downstairs below to the tunnels. There, a scary guide escorted the students.

The haunted house included scares such as being chased by a headless monster, a surgery with guts spread all around, and a head without a body that tried to talk to the students. There were monsters, spider webs, a crazy doctor doing surgery (Jesse) and much more. It was quite an elaborate haunted house, set up entirely by the staff.

It was interesting to see the students' reactions to the different components of the frightening corridors. Some screamed, many laughed nervously and a few were looking for another student to hold onto. Mike was dressed as a ghost and, as an escort, his job was to scare the groups just enough to keep them moving through the tunnels. He had as much fun as the students.

After going through the haunted house, the Pinger Home students were wound up when they arrived home. In describing what they saw to Kim and Mike, they laughed and tried to guess which staff members were present. No one mentioned being scared but Mike had heard that Kyle was one of the students who tried to run away when the van was taken over.

Kim, who stayed back in the home with the younger students, was eager to hear everyone's account of the evening. When the older kids arrived, she bombarded them with questions.

"Kyle, were you scared when you were at the haunted house?" Kim asked.

Kyle replied, "Sheeze, are you kidding me? I could beat up any of those monsters."

Kim wasn't buying it. "I heard you almost cried."

"Na huh," he said. "I had to save everyone in the home. Lucky I was there."

Sage was quick to tell Kim excitedly, "It was set up really cool. We had to walk through all those scary tunnels. There were so many monsters."

Kellie added, "Yeah, that one monster's head fell off and then they were operating on some other guy. It was gross but fun."

Cott added, "I didn't see that, because that ghost kept chasing us. Was that you Kim? It was you, wasn't it?"

Benny then said, "No, that was Mike chasing us. He was trying to scare us."

Steve chimed in, "I covered my eyes when those two guys got into the van. That was scary."

Later that night Eli told Mike, "That was fun! Can we go again tomorrow?" as he and Mike both laughed.

When they heard the older students talk about the haunted house Sweets, Vera and Sadie felt left out. They complained but the older kids weren't buying it.

Sweets complained, "It was unfair. Why didn't we get to go?"

Mally shook his head. "Sweets you would have… never mind. You would not have made it through there. A few older kids didn't even make it. It was way too scary for you."

Vera asked Kim, "Why couldn't we go?"

Then Sadie jumped in saying, "Yeah. We missed out on all the fun."

Hearing this, Sage put her hands up and said to her sisters. "Don't say that. I know you think you missed out, but you wouldn't have made it through. You can go next year."

Later that night Mike said to Kim, "I'm amazed. Some of these kids seemed scared to death. Yet, every one of them asked 'When are we having another haunted house?'"

Two days later, on the actual day of Halloween, students trick-or-treated across campus. There was also a contest held at the Rec Center where costumes were judged.

Many staff also dressed up. Kim went as a wicked witch. She was accompanied by the four Pinger Home girls who were also witches. Jesse and Jeannie transformed Jamie into a miniature ET.

Mike dressed as Sally, his supervisor. "That's the worst costume ever," Sally told Mike with a good-natured laugh when she figured out who he was supposed to be.

Halloween turned out to be a fun day for the students who participated. Wayne and Benny were too cool to dress up, but Kyle and Cott enjoyed themselves going as the Blues Brothers. All the other students were in costume. Once back home, much of the candy was traded which allowed everyone to select their favorites.

"Vera and Sadie, I'll give you a million dollars for a few candy bars," Mike said.

Sadie grabbed a 100 Grand bar. "Here take this," she laughed.

That night a sugar-high kicked in and there was excess energy in the home. Later, the students seemed to hit the wall as they each came down from the sugar rush. There were even a few gut aches before bedtime. Mike had one too.

Kim shook her head asking Mike, "Who are the kids around here and who are the adults?"

Since Halloween was on a weekday, Mike and Kim did their best to get everyone to settle down at bedtime. They understood the students being wound up and gave them extra time and space. They also knew that tomorrow morning everyone would be moving slowly.

Mike wrote in the log that night:

Everyone had a fun Halloween. The students really enjoyed the haunted house and talked about it for hours.

CHAPTER TWENTY

Fire Alarm

THERE IS ALWAYS A FASCINATION with firsts and early November brought the first dusting of snow. It was only an inch or two, but in the morning each student looked out the window with great anticipation. On this day the snow came down slowly, bestowing an aura of peace.

"Isn't that snowfall cool? Look at those big flakes coming down," Mike said to Mally and Eli as they were standing at the window staring outside.

Eli asked, "Can we go sledding after school?"

Mike replied, "Sure, if there's enough snow. But the ground is still warm, so it'll probably be melted by the end of school."

Several days later more snow fell. Six to eight inches covered the ground this time. After the normal Saturday morning routine, it was decided the home would go outside.

"We're going to go sledding," announced Kim. "Everyone has to put on warm clothes because we'll be out there for a while."

The process of twelve students getting ready took time. Different age levels meant different decisions on clothing. A variety of sizes meant clothing could not be easily shared. Since it was the first sledding experience of the year, no one had prior practice to draw from. Organized chaos ensued.

The younger students didn't seem to mind wearing snow gear such as snow pants and heavy coats. In Sweets' case though, getting dressed was time-consuming. From not being able to follow directions to not fitting into his boots and overalls, his frustrations grew. The rest of the group continued to tell him to hurry up but offered little help. This caused him to complain that everyone was picking on him.

Once Sweets was dressed Mally commented, "Hey Sweet Grass, you look like a stuffed mummy. The good thing is you won't need a sled because we'll just slide you down the hill."

Even Sweets laughed at this comment.

The older students, the eighth-grade boys in particular, were too cool for snow gear. They dressed minimally in jeans and windbreakers. Cott decided to wear his leather coat. Mike was just glad they didn't put up a stink about going, so he chose not to confront them.

However, Kim reminded them, "It's cold out and you'll freeze, but it's up to you what you wear."

Kyle replied, "We're Indian. We don't get cold!"

The students grabbed sleds and everyone headed for the hills on the north end of campus. Here, the long rolling hills flowed out onto the football field. With the proper speed, a sledder could travel nearly the entire width of the football field. Students used plastic sleds that provided little support for the body. Mike learned this the hard way, feeling every bump and rough patch on his back when he took a turn.

Everyone participated, trying to have the fastest sled, or traveling the farthest, or piling as many people on a sled as possible. Kim and Mike went down alone or sometimes with another student. Mike was pleased to notice that all of the Pinger Home kids willingly shared. Naturally, many races were held. Sometimes those sledding ran into someone else, taking their legs out from under them.

Other homes were also on the hills that morning which led to more competition. Mostly, it added to the congestion and made crashes inevitable. Yet, it also added to the excitement and enjoyment of the day.

Eli challenged Mike to a race. He and Mike lined up, got a short running start, jumped on their sleds and headed down the hill. At one point, their sleds ran into each other as they coasted. Mike, being fiercely competitive, was able to reach out and tip Eli's sled over, leaving him behind.

Eli yelled, "Hey, sheeze! That's cheating."

"Not if you don't get caught," Mike yelled.

As Mike looked back he laughed. Not paying attention, he then ran into Kim and Sweets who had finished their run and had just stood up. Of course, Mike undercut their legs and they both toppled over as their plastic sled flew up in the air. Sweets was now on his back struggling to get up.

"Mike," Kim yelled from her knees, "you're going to kill someone. Don't be so rough."

Mike went to attend to Sweets. As he helped him up, Mike apologized and asked if he was okay.

Sweets responded with a big smile, "I'm fine. Glad I had my padding on."

One incident put a damper on the day as the sledding wound down. Mike noticed Wayne had chew. It happened as Mike followed Wayne and Mally's sled down the hill. At the bottom, Mike noticed Wayne coughing. He went over to check on him.

As he approached the boys, Mike saw chew coming out of the side of Wayne's mouth. Mike quickly realized that Wayne's coughing was the result of swallowing chew. Mally tried to discretely point this out to Wayne before Mike got there. However, Wayne could not keep from coughing in time.

"Wayne," Mike asked out of concern, "are you all right?" Noticing the chew Mike then said more harshly, "I know you have chew. We'll deal with it back in Pinger."

Wayne was angry and puffed out his chest looking at Mike. Then his eyes teared up. Finally, he dropped his head.

After the sledding finished and the students arrived back at Pinger, Mike and Kim visited with Wayne.

"Wayne, we didn't think this was a problem anymore, after the pow-wow incident," Kim said. "You know the consequences are supervision and loss of privileges for two days."

"You know that stuff isn't good for you," Mike added.

Wayne had his head down and shrugged his shoulders. He didn't say anything as he sat there with his hands shaking.

After the meeting, Mike went upstairs and checked Wayne's room. Under his bed in the back corner, were two empty bottles with spit in them. In his clothing drawer, tucked behind his socks and underwear, was a container of Skoal. Mike and Kim were less angry with Wayne and more surprised they hadn't noticed the contraband sooner.

"I should have been more thorough when I check his room after pow-wow," Mike said to Kim. "This is kind of on me."

As Thanksgiving approached, Mike and Kim were looking forward to the break. Fall break was a week where students went home and staff had time off. Their hope that things would run smoothly until then did not pan out.

Mike remembered how quickly things became unraveled and unsettled. It was partly because he and Kim were unaware that some students needed an adjustment period before break. Andi and Gene gave some perspective.

At a changeover meeting, Andi explained it to Mike. "Our students have to prepare themselves for another environment. Think of the difference between St. Joe's and where our students are from. At home, there can be a lack of food, overcrowding and poor housing. It makes sense they might need time to prepare or adjust to things back home."

Mike nodded. "I hadn't thought of that."

Gene added, "Since our kids don't have the ability to express this, the adjustment comes out through their behaviors. Most often, it's negative behaviors we see at this time of the year. Sometimes it comes, almost out of the blue, from students who seem to be doing well here."

About two weeks before break, the adjustment period began with testing and disobedience. Behaviors included talking back, being disrespectful and questioning various routines in the home. Kim and Mike were a bit surprised when it happened.

After one particularly long day, Kim admitted to Sally, "The student's behaviors kind of caught us off-guard. We thought things were coming together."

The tension in the Pinger Home was now back, and the "us versus them" mentality was apparent. It was worse with some students. Mike recalled Eli becoming unsettled and even uncooperative. Before this, he was mostly fun-loving, happy and interested.

That is why Mike couldn't believe the day Eli angrily yelled, "No, I don't have to. You can't tell me what to do," when he was asked to assist with kitchen charges.

Mike confessed to Kim, "My feelings were somewhat hurt by Eli's bad attitude and disrespectful behavior."

Mike and Kim were forced to deal with a more negative environment again. They increased structure using early bedtime and other consequences. Mike was further confounded when several days before the break, the home reverted back to functioning fairly well.

A few days before break, Kim was not feeling well so Mike offered to cook dinner – a rare occurrence. After school, while the students watched television, Mike prepared the meal. He worked on his signature dish of hotdogs and macaroni.

At some point, Mike took a potholder out of the drawer so he could move a hot pan off the stove. Unbeknownst to Mike, he had touched a corner of the potholder to a heating element on the stove. Not realizing he'd done this, he put the potholder back in the drawer.

A few minutes later Mike noticed smoke coming from the drawer. He opened it and saw flames. Quickly he threw the potholder into the sink. Too late. The fire alarm went off.

"Kim's never going to let me live this one down," Mike muttered as he heard Kim running toward the kitchen.

"What did you do?" Kim demanded with several students right behind her.

Hearing Kim's comment, Cott added, "Mike, we should've just had cereal for dinner."

Now Mike found himself pouting a little as he and Kim made sure everyone headed outside.

On a cold, blustery November day, the students, along with Mike and Kim stood waiting for the "all-clear" to be given. Worse yet, other staff and students watched them from nearby homes.

"This is embarrassing," Mike said under his breath to Kim.

Jesse had heard there was a fire alarm ringing and came over to check it out. Once he saw Mike and figured out it was a false alarm, he made a few jokes about cooking and even smoking.

Jesse teased, "Rumor is, you were smoking on the job. Best to do that outside next time."

Later that evening, Sage happened to be doing her eyelash-trick up in her room, using ash from the matches. Her sister Kellie was with her. Sage accidentally dropped a lit match into a nearby garbage can starting a small fire. As she and Kellie quickly doused the flames with water, the fire alarm once again went off.

Hearing the signal, Mike and Kim at first hesitated, wondering if it had something to do with the earlier event. Mike quickly headed upstairs, where he smelled something burning but didn't see any smoke. Then he saw Sage and Kellie coming out of their room.

"I smell something burning up here. Better head outside. Now!" Mike barked.

Everyone once again raced outside with the fire alarm blaring. This time the fire department responded with two fire trucks coming onto campus and stopping in front of the home. Mike pointed towards the home and mentioned smelling smoke upstairs. A couple of firemen headed inside.

While standing outside freezing, Mike, Kim and Sally tried to sort out what happened. They make a quick decision to have the students go to several nearby homes and wait. Houseparents from other homes came and made sure everyone had a place to go.

Mike, Kim and Sally stood shivering and waiting. The firemen came out a few minutes later explaining they had found a garbage can upstairs with some burnt paper in it. After describing where it was located, Mike knew it was in Sage and Kellie's room.

Shortly afterward, the firetrucks left. Having received the all-clear, Mike rounded up the students and they headed back to the home. Once inside Kim and Sally spoke privately with Sage and Kellie.

Kim told Mike that Kellie quickly "ratted out" her sister, after one simple question. "What happened guys?"

"Sage had matches, not me," Kellie quickly answered.

Sage then admitted to lighting matches, explaining she was using the ashes to darken her eyelashes. She also admitted to doing this several times over the past couple of months.

"She cried hard while admitting this, so it was difficult at first to even understand. I felt kind of bad for her," Kim reported.

Discipline was administered swiftly and included a week of supervision that would carry over after the break. Sage cried even harder as she was lectured on everything from safety to being a role model.

"I'm sorry," Sage muttered as tears rolled down her cheeks.

Kellie on the other hand, received two days of early bed for not reporting her sister and being an accomplice. Her punishment was less because she was not considered the instigator. Kim said it did not phase Kellie as she shrugged and seemed content with her consequences.

"Whatever," Kellie's response came, mostly out of indifference.

Knowing that the girls, especially Sage, were mindful and sensitive about their appearance, Kim felt bad for Sage. The next morning she took her aside and they visited about what happened.

At the end of their talk, Mike heard Kim tell Sage, "I'll pick up some real mascara for you and your sisters. I'll bring it back after the break and show you how to use it." Then Kim and Sage gave each other a big hug.

After two fire alarms, Mike and Kim were now sure they would be fired. Fortunately, for some reason, they were not.

Mike wrote in the log:

Only the Pinger Home could do the impossible. We set the fire alarm off twice in one day. I think the students need a break from us.

CHAPTER TWENTY-ONE
Break — Finally

AFTER SEVERAL MONTHS OF WORKING with the students, the week of Thanksgiving break had arrived. It was not only time off from the house-parent work schedule, but also a mental break for Mike and Kim. The hiatus would allow them a chance to return to Illinois to see family and friends. They were both greatly looking forward to time away.

The students went home the Friday before Thanksgiving. Some students were picked up by their families, while others were transported by school personnel. Sally had told Mike that the day before break could be chaotic as staff tried to make sure all the students had a way home. So Mike and Kim were ready for anything.

Houseparents had to assist with the driving responsibilities for those students who needed a ride. Since Mike and Kim were new houseparents, they didn't have to transport students this first break. A side benefit of not having to drive allowed them the opportunity to visit with those family members who picked their students up.

Kim and Mike tried to make sure all the kids had proper clothing to go home. They loaded everyone up with additional snacks such as granola bars, cookies and chips, worried they would get hungry on the journey and at home.

Grandma Ancel, driven by Levy in the old dinged-up station wagon, arrived mid-morning to pick up the four boys. Ancel got out of the car slowly and Levy came around to assist. She was now using a walker. As she and Levy slowly made their way up to the home, Kyle and Steve ran out to meet them.

"Hey grandma, I missed you," Steve said as he hugged her. "We're ready to go home."

Mally and Wayne grabbed all the bags, taking them out and placing them in the back of the station wagon. Ancel came in and sat down to catch her breath as she sipped on a cup of coffee.

Kim gave a quick update on the boys. Her report was generally positive as she felt that Ancel was too frail to hear anything bad. Besides, at that point, any behavior issues the boys had didn't seem to be a big deal.

Kim jokingly commented about Kyle saying, "He sure likes to question things, but we still love him."

Mike could tell this comment embarrassed Kyle. When Kim said it, he lowered his gaze and tried to hide a half-hearted smile.

"The other three have been fine. Everybody's working hard trying to figure out the routine," Kim continued.

"That's good to hear," Ancel said. "I hope they listen to you."

There was additional small talk about the boys and a few questions about other kids in the family. After a short visit, the group headed to the vehicle. Kim made sure she hugged everyone as they left.

Mike was surprised, then dismayed, as he watched everyone load up. As he looked out the window, he noticed Levy handing Wayne a round container of chew. Mike shook his head.

"Did you see that?" Mike asked Kim. "It looks like we'll be dealing with Wayne's addiction to chew again when he gets back."

Transportation for the four girls arrived shortly thereafter. The sisters and three other students were being driven home by another houseparent. Their travel route would take them to Sioux Falls, then north to Flandreau. The trip would take over three hours for the girls, and another three hours for the driver to return to campus.

Kim hugged the girls. Each had a small bag but not many clothes to bring home. Kim told them, "Don't forget your coats and please be careful. Okay? We'll see you next week."

The girls seemed happy to be going home. They had spoken of missing their mom many times over the past months. Mike walked them out to the vehicle visiting with the houseparent who was driving. The girls piled into the van and Mike waved as they headed out.

Mike didn't have a good grasp of the girls' home situation. Knowing they were happy about going home, he assumed things were fine there. As he said goodbye, his main worry for them was fitting all their bags, the few they had, into the vehicle.

Eli's mom, Vinnie, and his Uncle Moore pulled up around noon. Vinnie, cheerful as usual, came in while Eli's uncle stayed in the car. Kim welcomed her and the two had a pleasant conversation about Eli.

Kim shared, "He's a great kid. He and Mike get along well."

Vinnie smiled, saying, "Elijah's very responsible at home."

"How are your two daughters doing?" Kim asked.

"They're in school today, back in Oglála. I hope to enroll them at St. Joe's maybe next year or the year after. They're too young to stay in Chamberlain and I feel like they need to be at home a little longer," Vinnie said.

"That makes sense," Kim agreed.

"I do like that this school provides a good education. It was good for me when I went to school here. And Eli is doing well and he likes it," Vinnie added.

Mike then inquired about Eli's uncle. "Does Moore want to come in for coffee, or something to eat?"

Vinnie said, "No, it's a four-hour drive from Oglála and he's kind of tired. But I'm sure he'll take a cup of coffee for the ride home."

Kim grabbed a cup and filled it with coffee, which Eli ran out to his uncle.

When they were ready to leave, Mike walked Eli and Vinnie outside. As they approached the car, Mike went around to say hello to Moore. As Moore rolled down the window, the strong smell of alcohol hit like a punch. Mike realized he was drunk.

Mike wasn't sure what to do as the family quickly said goodbye and left with Moore driving. Mike immediately told Kim when he went back into the Pinger Home.

"Moore seems really drunk to me. He smelled like liquor," Mike said.

"Really? What should we do? Do you think Vinnie will drive?" Kim said.

"I'm not sure why she wasn't, or even why Moore was driving. This isn't a good situation. Maybe Sally has some ideas," Mike suggested. "I'd better go tell her."

Mike visited with Sally who said she'd refer it to Wally. Sally said he would most likely contact the police.

Sweets' grandmother came to pick him up while Mike was still meeting with Sally. His grandma was happy to see him.

Later Kim told Mike what Grandma had said. "Sweet Grass told me on the phone that he doesn't always get enough to eat. Can I send some food back with him?"

Kim laughed, telling Mike that she told her, "Thanks. You're always welcome to send some snacks but, I assure you, Sweets gets plenty to eat."

As Mike came back from visiting Sally, he ran into Sweets and his grandma on their way to the car. She was struggling a bit, carrying both of Sweets' bags. Mike said hello and grabbed the small suitcase and duffle bag.

"Here Sweets, carry this," Mike said handing him the duffle bag.

After putting the luggage in the car, Mike quietly told Sweets, "I don't want to see your grandma carrying your bags again. You need to display good manners and respect for her. That's what gentlemen do."

"Oh, all right," Sweets groaned as he got into the car.

Benny's ride showed up at 3:00. His aunt couldn't make it, so Benny ended up riding with another family member who was coming to Chamberlain that day. The woman drove an old Vega and seemed to be in a big hurry.

When the driver of Benny's ride came in, she asked for money for gas. Mike again ran over to see Sally. She was able to provide the woman with a gas voucher redeemable at the local convenience store.

Mike walked Benny and the woman out to the car after getting the gas certificate from Sally. At the car, Mike wished Benny a good break.

Benny jumped in the car saying, "Maybe I'll see you next week and maybe not."

Mike, standing near the car smiled. "You can't fool me," he said "You want me to beg you to come back. See you next week, Benny."

"Doubt it," was Benny's reply as he shook his head in defiance.

Cott's ride didn't show up until after dark. His aunt did not leave until late and then had a flat tire. Somewhere along her route to the school, she stopped and called. She let Kim know she was having car trouble.

Mike worried about Cott who looked forlorn, as he peered out the window many times throughout the afternoon. The longer he waited, the more anxious he became. Besides watching TV, Cott and Mike played several games of finger football to pass the time.

When his aunt finally arrived, she apologized for being late. Cott joked with her but seemed quite relieved that his ride had shown up.

"Whew!" Cott said, "I was worried I'd have to sleep out there in the front yard in my teepee. I'm glad you made it."

Kim chimed in, "It's cold outside, Cott. We'd make sure you had enough hot chocolate to stay warm."

Kim gave Cott's aunt some coffee and something to eat. Then, as she stood up to leave, Kim hugged Cott and said goodbye.

"You be careful, Cott. We'll be here waiting for you next week," Kim said.

"Don't tell any bad jokes while you're gone," Mike teased shaking Cott's hand.

In the log that night, Kim wrote:

All the students left today. We made it to break!

CHAPTER TWENTY-TWO

Homeward Bound

Train to Chicago
June 9, 1986, 7:12 am

THE TRAIN SHOOK SLIGHTLY AS *it moved into the station at Oak Forrest. It slowed then stopped. Mike was nudged back into reality as he watched people rush on and off the train. He watched as the doors opened, then closed. After a couple of minutes, the train jerked forward slightly and again began to move.*

Mike thought about his behavior over that break period, seven months earlier. They had visited with many family and friends. He was now slightly perturbed with himself at how he portrayed his South Dakota experience.

It was a great case of having just a small part of an experience, only to think that you've had the whole thing. Later, you realize that what you told people was woefully inaccurate. The regret came from not being able to go back and retract, or at least restate what was said.

Mike reflected back to November the year before.

Kim and Mike headed for Illinois the morning after the students left. They were up early and out the door before 6:00. The day was still enveloped in darkness. Fortunately, the weather was not bad for driving. It was cold and windy, but there was little snow on the ground.

As they headed east Mike realized that there were no other cars on the interstate.

Mike said to Kim, "Just think, 700 miles down this same interstate, people are stopped, sitting in a traffic jam. I don't miss that."

In the first hour of the drive, they were treated to a spectacular sunrise. The red ball on the horizon cut through a sky shaded with colors of yellow and orange. Puffs of clouds billowed around, shadowing part of the sun as its rays streamed out. It seemed like the clouds were dancing with joy for a new day.

As he looked over to Kim, excited to share what he was seeing, he found her sleeping peacefully in the passenger seat. He smiled.

As the Nova crossed through South Dakota, Minnesota, Wisconsin and Illinois, more towns appeared with fewer stretches of farmland in between. They arrived at Mike's parents in Joliet in the early evening. Mike's parents, Ann and Don, were happy to see them.

Over the next few days, many of Mike's siblings came to visit. They shared and updated each other on life's events as well as talked about the job of being a houseparent. Both Mike and Kim shared what had transpired, or at least their interpretation of what they had experienced in South Dakota so far.

Mike reflected on several discussions, feeling that the way he spoke about the students was too negative. He remembered too often describing the students as disrespectful and ungrateful. Sure, he related positive events and anecdotes, but what he portrayed in general about the students was not flattering.

On the first night home, Mike and his dad got a chance to sit down and visit. Mike knew the drill. His dad would sit in his favorite chair in the small living room while smoking his pipe. Then Mike or one of his siblings would sit down and have a back and forth discussion on different topics. At times it might be one or more of Mike's siblings participating in the discussion – sometimes even his friends.

Tonight's topic for discussion was Kim and Mike's work at St. Joe's. Mike respected his dad's opinion and always appreciated these talks. Eventually, Mike brought up the students' behavior.

"You know the kids can be very disrespectful and even ungrateful. I'm surprised they don't appreciate what the school gives them," Mike said.

His dad, after taking a puff on his pipe, responded, "Kids will be kids. You can't forget that. Is the behavior that bad? Plus, you made a year-long commitment."

"I know. We've had some good things happen, but it hasn't been easy," Mike replied. "The environment in the home hasn't always been very good."

"So figure it out. Lots of things are hard. You should be asking how can you honor your commitment and make it work for the students?" his father challenged him.

Later that week, Mike and Kim met with Mike's high school friends and their wives. More updates took place over multiple drinks and Mike was pleased to see everyone. Later in the evening, Mike overheard Kim talking with one of his friends about a dog. Upon hearing this conversation Mike was glad he and Kim didn't have a dog to worry about, on top of everything else.

On Wednesday Kim and Mike headed to Waukesha, Wisconsin to spend Thanksgiving with Kim's parents. In addition to Glen and Doreen, Kim's sisters Kelly and Kerri were there, along with their families. The family basset hound, Dudley, also welcomed Kim and Mike.

When they arrived, there were hugs all around for Kim and high-fives for Mike. Over the next few days, Kim caught up with her sisters.

Mike recalled the Thanksgiving meal. It began with everyone taking turns to express their thanks for people or events that were important in their lives.

Kim said, "I want to pray for Wayne, Steve, Kyle, Mally, Eli, Sage, Kellie, Vera, Sadie, Benny, Cott and Sweets. I hope they're all okay."

As Mike listened to the prayers being offered, he secretly hoped he and Kim could hurry up and finish their commitment at St. Joe's. He was looking forward to coming back to Illinois. His friend Arthur had called him the day before and offered him a job. And he knew he was taking it.

"Besides family, I also want to pray for the Pinger Home," Mike stated when his turn came around. His other thoughts remained unspoken.

Kim and Mike headed back to Chamberlain on Saturday. Before leaving, Kim's dad handed her an envelope containing one hundred dollars.

"We know Christmas is coming up," Glen said. "Maybe this will help you to get something decent for the kids and the home. It's from your mom and me."

"Thanks Dad," Kim said as she hugged him. "This will help a lot."

The trip back was again uneventful as the radio continued to fade in and out. The weather remained perfect – bright and sunny. Kim and Mike were thankful there was no rain or snow to contend with during the drive.

They arrived in Chamberlain at sunset. As they drove up the hill out of town, Mike noticed the fields were covered with a white icing of snow. As Mike and Kim headed down the dirt road to their house, they stopped the car for a minute. The sunset of reds, orange, gray and blue spread out across the western horizon. It was beautiful.

After a moment of silence, Kim said, "Let's get home and see if the barn fell over," breaking the spell.

Mike laughed, "Hope not."

When they arrived home, they entered to find the house freezing. The heater wasn't working.

Once inside Mike's first words, were, "Sheeze! The damn heater is off."

"Well, at least the barn is still up," Kim said lightheartedly. "We should start the barn on fire for warmth."

Ignoring the comment, Mike said, "I'm glad we turned the water off when we left so there aren't any broken pipes. But it's freezing in here. Can you call Nellie and ask if we can stay there?"

Kim went to the phone and dialed. "Nellie, our heat is out. Can we stay at your place tonight?" Mike heard Kim ask. Then she added, "Yeah, that's what I'm thinking."

When Kim got off the phone, Mike asked what Nellie said.

"She said sure, we can stay there," Kim reported. "She also said we should use the barn for firewood."

Mike and Kim got back in the car and headed downhill to town. On the way, Kim told Mike they were supposed to meet Nellie at the Rush, so that's where they went. As the two entered, they saw Nellie and her husband Dan in a booth in the corner. They went over and joined them. Mike recognized Dan.

After being introduced Mike said, "Nice to meet you. You're the owner of the convenience store in town, right?"

As the conversation ensued, Mike didn't say much. Secretly he was stewing, irritated that the heater in their house wasn't working.

When the topic of the heater came up, Mike felt better when Dan said, "I'll look at the heater tomorrow. As long as your pipes didn't break you should be okay."

After Dan's comment, Mike felt his mood lighten. The heater wasn't going to be a problem, he hoped. At least not tonight.

Nellie, Dan, Kim and Mike ran into other St. Joe's staff at the Rush. Everyone seemed eager to catch up. Mike found it interesting that nearly everyone had traveled during the break. After the initial banter, the talk eventually came back to the students, as it always did.

Jesse and Jeannie, who had gone to the Black Hills for a few days, arrived later that night. Jesse was "revved-up" even though he drank little. Throughout the night, after a lot of back-and-forth with Mike, Jesse began to insist that their home could beat the Pinger Home in any kind of competition.

Jesse said, "Jeannie and I, and our kids can beat you and Kim and the Pinger kids in everything. We could even set the fire alarm off three times in a day if we wanted to."

Mike later challenged Jesse, "Let's plan to swim across the river when the water warms up in the spring. I know I'll beat you."

Jesse said, "No way. I'll win, hands-down."

The night ended with the song *Paradise on the Dashboard Lights* playing on the jukebox. Jesse and Jeannie had gone home earlier. Now Kim and Nellie were dancing all by themselves on the makeshift dance floor. Dan and Mike were finishing a discussion about guns, hunting and fishing in South Dakota. When the song ended, the two couples left the bar.

As Mike and Kim headed over to Nellie's, Mike reminded Kim. "The kids come back tomorrow?" There was a bit of apprehension in his voice.

Kim responded quickly. "I kind of miss everyone." Then there was silence.

After church the next morning, Dan went out and looked at the heater. A valve had stuck and no fuel oil was getting into the furnace. Dan set up a manual override. Now the heater could temporarily run on either a high or low setting.

Dan promised Kim he would come up during the week and put in a new valve.

Before noon, Mike and Kim left for the Pinger Home knowing their white house in the country had at least minimal heat. That was good enough for Mike, the guy who could not fix anything.

CHAPTER TWENTY-THREE

Starting Anew

THE BREAK HAD OFFICIALLY ENDED and Mike and Kim were back to work in the Pinger Home. Ten of the twelve students returned that Sunday afternoon. The four girls arrived at noon, coming back in a St. Joe's van. Vera and Sadie came in first. "Hey Kim!" Vera and Sadie said almost in unison, followed by a laugh. They each hugged Kim.

Kellie came in next and said angrily to Sage, "You should've taken time to make sure you had your stuff. It's not my fault that some of your clothes aren't in there. It's your problem, not mine."

Sage yelled at Kellie, "Well, you could've helped me out and thought about what I would want to wear. You know what I like."

Kellie grumbled under her breath at her sister then smiled saying, "Hey Kim. How are you? Can I put my stuff away and take a shower?"

Sage snapped back at her sister, "You always say mean things."

After glaring at her sister, Sage turned to Kim smiling, "Hey Kim, can I put my stuff away too?"

Kim said, "Hello girls. Glad to see you two had a nice ride here. Let me check your heads and then you can go upstairs."

After head-checks, Kim told the two oldest girls they were good to go. They quickly went up to put their things away and showered. Kim then checked Vera and Sadie. To her despair, they both had nits.

"Okay girls, you have nits. You know the drill," Kim said.

Mike noticed the exasperation in Kim's voice when she said to him, "Mike, you're now in charge of nit combing."

Mike noted Kim's frustration, understanding that cleaning heads was hard work. Kim did not hesitate though. She went ahead and applied the special shampoo to the girls' hair. After waiting fifteen minutes, she sent Vera and Sadie up to shower.

By this time Sage and Kellie had come back downstairs. They now seemed more content with one another. They sat at the table and ate lunch while Kim visited with them. Throughout the short conversation, both girls revealed tidbits of news about their break.

At one point Sage got up to get something from the refrigerator in the kitchen. Kellie whispered to Kim, "Sage stayed out the last two nights with her boyfriend. She almost missed the van back to campus."

Sage grimaced as she came back into the room sooner than Kellie anticipated. She was not happy with her sister reporting her.

"Yeah, but Kellie got punched last weekend and got a black eye. She's always talking back to everyone. I'm glad she got pounded," Sage said meanly.

Kim looked at Kellie's eye. Though the eye was healed, there were still faint traces of discoloration on the left side of her face.

Kellie said, "I could say a lot more about you and Curtis, but I didn't. Thanks for being a tattletale."

"You just told on me. Why can't you just mind your own business?" Sage shot back.

At this point, the two girls stopped talking. Kellie got up and moved to the other side of the table. From then on, they just ignored one another. After eating, they separated even further, with Sage going up to her room and Kellie watching television with Mike.

When Vera and Sadie came down from the shower, Kim set them up to be combed out. Sadie went first as Vera sat nearby and ate lunch. Once Sadie was finished she ate and Vera was combed next.

Although Kim had threatened Mike with combing duties, she wasn't about to give up this task. Combing was her time to find out what had happened to Sage and Kellie over break. She went right to work with her questions.

During the combing, Vera and Sadie were a wealth of information as Kim listened intently.

"How was break?" Kim asked as she began combing Sadie's hair.

"It was okay," replied Sadie. "We didn't have a lot of food so we went to our auntie's a couple of times."

Kim continued, "How's your mom?"

"She's good, but we don't like her boyfriend," Vera replied.

"He got drunk a few nights and isn't nice to our mom when he drinks," Sadie said.

"When that happens we try and leave; go to our auntie's," Vera added. "It's better there."

"But one night Kellie stayed behind and started yelling at him. We had all left and then Kellie went back." Sadie stopped talking as she noticed Kellie come into the room.

"And Kellie then came over later, crying and..." Vera then noticed Kellie.

"Maybe you guys should shut up," Kellie said as she walked in and angrily glared at her two sisters.

Mally, Steve, Kyle, Wayne and Benny arrived mid-afternoon. They returned in a van driven by a houseparent from another home. Grandma, along with Benny's aunt, couldn't get the boys back so she arranged to have them picked up.

Each of the boys returned with their belongings in a garbage bag. When they came into Pinger Mike knew their clothes needed to be washed. Steve's in particular smelled like urine.

"Hey guys," Mike said. "Good break? Let's get your wash going."

After leaving their clothes in the laundry room, the boys sat down and ate. By now, Kim had finished combing the girls' heads and was talking with the boys and listening to their accounts of break.

"We missed all of you. Kyle, I hope you missed me," Kim teased.

Mike listened in as he wandered back and forth between the laundry, the dining room and the TV room. The Bears game was on TV and he was trying to keep up on the score.

The boys' recount of their break was muddled. Knowing the right questions, Kim sorted things out.

"How's your grandma doing? Were you kind to her and did you follow the rules?" Kim said looking directly at Kyle.

Kyle responded, partly irritated at Kim because she picked on him and partly appreciative of the attention.

"Sheeze. Why are you looking at me? What about everyone else?" After a quick pause, Kyle added, "Yeah, grandma's fine and we were nice to her. We didn't backtalk her. We all took care of the younger ones and made sure everyone got something to eat."

"Levy was mean to me. He wouldn't let me eat a few times," Steve chimed in.

"That's because you were irritating him and everyone else. All you had to do is what Levy asked you to do," Mally said. "And then you took off and no one could find you for that whole day. You were just being a baby."

"Nah-huh," Steve replied. "You complained about Levy hogging the food too. You were hungry when I was."

Wayne added nothing to the conversation. He sat there quietly eating his lunch and watching everyone else.

"It was a fun break for me. Having no rules is always fun!" said Benny ignoring the boys' bickering. "I'm surprised I decided to come back."

"We're glad you did Benny," Kim said. "I hope you were good on break."

"It was great!" said Benny with an odd laugh.

A little later Mally told Kim in a private conversation, "Benny got high a couple of times. Huffing stuff, saying weird things and acting all out of it. We laughed at him, but I was kind of worried he might get hurt."

Mike figured that supervision was lacking at home and the kids had to fend for themselves. The older siblings, who were only kids themselves, attended to the younger ones who were preschool age.

Overhearing the conversation, Mike got the impression that Kyle was happy to be back. This was not apparent unless you knew his personality. When Kim asked, or more to the point, peppered him with questions, he came forth with a lot of information. From Mike's perspective, it wasn't hard to see that Kyle enjoyed Kim's attention.

The good news was that four of the boys were nit-free. The bad news was that Steve had nits. Kim shampooed his head and sent him to the shower. Then she combed him out.

While being combed out Steve whined, "You're pulling my hair. It hurts."

Kim ignored him and kept on combing. "We've got to get these bugs out," she said.

Eli arrived in the early evening and both his mom and uncle came in.

Eli's mom, Vinnie, said, "Eli was bored at home. He hung out with cousins and they played a lot of basketball."

After a short visit, Vinnie and Eli's Uncle Moore ate, drank coffee then headed on their way. After they left Eli asked Mike, "Did Notre Dame win their last game? I didn't get a chance to watch."

"No, Eli. They had a bad year and that means they didn't make a bowl game," Mike answered. "But the Bears are playing well!"

Sweets and Cott didn't make it back that Sunday. The school social worker had been in touch with Sweet's grandma and Cott's aunt. He let Kim and Mike know that they were set to arrive the following day.

That Sunday evening was relaxed. Most of the students seemed tired but happy to be back. A dinner of sloppy joes served buffet style, made the meal less formal than usual. As everyone sat to eat Kim asked "Would you rather?" questions.

"Mike, would you rather have a golden retriever or a pit bull?" Kim began questioning.

Mally chimed in before Mike could answer, "Mike deserves to have a big tough dog like a pit bull."

Kim said, "Wrong. He looks like a golden retriever guy!"

The questions Kim asked that night were quite funny, drawing the occasional laugh or cringe from the students. Mike, from his side of the table, marveled at Kim's ability to draw everyone in and make them feel they were part of the Pinger Home. It was another small, important step allowing everyone to trust the environment while having some fun.

Sweets arrived on Monday morning after the others left for school. Kim and Mike were still in the home when he and Grandma arrived. Kim and Grandma spoke briefly, then she hugged Sweets and left.

Sweets then said to Mike, "Since I'm late, I guess I don't have to go to school today."

Mike said, "Okay, but we have to do the laundry and clean the house from top to bottom."

Sweets quickly said, "I'm ready for school."

Kim checked his hair and happily reported, "No nits!" as Mike hustled him out of the house.

Cott arrived on Monday around dinnertime. His aunt Malinda explained that they had car troubles. She apologized for not getting Cott back on Sunday. Since it was time, she stayed and ate dinner with the home.

Malinda was average size in height, on the heavy side, with a round face. She had short black hair, was well-spoken and chatty. She wore jeans and a sweatshirt. Mike guessed her to be in her early thirties.

Malinda was not shy in visiting with everyone over a meal of tater-tot casserole. She told everyone about her life mentioning that she had been in the military.

Malinda said, "I had to get a GED to get into the army because I dropped out of high school. As you guys get older, you're going to have real-life problems and hard decisions. Best you stay in school because that's the easiest way to get ahead."

Mike was surprised at Eli's interest in Malinda's military experience. He asked her several questions. "Was it hard to get into the army?" He then followed up with, "Was boot camp tough?"

The other students were respectful but mainly quiet during the meal. Mike could tell they were listening to what Malinda was saying. He also tried prompting the students, hoping they would ask their own questions but, other than Eli, no one said anything.

While they ate, Cott acted disinterested, even embarrassed. He didn't add anything to the conversation and seemed relieved when the meal ended. After Malinda left he was more at ease, finally hugging Kim.

"Cott, are you doing okay?" Kim asked.

"Yeah, just tired," he replied.

"How did break go for you?" Kim asked sensing there was more to his story.

Cott's eyes filled with tears. "Well, my mom's in jail again. She got caught drinking and driving. There wasn't a lot of room at grandma's so I slept at my uncle's place a few nights."

"Well, we're glad you're back and there's a nice comfortable bed waiting for you upstairs," Kim said smiling.

Mike listened to Kim and Cott's conversation, remembering that Cott lived with his grandma, her two daughters and several of their children in a small house in Cherry Creek. Cott was older than the other kids and often left on his own. Sensing his disinterest during the meal, Mike was fairly sure that Cott did not feel close to his aunt Malinda.

The struggles of the first few months were Mike and Kim's only experience at setting a home routine, so Mike was surprised by how smoothly the restart was. The students now easily embraced the expected dinner, prayer and bedtime practices. Charges were now simply a regular activity that needed attending to.

On the drive back from break, Kim and Mike discussed the importance of the Pinger Home routine. They re-dedicated their effort to maintaining consistency in the home environment. Expecting the students to be respectful at weekly Mass, having students help with meal preparation, family-style meals as a norm with the students using proper table manners, even lowering the lights after 7:00 p.m.as a means of calming everyone, were expectations and practices Kim and Mike recommitted to.

Mike celebrated a simple, yet profound breakthrough that first week back. The normal bedtime routine entailed the students going upstairs to their rooms at the assigned time. Mike would either go with them or head up a few minutes later. Upstairs there was the normal practice of settling down, as twelve students, in six bedrooms, got ready for bed.

As Mike would walk down the hallway, he'd look into the students' rooms giving everything the once-over. During that simple check-in, there might be a short discussion about the day's events, a reminder about something coming up, or some other small exchange. Then Mike would turn out the lights, ending with "good night."

Not always, but most often the students would reply with "good night" or some other acknowledgment. Mike wasn't sure why this was the exact routine, but he liked it as the last connection before the students went to sleep.

Throughout the fall Mike began to realize that Benny had never actually said the words "good night" to him. Benny and Cott roomed together and Cott was always quick to reply, usually with "good night." On a rare occasion, Benny might say something funny, but most often he was silent.

Mike was not sure when he came to this realization during the first months of the semester, but he had a discussion with Kim about it. They agreed it was possibly something in Benny's background – maybe a safety or trust issue. But they also felt it was personal to Benny, so it would be best to monitor but not approach him directly.

Then one night during that first week back, Mike was going about his normal bedtime routine. After turning out the lights in Benny and Cott's room, Mike said quietly, "Good night, Benny. Good night, Cott."

Mike then heard Cott say, "Good night."

As Mike began to move along to the next room, he quietly heard Benny say, "Good night, Mike." Mike stopped, paused, smiled and kept moving. He didn't want to give Benny a chance to retract his three words.

After Mike monitored the hallway for a while he went downstairs where he found Kim and Sally visiting.

"Guess what?" Mike said, giving a fist pump, "Benny just said 'good night' to me."

The week flew by and suddenly, Mike and Kim were off for three days. The December weather on that Sunday morning had turned cold and the South Dakota winds blew hard. At the house, the heat was working but there was no middle setting for the temperature. When Mike turned it up, it was extremely hot. When he turned it down, there was minimal heat.

"Damn!" Mike said to Kim. "This thing is crap. I wish I knew how to fix it."

That night, Mike got his first chance to go fishing on the Missouri River. Dan invited Mike to go out on his boat. Dan, who grew up in the area, promised Mike he would take him out sometime.

Dan drove up as the sun was setting, came into the house to get Mike and say hello to Kim. As he entered, he noticed it was extremely warm.

"It's hot in here!" Dan said. "Didn't I get the setting right on the heater?"

"We didn't want to bother you, but it seems as if there is no middle setting," Kim said.

"Well, you should've told me. Let me look at it for a second," Dan responded.

He went over to the furnace and began to tinker with something on the heater. He then went out to his truck and came back with a screwdriver.

"Darn," Dan said. "I can't get this dial to stop on the middle setting."

Dan then used the handle of the screwdriver and tapped the dial two times, using force. Suddenly, the fan turned off. Mike wasn't sure what to think.

"I think that did it," Dan stated. "It looks like the heater is now working on all three settings."

"Wow," Kim laughed. "If I had known that all you have to do is smash it, I would have done that myself."

It was dark with light snow blowing around when Dan and Mike left to go fishing. Though cold outside, the river was not yet frozen over. Once they arrived at the marina, Dan had a small boat that he and Mike put into the water. He told Mike he'd had success at this spot, explaining that they would stay in the inlet leading to the river, but not go out onto the main channel.

The wind caused the boat to drift. To slow the movement of the boat, Dan threw a bucket into the water. This slowed down the boat's drag as they drifted toward the main river channel. When they floated too far, Dan would start the motor and pilot the boat back to where they started. Then the process would repeat and they would begin to slowly drift out again.

On a cold December night, in the dark, Mike and Dan fished.

Fending off the cold, Mike got a few bites while Dan caught two wall-eyes right away. They restarted the process several times as their success slowed. Finally, Mike got a hit on his line and it was big. He began to reel in the line as something tugged hard on his fishing pole.

"This fish is fighting me pretty good," Mike said. "I think I have a big one!"

"Reel it in, nice and steady," Dan instructed. "I'll use the net when it gets close."

When Mike got home later that night, he was freezing. The first thing he did was stand directly in front of the heater to warm up. Kim asked how he did. Mike smiled.

"I caught a bigger prize than Dan," Mike said.

"Really?" Kim said. "Wow, good to hear!"

"Yeah. It turns out I hooked the bucket we used to slow the boat from drifting," Mike continued. "I struggled to reel it in for about five minutes."

"So Mr. Fisherman," Kim said barely containing her laughter. "Your first time fishing and you caught a bucket? I'm so proud!"

Kim and Mike stayed home for the next two days, and Mike went on a couple of long walks. He enjoyed traipsing around in the fields adjacent to the house and hiking among the shelterbelts. He found the crunch of the snow, the wind and the cold invigorating. It was peaceful, even prayerful for him.

Over their time off, Kim read a trashy novel and spoke on the phone with family and friends. Together, Mike and Kim watched four movies. Mike remembered it being their first real relaxing set of days off.

CHAPTER TWENTY-FOUR
What a Year!

THE CHRISTMAS SEASON WAS AN exciting time for the kids. Two weeks before Christmas break was to begin, the students helped put up the home's Christmas tree. Kim and Mike had moved furniture around in the great room, making space for a tree in corner of the living room area. They liked the idea that the tree would be visible when they all sat at the table for dinner.

The tree was what Mike called fake, meaning it was not a real tree. Once assembled though, he admitted it looked presentable, and he appreciated that it was easy to put together. He made sure the lights worked before the students strung them around the tree. Then came red and silver ornaments to finish off the decorating.

Realizing that the tree in the Pinger Home basement crawl space was in bad shape, Mike and Kim had resurrected this tree, having found it in a storage place maintained by the sewing ladies. They had sweet-talked Ruth and Mary into allowing them to go through the storage room that contained discarded items. Sally had mentioned being in the room a while back.

"I remember seeing Christmas stuff in there. You and Mike should talk to Ruth and Mary and see if they will let you check it out," Sally suggested.

In exploring the space, Kim and Mike also found old Christmas decorations such as stockings, a wreath, lights and ornaments. They cobbled together what they could and brought their bonanza back to the home.

Besides the tree ornaments, other decorations were placed around the room. The students added a paper chain, stringing it together using red and green paper. They glued the loops together and strung the garland up on the walls. Kim hung mistletoe over the doorway between the dining room and kitchen.

Kim explained to the students, "Two people have to kiss when they stand under the mistletoe."

"Nah-huh," Kyle said. "That's not true. Why would you do that?"

"It's a tradition," Kim said. "For you, it's a chance to smooch your honey!"

Mally was the first to say to Mike, "Come on, stand there and kiss Kim."

"Why would I do that?" Mike asked jokingly.

Most of the students enjoyed decorating. Mike realized that few of them had much opportunity to do this away from campus. The younger students like Sweet Grass, Sadie, Vera, Mally and Eli were the most excited about the home decorations.

The older students were not as thrilled. Wayne seemed totally disinterested in decorating activities. Benny and Steve watched TV after a half-hearted effort to help. Kyle and Cott watched and made negative comments, but eventually jumped in to help with the paper chain.

Sage and Kellie played with ornaments at the table. They seemed happy just chit-chatting with Kim while decorations were going up. Throughout the course of the evening, everyone seemed to find their place.

Kim was a master at finding Christmas gifts for the kids. She was able to utilize the money her dad gave her while shopping in Sioux Falls. She also found other goods in the donated items area. This required schmoozing with the sewing ladies.

Kim secured one nice gift for each student along with other smaller gifts. She used clothing items to round out what each student was to receive for Christmas.

Mike told Kim, "Your shopping abilities came in handy, finally! I never thought I'd say that."

"And I never thought I'd hear it either," Kim responded, happy her shopping skills were put to good use.

Pinger Home had its Christmas celebration on a Friday morning, prior to break. Across campus, each home was to set up its celebration deciding on a schedule for Christmas activities. Kim, Mike, Gene and Andie decided on an early morning event, thinking it would surprise the students.

On the selected Friday, Gene and Andie arrived before the students woke up. They moved furniture and helped set out presents in the middle of the great room. Gifts were laid out in a big circle, in separate piles for individual students.

Mike woke the students before 7:00 saying, "You have seven minutes to get dressed. Then wait up in your rooms and I'll come and get you."

Benny questioned, "Sheeze, are we late for school? Did you sleep in again?"

"Just hurry up, Benny." Mike smiled, appreciating Benny's humor for once.

When everyone was dressed in their school clothes, Mike lined the students on the steps, youngest to oldest. The students looked at him inquisitively. The older students had heard about other homes' Christmas celebrations, so they knew what was going on. The younger students were more curious.

Sweets asked, "Are we in trouble?"

"There's a surprise downstairs. It's not bad, Sweets, so you can relax," Mike replied.

Eli rubbed his hands together and said, "I hope Santa came."

All the students excitedly followed Mike as he waved the group forward. Once down the stairs, they stood in the center of the great room area. Surrounding the students were twelve individual groupings of gifts with a stocking on top. Each stocking had the student's name on it. As the students looked at the gifts, Mike noticed everyone was smiling.

"Can we open our presents?" Sweets asked impatiently.

Kim, holding up her hands said, "Wait! We're going to open these up after you do your charges. Or maybe we should wait until after school."

"What? Sheeze, no way," said Kyle.

"I'm just kidding," Kim said with a smile. "But we're going to open presents one at a time. If you aren't opening a present, you have to watch the person who is. We'll start from youngest to oldest. Now go and sit near the stocking that has your name on it."

Everyone took a seat in a large circle around the great room, sitting on the floor. Mike, Kim, Andie and Gene were seated just outside the circle in various corners.

"Each of you is to open the wrapped gift on top of your pile. Sweets, you're first." Kim instructed.

Sweets tore the wrapping paper off his gift. It was a shoebox, which he opened quickly. Inside were two G.I. Joe action figures. He held these up.

"Pow, pow! Wham!" Sweets immediately made the two action figures fight. Everyone laughed.

Sadie was next. She received a knock-off of a Cabbage Patch doll. She had a big smile when she saw it. "I love it. Thank you everyone," Sadie said hugging the doll.

Kellie chimed in. "That doll looks just like you," and there were more laughs.

As Vera opened her gift, Mike figured she would assume it was going to be another Cabbage Patch Doll. When she saw a toy resembling a Pound Puppy she giggled. As she hugged the dog Vera said happily, "Thank you Kim, Mike, Gene and Andie. Now I have a puppy that loves me."

Mally went next. He got a pogo ball. Showing everyone, he then looked at Mike.

"Hey, Big Guy, do you want me to teach you how to bounce on this? Oh wait, you might pop the ball." Mally called out in his raspy voice. Laughter followed.

Eli quickly opened his present next. He immediately threw his new football to Mike yelling, "Go Irish!"

"That'll give you a chance to improve your throwing. If you want to get better, you have to practice," Mike responded with a thumbs-up.

"Always the coach," Kim said smiling and rolling her eyes.

Kellie received a Rock 'Em Sock 'Em Robot game. She laughed a bit perplexed. "Thank you Kim, Mike, Gene and Andie. It's just what I wanted. I think?"

Andie said, "Now you can take your frustrations out by playing the game, instead of fighting other kids. This way no one will get hurt."

"That's a good life lesson," Gene added.

Steve got a Transformer. After opening the toy he did not say anything. He just started to play with the toy, oblivious that the group was watching him.

Gene chided good-naturedly, "Steve, you forgot something. What do you say?"

"Oh yeah," Steve said, "Thanks everyone!"

Benny was up next. After seeing his new skateboard he joked, "Who wants to trade? Anybody interested?"

"Funny, Benny," Mike said. "I'll have to show you how to use that."

"No way," said Benny. I'll figure it out myself so that way you won't get hurt."

Sage's present was make-up, including mascara. She looked Kim's way and smiled. Kim winked back.

"Hope you like it," Kim mouthed to Sage.

Sage mouthed back, "It's perfect!"

Cott, Wayne and Kyle were last to open gifts. They each received a backpack for books. Once their gifts were opened, Cott and Wayne were quiet, not saying much. Overall they looked appreciative. Then they both stood up and put them on their backs.

"How's this look?" Cott asked everyone. "I'm a school boy."

Kyle, not looking happy said, "Is this all I get?"

He then dropped the backpack on the ground and began looking at the other items in his pile of gifts.

"Sheeze," Kyle grumbled, quietly under his breath, "my gift sucks!"

Kim, Mike, Gene and Andie ignored his behavior.

All the students got additional gifts, including items like socks, sweatshirts, hats and gloves. The younger kids received a few more small toys. Everyone also had candy in their stockings.

Mike looked at the clock and was shocked at how quickly the time passed.

"Hey, everybody," Mike said. "We've got to get going to school. We don't want to be late a second time this year."

The students ate a quick breakfast and headed out. Mike visited with Kellie along the way talking about her gift.

"Kellie, fighting out of anger or meanness isn't right and shows that a person is a bully. But defending yourself and others is a different story. We got you the game to remind you that there's a difference," Mike said this as Kellie nodded, seeming to understand.

Before leaving for school Gene and Kim asked Kyle to stay back. He was still grumbling about his gift when they sat down.

"Kyle," Kim said sternly, "I don't appreciate your behavior. You may not have liked your gift, but you need to be more respectful. We were hoping the backpack might signal to you that high school is coming up and you need to start thinking about that."

Kyle got tears in his eyes and dropped his head. "I know. I kind of liked what everyone else got. I never get anything fun for Christmas. Never have, never will."

Kyle then took a few minutes to compose himself and headed out the door to school. When Mike returned, Kim told him what Kyle said.

"You know we probably could have handled that better," Mike said.

With an enlightened look, Kim said, "I have an idea. Get those two gift certificates you won for that firemen's fundraiser. They were for the convenience store, right? I'm going to need them."

Kim immediately went to the kitchen and started baking cookies. After finishing two dozen, she left the Pinger Home, heading over to see Ruth and Mary.

Arriving at the donated goods area, Kim said, "Good morning ladies! We're short three presents and I was wondering what you had left for student gifts?"

Mary replied, "Sorry, Kim. We're pretty much out since all of the homes have had their own Christmas celebrations. Not a lot of toys donated this year."

"Okay. Well, the Pinger Home wanted to say thank you for the gifts we received. Here are a couple of cards for each of you. The students helped me bake some Christmas cookies as a way to say thanks for all you do for everyone," Kim said knowing she was stretching the truth.

"They look yummy," said Ruth as both women opened their cards. "Wow! Gift certificates! Thanks, that's very nice. We usually get forgotten down here once the gifts are opened."

"You know, Kim, it turns out we did get a few donations just yesterday. We were storing them up for birthday presents. Let me show you what we got. Maybe you can use something from these items. But please don't tell anyone since there's not enough for everyone," Mary said leading Kim to a locked door.

When the students arrived home from school, two wrapped gifts were sitting on the dining room table along with one envelope.

"Who are those for?" Sweets asked when he came in.

"The eighth-graders," said Kim.

"I'm going to go get my G.I. Joe," said Sweets, now uninterested

As other students came into the great room, Kim and Mike asked Kyle, Cott and Wayne to sit at the table by two wrapped presents and the envelope. The other students took notice but not enough to stop. They were more interested in checking out what they'd received in the morning.

"You know, Santa brought you more than just those backpacks. What you received this morning were pre-graduation presents," Mike said. "Wayne and Cott, open your packages."

Each boy grabbed a wrapped present with his name on it and started unwrapping it.

Cott unwrapped his first to discover it was the game Monopoly.

"Wow, thanks! Maybe we can have a game night sometime. Here in the home?" Cott suggested. "I'll beat you, Mike."

"We'll see about that, Cott. As a businessman, I happen to be an expert at that game," Mike bragged.

Wayne opened his gift next, finding a drawing kit. He studied the pencils and drawing pad. Quietly he said, "Thanks. Can I draw a picture for you, Kim?"

"I'd like that, Wayne," she said. "But if it's a picture of me, please make me look thin."

Sitting in front of Kyle was an envelope with his name on it. Mike and Kim figured he'd think his complaints from the morning meant he didn't get a present.

"Kyle, open the envelope and read the card," Kim said.

Kyle picked up the envelope and read the card to himself. He looked puzzled.

"Who are your favorite houseparents?" Kyle read slowly, out loud, with a puzzled look.

Just then, as Kyle looked up, Kim brought in a used Coleco Table Hockey game from the kitchen. She set it on the table in front of him. Then Kim spun some of the players and tossed a small, black plastic hockey puck onto the game surface.

"That's for you," Kim said. "Merry Christmas! And what's the answer to your question?"

Kyle, now smiling, answered quick-wittedly, "Gene and Andie."

As the table hockey game sat on the dining room table, Kim took command of the controls on her side of the table. She turned the dials and moved the metal hockey figures via rods that ran under the surface of the game. Kyle then stood up by the dials on his side of the table. Before he could figure out exactly what to do, Kim shot the puck into the net on his side of the table.

"Goal!" Kim shouted.

Before he could catch himself, Kyle looked up and said, "Hey, this didn't come in a box. Is this a new game?"

"We can give it to someone else," Kim quickly responded as Kyle popped the puck out of the goal.

"No, no," said Kyle trying to backtrack. "I wasn't complaining, really. I like it a lot! It seems cool. But first, teach me how to play!"

"No way," said Kim. "You'll figure it out after I beat you a few hundred times!"

The days between the students returning from Thanksgiving and the beginning of Christmas break went quickly. Mike described it as three weeks of high intensity due to its short length of time. Along with the home and classroom celebrations of Christmas, the regular school routine and campus activities like basketball, there was the mental preparation that some students needed to make before going home. This also added to the level of anxiety across campus.

As quickly as this busy period moved along, Mike and Kim were happy there were no real problems in the home. Even the students who faced the prospect of going home with trepidation didn't seem to be as troubled as before Thanksgiving break. It was as if the routine, along with Mike and Kim's return from the break, signaled something positive to the students. Maybe they're glad we didn't abandon them, Mike wondered on the day Christmas break arrived.

Mike was assigned to drive students home for break. After dropping three kids off in Sioux Falls, Mike drove north for forty miles to deliver the Sage, Kellie, Sadie and Vera home. When he arrived at the trailer where the girls lived, he was surprised at how small and rundown their place was.

As the girls climbed out of the van Mike helped them get their bags. After gathering their stuff, they all quickly went into the trailer. Mike nearly slipped on a patch of ice as he tried to follow along.

As Mike neared the trailer, he was able to see in the window. There in the bare-bones kitchen sat a frail-looking, Native American woman. With thinning grayish hair and glasses, Mike guessed she was in her thirties. He could also see beer cans on the main counter in the room. The girls were now inside, hugging her.

As Mike entered the trailer, he noticed the woman was in a wheelchair. She was missing a leg. Mike was surprised he didn't know this.

Interrupting the girls' hugs, he said "Hi, my name's Mike. I'm one of the houseparents of your daughters."

"My name's Bev. Glad to meet you." She said shaking Mike's hand.

"The girls mentioned a cute blonde woman and a bald white guy being their houseparents. You're obviously not blonde," Bev said with a smoker's gravelly laugh, as the girls laughed too.

"How've they been doing? It's nice to hear their voices on the phone, but I miss them being here with me," Bev said in a more serious tone.

"The girls are doing well in both the home and the school. They make friends easily. Vera and Sadie are fun to be around. Kellie, as you know, isn't afraid to speak her mind and Sage is a wonderful young lady. Kim, my wife, loves the fact they're in our home. She spends a lot of time with them," Mike said answering Bev's question.

"That's nice to hear," Bev said.

After visiting, Mike said to the group, "I've got a long drive back so I'm going to head out. I'll see you guys in a couple of weeks. Merry Christmas!"

Leaving the trailer, Mike suddenly realized there were no Christmas decorations inside. As he walked to the van, he wondered what kind of Christmas the girls would have. It will probably be bleak he thought, shaking his head.

After leaving the house Mike got on the road back to Chamberlain. As he traveled on the interstate through Sioux Falls he was pulled over by a state trooper and received a speeding ticket. The trooper was polite but still issued a $100 fine.

"Where's a blonde wig and fluttering eyelashes when you need them?" Mike muttered to himself as he drove away.

Later that day Mike ran into Jesse who had also taken students home. Like Mike, Jesse's route took him through Sioux Falls where he also got a ticket.

"You got pulled over too?" Mike asked Jesse somewhat shocked.

Jesse said, "After being stopped, the trooper came up to the vehicle to get my license. He asked where I was from before going back to the squad car. I told him I was from Chamberlain transporting students who attend St. Joe's."

When he came back to my vehicle he asked, "Do you know Mike Tyrell?"

Jesse laughed and said, "I told him 'yes.' He then gave me the ticket and left without saying anything else."

"No way!" Mike said. "You're messing with me.

"No, it's true," said Jesse. "Are you in some kind of Witness Protection Program?"

Mike laughed saying, "Just don't tell Kim, okay?"

Kim and Mike spent Christmas break in Illinois, moving between both of their families. It was a welcome time away. Even in the usual rush of Christmas, there was time to reflect on their South Dakota experience. As challenging as the fall had been, the last few weeks were much better. Now, Mike found himself worrying about the students.

Mike noticed that over this break, he and Kim talked a lot more about the kids and their work. After thinking about it, he realized that his negative comments about the students had disappeared.

Heading back to South Dakota, Mike found himself irritated by the panting coming from the backseat of the Nova. This was the result of Kim pulling a fast one on him.

As they were preparing to leave Joliet, Kim had taken the car, telling Mike she needed to go to the store. Instead, she had driven over to the home of one of Mike's friends and picked up a Golden Retriever named Angie. The dog had lived with his friend's mom and spent most of her time outside in a kennel.

When Kim returned with the car, there was now a large dog in the back seat.

"What the heck?" Mike said angrily. "I'm not going anywhere with that dog."

Kim confessed to Mike that his friend Joe had talked to her about the animal back in November.

"He said Angie's a good-natured dog, but she doesn't get enough attention or exercise. 'It'd be cool if you could take her to South Dakota where she'd have space to run around,'" Kim reported.

Mike was perturbed that Kim hadn't said anything to him about this. Mostly though, he was irritated that he had to drive all the way back with an unfamiliar animal. Not being a dog lover, he found himself pouting and fearing the dog might jump into the front seat with him. Angie's panting and bad breath were continuous reminders of the dog's presence.

Mike told Kim more than once, "We have to deal with eight hours of this dog panting in the back seat. This is a dumb idea."

There was snow on the ground the entire drive. It was as cold and windy as one would expect in late December in Wisconsin, Minnesota and South Dakota. Kim, Mike and Angie arrived back home in the dark on December 30th. As they turned off the oil road, they were relieved to find the gravel drive to their house was open.

"Thank God Johnny plowed," Mike said quietly.

Mike and Kim were happy to be back in South Dakota. Once at the white house in the country, Kim opened the rear-side door and Angie jumped out running three laps around the house. All the while her tail was wagging and snow flying. The seven-year-old dog seemed to enjoy her freedom. After a short while, Mike noticed the neighbor's dog had come to say hello.

As Mike and Kim entered the house, they found it cool inside, but the low-heat setting had kept the house at a sufficient temperature. They gratefully kicked the heater up to high.

"It worked!" Mike exclaimed.

"Alleluia!" Kim sang.

The next night Mike and Kim met Jesse, Jeannie, Nellie and Dan at the Rush. As expected, the place was crowded for New Year's Eve. Other school staff were present as well, with many still out of state for the break. Everyone was in a festive mood.

As midnight approached there was a toast. Jesse raised his glass and said, "Well, it looks like Kim and Mike survived 1985. Here's to 1986. May it be a great year!"

Everyone raised a glass, smiling as they thought about past experiences and the adventures ahead. It was then the clock struck midnight.

Mike thought, what a year 1985 had been, as *You're a Friend of Mine* played loudly in the background.

CHAPTER TWENTY-FIVE

Second Act

Train to Chicago

June 9, 1986, 7:33 am

As THE TRAIN JOSTLED MIKE *back and forth, he noticed a mother and young son. They had boarded at Oak Forrest and sat down in seats facing him, about three rows ahead. They were now in the process of changing seats. They passed Mike and then sat directly behind him.*

"This is better, Mommy," Mike heard the boy say. "I like to see where we're going, not where we've already been."

Mike took a deep breath as memories of the last half of the school year played out in his head.

Winter was definitely in the air. A legion of snowdrifts on the ground, a white frozen river, snow covering the bluffs on both sides of the river and temperatures dropping to zero were signs of a South Dakota January. It also signaled the second half of the year was about to begin.

All the students made it back from break on the assigned Sunday. Mike and Kim were relieved and happy to see everyone. Mike felt fortunate that he and Kim didn't have to drive and pick up students, so they were both there to greet the kids and their families as they arrived.

Pinger Home spent the day doing the customary check-in activities like head inspections and laundry. Kim made sure there was food for both the students and their families. Mike was pleased, sensing that all the students were happy to be back.

Throughout the day, Mike and Kim caught up with the kids trying to gauge what their breaks were like. Knowing them better gave Mike and Kim improved insights, not only based on what the students told them, but also on what was not said.

Driven back to school by St. Joe's staff, Wayne, Kyle, Steve and Mally had had a tough break. This was partly due to a longer break period (two weeks at home) and cold weather forcing everyone to live in close quarters. The boys came back tired out. This led them to be short-tempered and mean to one another.

Mike thought it was interesting that the first thing Kyle asked was if he could go upstairs and shower. All the other boys were hungry and ate as soon as they could.

Later, when Kim asked Kyle about break, he responded with some irritation, "You don't want to know," as he shook his head.

Before Benny arrived, Mally and Steve spoke to Kim about Benny's huffing.

"Sheeze, it was really bad," said Mally.

When Benny's aunt dropped him off, Mike noticed that Benny left the car first. His aunt trailed him toward the home, leaving the car running. It looked to Mike as if Benny and his aunt were having words as they walked toward the house. As Benny came up the front steps and into the home, his aunt stopped at the front door. She didn't come in.

As Mike held the door open and greeted her, she fumed, "He's all yours." She then turned around and left.

Benny didn't say anything about the incident, telling Kim, "I had a great break. Then he asked, "Is it okay if I get kicked out?"

"It sure is," was Kim's reply. "But why don't you get something to eat first."

The four girls came back as usual in a van that belonged to the tribe. Upon arrival, they each gave Kim a big hug. On the surface it seemed as if their time home went well. They spoke of their mom and indicated they had a good time. They even reported getting a few Christmas presents.

The following day Kim discovered, through Sadie and Vera, that the two older girls had one, or possibly two drinking incidents. It wasn't clear. They had gotten into their mother's beer. Kellie had another run-in with her mom's boyfriend. Although it didn't get physical, it included a verbal altercation. Since Kim and Mike knew the girls were sensitive to their sisters' tattling, they didn't say anything to Sage or Kellie.

Eli was brought back by Vinnie and his Uncle Moore. Vinnie reported that Eli had a good break, but was bored after a week. Vinnie and Moore didn't stay long, just enough to get a sandwich and some coffee.

When Eli saw Mike, the first thing he said was, "Go Irish!"

Mike was glad to find that Moore seemed sober. Earlier in the day, as he and Kim came back to work, Sally had passed along information about Eli's trip home at Thanksgiving break.

Mike and Kim had not forgotten that Moore was intoxicated and driving the day Eli was picked up back in November. It turned out that when Eli, Vinnie and Moore left the campus, they stopped at the rest area just outside of Chamberlain so Moore could use the restroom. While he was gone Vinnie told Eli, "Hurry up. Get into the driver's seat before he comes back."

When Moore returned, Vinnie told him to get into the back seat. Then Eli, all of twelve years old, drove over 200 miles back to Oglála.

Hearing the story, Mike shook his head. "I never should've let them leave campus that day," he said.

Sally, Kim and Mike decided they would not tell Eli they had heard the story unless it became necessary for some reason. It never did.

Malinda brought Cott back. Like the others, she came in to grab a quick bite and some coffee. She kept the car running, saying the heater wasn't working very well.

"I better not stay too long. See you, Cott," Malinda said giving him a quick hug, then exiting the home.

Mike noted that once Malinda left, Cott gave Kim a big hug. In the discussion that ensued, he told Kim his break went okay but boring. Mike noted that he seemed to have all his clothing, so that was good.

Sweets was last to arrive. Mike didn't notice the car pull up until he and his grandma were already in the house. Of course, his grandma was carrying his bags.

"Sweets," Mike said. "I told you I expect you to carry your own bags. Not your grandma."

"Okay," sighed Sweets, then he quickly changed the subject. "Got anything to eat?"

Kim and Sweets' grandma visited as she drank a cup of coffee. As she had inquired in the past, she asked if Sweets was getting enough to eat. She also wanted to know about Sweet's roommate, noting that Sweets said they got along. Kim assured her they were good bunkmates.

Kim was happy that there was only one case of nits among the students.

"Piece of cake," she told Mike. "I'll have Steve nit-free in no time.

There was a sense of bonding that had begun to take hold in the Pinger Home. Mike marveled that it had happened based on how the year started. A solid connection had developed between the students and houseparents, growing deeper over the final half of the school year.

As Mike would philosophize, the relationship was a simple concept to achieve in theory, but much more difficult in reality. Mike looked at the bond not as a linear equation but more of an experience of the heart.

Mike remembered something Sally had told him and Kim in the fall when they were struggling, "I think it's mostly about perseverance," she said. "Perseverance, combined with shared experiences turns into trust. Trust then manifests itself into feelings and those feelings are simply love and belonging. I hope you get to realize that someday."

Mike further recognized how the Pinger Home environment, with its regular stable routine, helped the kids in many ways. In terms of education, the hour of study time each weeknight greatly benefited individual students' academic progress.

Sweet Grass was bright academically but didn't want to do the work. He made multiple excuses when it came time to do homework. He frequently needed to be redirected as he found ways to veer off track.

Sweets would say things like, "Aw Kim, this is too hard," and "Sheeze. Why do I have to know how to add and subtract? It's dumb."

Vera and Sadie completed their work without a lot of fuss. They sometimes leaned on each other, as twins often do. They did this by giving answers to each other when one was struggling.

Sadie read well for her age and was advanced while Vera struggled. Vera's poor reading skills impacted all her classes, but Sadie would bail her out, so the work was always completed. Together they had good attitudes, which made them easy to work with.

Mike remembered a time when Vera said, out of a sense of frustration, "Sadie's the smart one. I'm the dumb one."

Kim supportively said to Vera, "I assure you, you're not lacking brain power, just confidence. Don't sell yourself short. Mike and I believe in you and your abilities."

Sadie once asked Kim, "When it comes to you and Mike, who got the looks and who got the brains?"

"That's easy," Kim replied quickly. "I got both of them,"

Mally wasn't a great student. He needed additional prompting when it came to schoolwork struggling with both math and reading. He was often late with assignments or they were rushed and done sloppily.

Mike found the contrast between Mally's educational aptitude and his basic depth of understanding quite interesting. Mally was able to carry on conversations about topics that were well above his age level. He could talk about issues like racism and seemed interested in Native ceremonies. Mike also felt he had some sense of understanding group dynamics. Mike referred to him as being "wise beyond his years!"

Mike chuckled aloud thinking of a question Mally asked once. "Do you think the Indians could beat you old white guys if everybody just had bows and arrows?"

Eli was a good student. His athleticism inspired him to get his homework done so he could stay eligible for sports. He would talk about college or joining the military. Mike suggested to Eli that he could do both and used his interest in Notre Dame football to talk about the opportunities afforded through a college education.

"Eli," Mike said. "If you get to college, someday you'll be the next Joe Montana."

Eli quipped, "How about they call me Eli Lakȟóta?"

Steve was not a good student. His perceived role as a victim, because he was picked on, affected his academics. By always playing the injured party, he sabotaged his ability to enjoy success.

Steve did best completing academic assignments in small chunks, with simple compliments to keep him going. If the task was too big or the praise too broad, Steve would find a way to fail. It took Mike and Kim a while to figure this out, but once they did, it helped them work with him more effectively.

Kim told Mike, "I love to see that kid's cheesy smile when he gets a pat on the back."

When Kim would compliment Steve on doing a good job, he would sometimes say, "Hey Kim, as my reward, will you do my homework for me next time?" Then he'd smile.

Kellie and Sage both struggled academically. Kim found out they had missed a lot of school when they were younger. This meant they were behind in the basic skills of reading and math. They weren't a problem behaviorally but struggled with their schoolwork. They tried hard and tried to please. Their afterschool banter with Kim was always unique.

Kim would ask, "Hey girls, how was school today?

Kellie responded first, "It was okay. I don't like math very much. It doesn't make sense."

Then Sage, with a sigh, "School is hard and boring except for art, that's okay."

"I meant the boys in school? How are they?" Kim would say.

Kellie with a smile said, "Sheeze, I can beat up every boy in my class."

"All the boys are mean to me," Sage would add.

"That's because they think you guys are cute and they're intimidated," Kim would say as both girls giggled. "Remember, cute and smart together is a powerful combination."

Benny struggled academically. He saw no value in school, was the class clown and may have had mild brain damage due to his huffing. He tried to avoid work and used humor to hide the fact that he often did not understand the assignments.

Once, when asked about school Benny said, "I'm the smartest one in the class. Next year I'm gonna skip eighth grade and go right to high school or college. That way I don't have to come back here."

Wayne lacked a vision for his future. After working with him on his homework, Mike recognized that he didn't plan to attend high school. It became Mike and Kim's goal to get him through eighth grade. Praising his artistic ability could sometimes help him stay motivated.

Wayne, in his reserved manner, once said, "School isn't my thing so why should I go?"

Cott hoped to go to high school and play basketball. He was okay academically but did the minimum to get by. He was good at math but struggled with reading.

Cott told Mike, "All I want to do is stay eligible and make the basketball team. That's good enough for me."

After Cott's comment, Mike thought to himself, "That sounds like me in school. 'C's get degrees.'"

Kyle could have been the best student in the home, but he was up and down academically. When he was interested in the subject, he worked hard at it. Other times he put in minimal effort. One thing he did well was write. Kim encouraged him in this and, depending on his mood, he might deliver a good effort.

Kyle complained at one point in the spring, "The teachers don't know how to teach. If I wanted to, I could get all A's, but why try?"

After hearing Kyle's comment, Kim rebutted. "Sure Kyle. And what do you say about Mike and me?"

Kyle retorted, "I say I could be the best student on campus, if my houseparents knew how to, how to, ahh, ahh… houseparent." The last word trickled out as Kyle couldn't quite figure out how to end the sentence.

The teaching staff at the school worked well with the students, promoting consistency in the classroom learning environment. All the teachers had their challenges when it came to student motivation and academic ability. Since so many students were behind academically for a variety of reasons, curriculums were modified to meet individual academic goals.

Mike identified early on that none of the students in Pinger had a parent who had graduated from high school. This lack of role models didn't help matters. Since an understanding of how to succeed academically in school was lacking in the families, there was little enthusiasm or vocal support for education.

CHAPTER TWENTY-SIX
Coming Together

THE PINGER HOME STUDENTS HAD a lot going on in the second semester of the school year. Campus-wide interests like athletic practices and games, plus nightly study times in the homes, were part of St. Joe's formal programming. Other activities were unique to the Pinger Home, such as celebrating birthdays, hiking in the Chalk Hills, sledding, gym-time, pool-time, or game nights. Collectively, the array of pursuits provided Kim, Mike and the students with many bonding experiences.

There was a trip to Huron, South Dakota in January. Fortunately, the roads were clear as everyone loaded into the fourteen-passenger van to go to a basketball tournament. The eighth-graders, Kyle, Wayne and Cott, were playing for the eighth-grade team.

St. Joe's team played three games. The Pinger Home students watched and enjoyed each one. In between contests, the kids raided the concession stand. Kim and Mike were constantly counting heads to make sure they didn't lose anyone.

Cott was a good player and started all three games. He played well and was the high scorer on the team. To Mike, he seemed to have a knack for the game that included a desire to improve. In between games, Cott asked Mike how he performed.

"Mike, how did I do?" Cott asked. "I need to work on my shooting. What do you think?"

Kyle was more of a role player, filling in to play aggressive defense or to cover as other team members needed a break. Wayne subbed in also, but with his shy personality, he seemed embarrassed when he got onto the court. Both tried their best with the skills they had.

Kim was certainly the loudest fan as the whole home cheered for the boys. Mike was always amazed how she would shout her hoorays at the wrong time and make everyone laugh. Mike recalled how each of the three boys would react when they'd hear Kim yelling for them. Cott and Kyle would smile or laugh visibly. Wayne's smile was present, but it was more out of embarrassment.

The eighth-grade team lost a close first game and won the second. In the third game, St. Joe's was down by three points to Wessington Springs with ten seconds to go. Cott had been fouled and was preparing to shoot two shots at the free-throw line.

Mike knew the game was over. There was no way this group of eighth-graders could get the ball and score four points in ten seconds.

Kim yelled, "Come on, Cott, you can make this! We believe in you. You're the best!"

"Kim, let him shoot," Mike pleaded.

Cott made the first free throw as the crowd looked on.

"Yay, Cott!" Kim yelled loudly adding a deafening clap. "You've got this one, you can do it."

"Kim, shush," Mike said. "You're making him nervous."

Cott missed the second attempt but as the ball bounced off the rim it came right back to him. He grabbed it and threw the ball back at the basket while falling to the ground. At the same time, one of the other team's players accidentally fell on him. To everyone's amazement, the ball somehow went into the basket.

"That's a foul!" Mike now yelled, suddenly not worried about being too loud. The whistle blew and Cott was back on the free-throw line.

"You can do this, Cott!" Mike yelled. "Deep breaths."

"Mike, shush," Kim now said. "Don't add any pressure here."

Cott made the final free throw to secure a win. All the Pinger Home students cheered.

"Way to go, Cott!" Sage yelled.

"Sage has a boyfriend," Sweets ribbed.

"You did it, Cott," Kim said hugging him after the game, as the rest of the students looked on.

"Good job, Cott, Kyle and Wayne!" Mike added. "That was exciting."

Everyone seemed happy with the outcome of the final game. Even Sweet Grass supported the boys.

"Good job guys," Mike heard Sweets say to the boys.

Later, as everyone left the facility and walked toward the van, Sweets quietly asked Mike, "Did we win that game? I wasn't sure."

On the way back to Chamberlain, the plan was to go to Mitchell and eat at McDonald's. As the van drove down the highway Mike just missed several pheasants crossing the road. He maneuvered the vehicle, not quite swerving, to avoid the birds. With the movement of the van, there were a few yelps from the back seats.

Kim yelled out from the back of the van, "Do you think I should drive?"

To Kim's question, Mike heard a few "Yes!" responses coming from the group.

"Do any of you kids want to drive?" Mike asked.

To Mike's question, more cheers came from behind him.

As they continued toward Mitchell, Mike sensed they were getting looks from cars moving in the opposite direction. Mike figured it was "those friendly South Dakotans."

Eli, who was sitting in the front passenger seat commented, "People in those cars are looking at us!"

Mike asked, "What do you mean?"

Kellie, Sage and Mally happened to be sitting right behind Mike and Eli. At that point, a discussion ensued in which the students told Mike that they often felt watched, and it was white people looking at them.

"We told you about this," Kellie said. "You know, when we go to the Variety Store they watch us. They don't do that with anyone else. You don't get it because you're a *Wašíču,* a white man!"

Mally agreed. "Yeah, it's because we're Indian."

"It happens all the time," Sage added. "Not just in Chamberlain."

Mike found the comments interesting but wasn't fully understanding. "Okay," he said. "When we go to Mitchell, let's check it out and see if anyone at McDonald's stares at us."

As Mike drove on, it seemed to him that cars in the oncoming lane, as they whizzed by, really were staring at the van. He found this strange and unusual. Mike tried to ignore it, but he noticed there were even a few people actually pointing at their vehicle. Mike thought maybe what the kids said was true.

As they pulled into McDonald's in Mitchell, the stares and finger-pointing persisted. Mike parked the van and everyone piled out.

Mike whispered to Kim, "Are people watching us?"

Not hearing his discussion with the kids, Kim replied, "What're you talking about? We have twelve Native American kids with us. Of course, people are staring."

"That's not what I mean," Mike shot back.

As the Pinger Home walked into McDonald's, the overt looks continued, supplemented with smiles and an occasional laugh.

I'm sure I'm just imagining this, Mike thought. It's probably due to the conversation we just had. I'm just overly sensitive to something that isn't real.

As everyone lined up at the counter, the kids were prepared to do their own ordering. In the fall, the one time the home ate out, Kim found that most of the kids were not comfortable ordering food. It was a life skill they had not all learned. Often when ordering, the students would just say, "I'll have that," indicating they would have whatever the person in front of them had ordered. It was easy and took away the chance of embarrassment.

Two days before the trip, the kids practiced ordering with Kim. During practice, each student was supposed to order what they had already rehearsed. The plan worked fairly well until Wayne and Steve, the last two in line, were nearing the counter. Once there, they lost confidence and begged Kim to order for them. Kim initially told them no, but as they persisted she ended up placing their order. She was afraid that if she didn't assist, they wouldn't get anything to eat.

Fortunately, McDonald's had a large area to sit down and eat, so the home was able to secure a big booth where everyone ate in a big group. As in the Pinger Home, Mike and Kim sat at opposite ends and the students filled in between them. As everyone ate, there was a lot of talk about the games and the trip in general.

At one point Mike said to Eli and Mally, "I thought we were being looked at earlier. Now I don't believe so. What do you think?"

Before Eli or Mally could answer, Mike was distracted by other students who had finished their meals and gotten up to throw their trash away. Just then an older man came over to Mike and asked something about a limit.

"What?" Mike asked, with an initial concern the man may have had a beef with one of the kids.

The man again asked, "Did you get your limit for the day?"

Mike thought the man was being condescending and was concerned that this might lead to a confrontation. He stood up to try and get more clarification.

The man saw that Mike looked puzzled and said, "You have a pheasant hanging off the grill in front of your van."

Mike again asked, "What?"

After a brief explanation, Mike realized that one of the pheasants he thought he avoided was caught in the grill of the van. The poor pheasant had been stuck for fifty miles.

Mike thanked the fellow and now hurried outside to look at the van. He was hoping to see what the man was referring to before any of the students got to the vehicle. Of course, he was not fast enough. Every Pinger Home student as well as Kim quickly finished their meal and followed him outside.

As Mike went around to the front of the van, there was indeed a dead pheasant hanging from the grill by its claw. Mike immediately felt bad for the gnarled bird.

"Ew, that bird is dead," Vera said. "Gross."

Benny chimed in, "Good hunting, Mike."

"Oh my, your fishing and hunting skills are stellar!" Kim exclaimed. "But you better keep your day job!"

In his mind Mike was now dealing with a second issue he hoped to keep from the students, getting the pheasant loose.

"I don't want to touch that thing," he muttered under his breath.

Fortunately, Mally came to the rescue and quickly removed the claw without even asking. Then he walked over and tossed the mangled bird into the trash.

Sensing Mike's insecurity as he walked back to the group, Mally said, "I got you covered, Big Guy."

As Mike drove the van back to Chamberlain, he reflected on his earlier discussion with the students.

Later he told Kim, "Back in the fall I really should've been more understanding when they voiced their concerns about being watched. It's a good reminder to listen to the students before judging."

There were other indications that things were coming together for the Pinger Home. Some of the signs were complex but most were simple and subtle. There was the day that a strange car was driving on campus. It was probably just a supporter of the school, but Steve took notice.

"We'd better hide out in case they come after us. Mike, glad you're here to protect us," Steve said overreacting slightly.

In that remark, Mike understood that Steve was looking for security. Mike wasn't sure why, but also hearing the words "we" and "us" when talking about being kept safe made him feel appreciated. It was a simple thing but seemed to indicate that the trust level was growing.

Mealtimes became important to the group dynamics. In the fall Mike often dreaded these occasions. Now it provided everyone with a daily opportunity to interact, converse and share. As twelve students sat around the dining room tables, with Kim and Mike on each end, they had some great discussions. Even meal preparation, with Kim and one of the students, often led to special conversations.

Meals covered topics of interest to individual students, campus gossip, or any range of subjects. Some meals generated serious discussions and others humor. There were times where Mike felt he gained a better understanding of the students, or where he and Kim could share an experience. Sometimes it would be things the students said, but more often it was the way it was presented that revealed a true mindset.

Mike remembered an exchange about bars that took place at one meal. He found it gave him insight into what the students' experienced.

Kyle offered, "Anyone that goes into a bar comes out drunk."

"I don't think that's true," Mike said.

"Everybody comes out stumbling, doing weird stuff," Benny shared.

"Yeah," added Steve. "See it all the time."

Later, Mike reflected on what the boys had said. He realized they probably had never seen anyone they knew go into a bar and not come out intoxicated.

In another situation, Mike recalled the night Kim told the students that Angie was expecting puppies later in March. The students were excited about this and acted as if Angie was family.

"And Mike will be the puppies' grandpa," Kim said as the students laughed.

Remembering other dinner discussions made Mike laugh. At one meal Sadie asked how Mike and Kim met.

"You know Kim is a Canadian citizen," Mike said.

"Nah-huh," Kyle shot back. "No way."

"It's true," Mike said as everyone looked at Kim.

"Yep, I was born in Hamilton, Ontario Canada," Kim agreed.

"I was on a trip near the Canadian border and Kim was at the border on the other side. She was climbing over the fence, so I helped her out. After that we got to know each other, then got married. That's how we met," Mike explained.

All the students at the table looked at Mike then Kim, not knowing what to believe.

"Mike was lucky that day. I was trying to get a ball that had gone over the fence. I should've just left it in the U.S." Kim added as the puzzled looks continued.

Finally, Kim smiled saying, "Josh!" as everyone laughed.

"Sheeze," said Kyle. "You're not an American. You shouldn't even be working here then. Hey, is that why you know how to play that hockey game? Josh," he added with a smile.

Out of nowhere, Mally wrapped up the conversation with, "At least the Canadians didn't steal our land."

Mealtime conversations sometimes took an interesting turn. Like the night Mike and Kim were talking about the importance of college. During the conversation, Mike mentioned college campuses.

"All college campuses are different," Mike said to the group.

"What's a campus?" asked Sweets.

"It's the place you live and go to school. Like here at St. Joe's. Our campus has places to live and a school. A college would be kinda like this, just a lot bigger," Mike explained.

"Mike and I went to a college that had a big campus, including tall buildings to live in," Kim said. "Like Mike said though, every campus is different."

"Like Notre Dame, Eli. If you ever get there, they have a nice layout. One building even has the Golden Dome," Mike added.

"What's a dome?" Sadie asked.

"It's a roof to a building, but curved," Mike said.

"They have a roof that's gold?" Mally asked. "You mean it's just painted gold?"

"It's painted gold, but rumor is they put gold chips in the paint," Mike said.

"Nuh-huh," said Steve skeptically. "Who would put gold on a roof?"

"Sheeze. Like a golden necklace?" asked Sage touching her neck.

"Do people try and steal the gold?" asked Mally puzzled.

"I think they have guards around it," Kim jumped in with a wink to Mike. "Every once in a while they catch people trying to climb up on the roof and get the gold."

"That's stupid," Steve said. "Why wouldn't they just try and hide the gold? I'd try and hide it if it were mine, not put it on my roof. Unless that was my hiding spot."

"And who lives in the house with a gold roof?" Vera asked.

"It's an administration building. The president of Notre Dame and the department heads work there," Mike said.

"Oh, so the rich people live there," Cott said. "It figures. They don't want anyone to get their gold."

"Well, I'd like to go there and climb on the roof," Mally said. That would be cool to stand on gold. I'd have to wear moccasins so I didn't scratch it."

"But, but, Mike," Sweets said, trying to get in a comment. "What do they do when it rains? Cover the gold?"

"Yes, Sweets. They have a big tarp," Mike said laughing.

Kim and Mike tried to make birthdays special for each student. On the day of a birthday, there would be a poster hung up first thing in the morning acknowledging the student's special day. Students would be given their choice of food to be served at dinner. Siblings would be invited over for the meal.

At some point in the day, usually in the evening at snack time, there would be cake, ice cream and a gift or two. Kim used her talent, finding each student at least one special item. Of course, they always sang Happy Birthday, including a special middle-verse, which was a tradition in Mike's family growing up. Over time, the kids even picked up the words and tune.

Reflecting on Cott's birthday celebration earlier in the year, Mike felt they needed to emphasize the special nature of the day to a greater extent. Sure they had covered the basics, but Mike felt it was too much of the home just going through the motions. Afterward, he and Kim committed to celebrating the importance of the whole day. Mike even made a point of saying Happy Birthday, as the final words the students heard at bedtime, after Good Night.

"You know we have to make a fuss over everyone's birthday," Mike told Kim. "We don't know what past birthdays were like, or how future birthdays might be, so let's focus on the one we can celebrate. You know, a special day, just for each student."

As Mike and Kim became more comfortable in the houseparent role, Kim's nurturing characteristics naturally came forth. Mike observed that Kim could be firm, but acknowledged her street smarts to be able to sort out inaccuracies in the kid's stories. She also had a sincere love and bonded with each student in special ways.

Kim loved the girls and the "sister thing." She could joke with Sage and Kellie about boys and understand adolescent issues. Yet she had a certain tenderness with Vera and Sadie. She understood fights between sisters and never overreacted when they all would get testy with one another.

Kim would tell the girls, "I fought with my sisters all the time, but in the end we're sisters and that's a bond that can't be broken. You'll laugh about your fights someday."

"I hope so," said Sage. "Because Kellie sure can be mean."

"Yeah and don't you forget it or I'll beat you up," Kellie said, showing her fists. Then all the girls laughed.

Kim could be tough with Sweets and did not put up with any disrespect. He thrived on discipline and consistency. He also loved the attention.

"Okay, Kim. I know. I'm trying. Sheeze," Sweets would say with a sigh after being disciplined.

Mike related to some of the boys through sports. He would take them to the gym for basketball or throw a football around in a nearby field. He found the boys related better if there was activity with action.

Mike's relationship with Cott improved as time went on. Mike understood this based upon Cott's acknowledging him with funny comments or one-liners.

"Hey, old man," Cott would say, "You're too slow."

Mike worked well with Eli from the beginning and that never changed. They bonded over sports and discussing which teams were better. Eli was a good athlete and Mike took the time to compliment him on his athletic ability. Mike also knew Eli had an interest in the military. He spent time talking with him about self-discipline and how that might help him.

Kyle grew to be a favorite of Kim's and loved the attention. He would challenge her and question things. But Kyle also grew to know when it was time to relent if he pushed things too far.

One day Kyle said to her, "Let's arm wrestle. I'll beat you bad."

"Okay," Kim said as they squared off. "But if I win you have to say, 'Kim you are better than me.'"

"I'm not saying that!" Kyle said.

Kim then tugged his arm to the table in one quick yank.

"See, I'm better than you. I told you so," Kim bragged, not letting him lift his arm off the table.

"Okay, okay, you win. I give," said Kyle as Kim released her pressure.

Once his arm was free Kyle added, while quickly running away, "I let you win. You're not better than me."

Kim and Mike both had a fondness for Mally who was good-natured, loved animals and had a positive disposition. He was kind to Sweet Grass, his roommate, finding some good in whatever Sweets was doing. But he also had a toughness that was apparent after you got to know him.

Mally loved dogs and often told the story, "Everyone in my family has a dog. My dog Pogo is the best rez dog ever. He knows a lot of tricks but is tougher than every other dog."

Kim totally respected anyone who loved dogs. So she made a point to ask Mally about Pogo after each break.

Kim and Mike caught on to Benny who was always trying to do or say something inappropriate. They came to realize it was his way to get attention. They knew his regular threats to get kicked out were a ruse. The plan Kim and Mike deployed was to simply ignore his negative comments. They also tried hard to compliment him when he acted more appropriately.

Although Wayne was quiet and reserved, he eventually became more trusting. As this happened, he revealed more of himself. Kim and Mike, learning he could draw fairly well, were quick to praise his art. They would ask Wayne to draw something for a special occasion – often a poster or greeting card. He'd smile and always say yes.

At one point, Mike asked Wayne, "Can you draw me a picture of Kim? And don't forget to sign it. I'll hang onto it. If you become famous it might be worth something someday. Kinda like the Mona Lisa." After saying that, Mike was sure Wayne had no idea what he was talking about.

Wayne also drew Mike several other pictures always asking, "How's this look?"

Mike would reply, "I think this is the one. Looks great. I'll put it in my vault."

Kim and Mike recognized Steve's low self-esteem right away. As Mike and Kim acknowledged earlier in the year, this was exacerbated by the way his three siblings treated him. His acting like a victim was essentially playing a role expected of him. Kim and Mike worked to find the right balance in Steve's interaction with the other boys, intervening if the criticism was too harsh or excessive.

"You doing okay, Steve?" Kim would ask, trying to demonstrate her concern for his struggles.

Mike recounted an early February visit from Kim's mom and dad. They braved the cold weather to drive in from Wisconsin. While Kim's parents were at Pinger, the kids were on their best behavior. Although the students didn't always engage guests verbally right away, they did pay close attention.

One thing Mike noticed was how the kids observed the interaction between Kim and her parents, and their relationship with him. By his account, the students seemed interested in what Glen and Doreen expected from him. As the students warmed up to Kim's mom and dad, they asked more questions.

"Does Mike treat your daughter good?" Mally asked Kim's dad.

Glen responded, "Of course, that's what I expect out of him."

"Should we call you if he doesn't?" Mally asked.

"Absolutely. I'd expect a call right away, but don't call me if Kim is mean to Mike." Glen said somewhat seriously, then he smiled.

The students were curious about many things like how Kim acted as a young child.

Kyle joked with Kim's mom, "Did Kim get into trouble ever?"

Doreen answered, "No, she was an angel."

"Nuh huh, sheeze, that can't be true. I'm sure she got in trouble all the time." Kyle replied.

"Did you teach her how to cook?" he then wanted to know.

"I guess so. I'm a baker though. I like making pies, cookies and things like that. Kim is more of a cook, making meals for you in this home." Doreen responded.

"Well, one day I made a comment about her cooking and she got mad. I was just trying to help her cook better," Kyle said as Kim pretended to glare at him.

The four girls also were able to sit down and talk to Kim's mom. Mike remembered them all sitting on the couch in the great room listing to Doreen's stories about Kim.

At one point Mike overheard Doreen say. "Yes, Kim and her sisters did fight. They would fight over clothes, friends and even tattle on one another. I'm sure you don't have those problems.

Mike laughed as he noticed the girls look at one another and smile.

What Mike thought was funny was how interested the boys were in Glen's car. He drove a Lincoln Town Car and the boys referred to it as a "Caddy" or "limo."

Mally, Steve and Sweets peppered him with questions about the car.

"Where'd you get that limo?"

"How many people can fit in your Caddy?"

"Are you rich?"

Kim's dad enjoyed these questions, laughing and giving them answers like, "Save your money and get one yourself someday!"

Glen was an avid golfer. Although there was snow on the ground, Mike wanted to show his father-in-law the local nine-hole course.

On their return, after crossing the river, Glen pulled up at the only quasi traffic light, located in the middle of town. It was a three-way stop with blinking red lights affixed to each stop sign. At the intersection, Mike recognized Ruth from the sewing room in another car stopped at the adjacent stop sign.

As Glen drove up, exhaust billowed up from Ruth's vehicle. Sitting at the stop, she hesitated to drive through the intersection. This caused Glen to hesitate. This behavior went back and forth three or four times with each car nudging forward, then stopping. Glen became frustrated. Finally, Ruth made her way into the intersection. As she drove in front of Glen's car, he gave her the finger.

Mike quickly reminded Glen that he was in a small town. "Everyone knows everybody else," he said. "That lady works at St. Joe's. This isn't Chicago!"

In a log entry that March, Kim wrote:

Things seem to be coming together. We are enjoying the students more each day!

CHAPTER TWENTY-SEVEN
Winter Weather

THE OUTDOORS IN SOUTH DAKOTA, the vast openness, broad horizons, and ever-changing weather, affected everything from moods to the ability to travel. The landscape undulates from flat or slightly rolling plains, to the breaks of the Missouri River, to the wind-worn peaks and rocks of the Badlands, to the Black Hills. The countryside became something that both Kim and Mike appreciated over time. Mike, with fondness, would describe the open space as a place of rugged beauty.

Living in the white house in the country forced Mike and Kim to respect the outdoors for the good and bad it brought them. There were hot, 100-degree days in the summer. There were below-zero temperatures and cutting wind chills - sometimes 20 to 30 degrees below - in the winter. Summer's heat could be oppressive, while winter's biting wind chill could be downright painful and truly dangerous.

When it came to the cold and the students, Mike would laugh at the number of times the boys in the Pinger Home told him, "We don't get cold. We're Indian."

Mike thought about the difficulty of driving on the gravel portion of their road when it snowed. There were several times when he or Kim got their Nova stuck trying to make it home. It was the neighbor, one mile to the south, who dug them out with his tractor. Throughout the entire winter, he repeatedly cleared a path in the snow, so Kim and Mike could get through.

Dan was also a savior to Kim and Mike that winter. Several times, he pulled the car out of their circle of a driveway by way of a chain hooked to his four-wheel-drive pickup. Mike remembered that quick jolt as the chain would become taut, then the car would lunge forward. The movement was accompanied by a loud screeching of metal as the car would start moving.

Mike recalled a conversation where Dan warned him, "Stay away from driving in a blizzard."

"Really? I've driven in bad weather before," Mike replied. "You just have to take it slow."

"Trust me," Dan said. "Driving in the country when it's snowing with a thirty-mile an hour wind is dangerous. Doing that just once will give you a lifetime's respect for driving in bad weather. It's not only terrifying but life-threatening."

The worst winter driving situation Kim and Mike encountered that year happened on their day off. It was a school day in February and Kim had offered to assist Nellie in the infirmary by driving Sadie to Pierre, South Dakota to see an orthodontist. Kim had talked the administration into letting Vera go along for support.

At the last minute, Mike volunteered to go along with Kim and the girls. Since it was their day off Mike didn't have anything pressing. He thought Kim might appreciate another driver.

In the morning, instead of heading off to school, Sadie and Vera, along with Kim and Mike, loaded up in a school car and headed off to Pierre.

As they headed out of town Kim said to the girls, "Since Angie is having pups, we can't leave her alone. Would you mind if we picked her up and brought her along?"

Sadie replied with a smile, "Yeah. That would be neat," as Vera nodded in agreement.

Mike added conspiratorially, "I'm sure it's against school rules to have a dog in the car, so we'd better keep it hush-hush."

Vera held a finger to her lips, silently promising not to tell.

They picked up Angie, the golden retriever and headed to Pierre. Mike drove, with Kim in the passenger seat. The two girls and Angie sat in the back.

The forecast that day was for one to two inches of snow later in the evening. The temperature was cold, but not extremely so. When they left, the sky was blue with a few white, billowy clouds. Pierre was a ninety-mile drive from Chamberlain on the highway.

Mike had come to enjoy highway driving versus always traveling on the interstate. The traffic was lighter and the open road had a nice unbridled feel to it. In his limited experience, he felt that highways tended to roll across the open landscape and hills, whereas the interstate often cut through the flattest part of the terrain. Driving on these routes caused Mike to feel more in harmony with the land.

He was grateful that this particular jaunt included changing landscapes. Sometimes the view consisted of bluffs that overlooked a frozen white Missouri river. With recent snows, the ridges and foothills were also dotted with pockets of white. At other times, he drove on the open prairie, which was accentuated with patches of snow on this wintery day.

Parts of the drive were picturesque, while other long stretches of flat farmland provided Mike with a sense of inner peace. At one point the road took them through the Crow Creek Reservation.

Somewhere on the open road Kim said, "We'd better let Angie out."

"No problem," Mike said. "Only in South Dakota can we stop on the highway because there are no cars on the road."

They pulled off on the side of the road at a spot that provided an appealing view of the river. Kim took Angie for a quick walk while Mike stayed in the car with the girls.

"Look at the ice on the river," Mike said to the girls. "It looks neat with the river frozen over and covered with snow. Reminds me of vanilla frosting."

As they arrived in Pierre, light snow began to fall. Kim, Sadie and Vera went into the orthodontist's office for the appointment. They returned to the car a mere thirty minutes later.

Kim reported to Mike, "It went well. Sadie and Vera were great!"

"Since that didn't take long, how about we go to the State Capitol and look around," Mike suggested.

"That would be fun," Vera said, not really knowing what she was agreeing to.

As they drove to the capitol building Mike realized the legislature was still in session. There were large numbers of cars parked in the area. Mike and Kim decided they could look at the capital from the car. As they drove around the girls noticed the dome on top.

"Hey guys," Mike said. "Remember a discussion we had about a dome? Well, that roof is what you call a dome. However, it's not gold like the one we talked about."

"Boring," Kim chimed in. "But seriously girls, do you know what goes on at the capitol?"

Sadie said, "No, but it's a big building."

For the next few minutes Kim, then Mike, tried to explain how the government works. Mike realized he had gotten too technical in his explanation, so he started singing.

"I'm just a bill. I'm just a bill and live on Capitol Hill!" Mike belted out.

"Mike, your explanation is confusing to the girls and your singing is awful," Kim said as the girls laughed.

"Sadie and Vera, just know, when you grow up remember to vote. Vote for good people who aren't corrupt and you'll be fine. Oh, and marry someone who can sing," Kim continued.

"Kim, I'm sure the girls don't understand what corrupt means and my singing is fine," Mike interjected. "Remember, voting is a good thing and very important."

"Maybe someday one of you can hold office or even be the Governor. If you did, that's where you'd work. We'd come to see you here in Pierre. Promise!" Kim said.

"Since that is such a big building, I'd even do your charges," Mike added. "Because the Governor is always cleaning up everyone's mess."

"That's not funny," Kim said rolling her eyes as the girls looked at both Kim and Mike, now quite puzzled.

"Ignore him," Kim said, ending the conversation.

Next, the group went to lunch as the snow continued. It was snowing a little harder now, but not enough that Mike had any worries about getting back to Chamberlain. His goal at that moment was to find a place where he and Kim could sit down and eat with the girls.

They found a nice little restaurant in downtown Pierre. Once seated, Kim reminded the girls that it was proper to put a napkin on their lap, like at Pinger. Then she talked about using a menu. Sadie and Vera each found something they liked and Kim showed them how to order. When the server came around they both looked at Kim for approval, then ordered.

"I'll have a grilled cheese sandwich and soup," said Vera. "Please."

"I'll have a hamburger and fries, please," Sadie said.

When the waitress left Kim told them, "That was very good. Now you know how to order. You can eat at any restaurant."

Sadie and Vera both smiled as they sipped their pop.

During lunch, Kim peppered the girls with questions. Questions ranged from things at the school to asking about their lives back home. With Kim's gentle prodding Sadie and Vera seemed more than happy to answer. Mike sat back and mostly listened.

After lunch, Mike was impressed when they found Angie waiting patiently in the front seat of the car. Kim of course, had saved half of her hamburger and fed it to Angie as she opened up the car door.

"Hey, watch what you're doing," Mike warned Kim. "Don't get food all over the school car."

"Take it easy," Kim said. "She's having puppies. Right, girls? Let's give her a break." Sadie and Vera laughed at this exchange.

"Sadie and Vera, I'm going to take Angie for a quick walk, so she can take care of business. Do you want to come?" Mike asked.

"No, thank you," Vera said. "We're cold."

"Turn on the car so we can warm up," Kim said as they all piled in. "We'll wait for you."

Mike put a leash on Angie and proceeded to walk her down the block.

Finding a spot for the dog, Mike asked, "Are you enjoying your time with the girls in the backseat? This is a good lesson in motherhood. You can practice being their protector."

Mike then caught himself. "Man, I'm starting to sound like Kim," he muttered shaking off the cold.

By the time they left Pierre, the snow had been falling for several hours. Although it was light, about two inches had accumulated on the ground. Mike noticed the snowflakes getting bigger and the snowfall heavier. There was little wind though, so he still had no worries.

As the group drove into the country the snow fell more heavily. Then the wind came up and large flakes blew straight across the windshield. The snow began to stick to the road and Mike felt the car fishtailing slightly. The weather continued to worsen the farther away they drove from Pierre. Mike estimated that six inches of snow had now fallen.

He asked Kim, "Do you think we should turn around?" Before she could respond, Mike said, "Nah, we'll be fine."

They drove on. Mike guessed they were about halfway between Pierre and the Crow Creek Reservation when the wipers began to freeze up. He was having a hard time seeing out the windshield. It was now snowing harder and with the wind, the road conditions worsened. The car could only crawl along slowly.

At some point, it became apparent to Mike that despite the treacherous situation, they only had one option. He swallowed hard.

As quietly as he could, Mike whispered to Kim, "We can't turn around because if we try a side road, we'll get stuck. There's too much snow. And with this visibility, we can't make a U-turn. Another car might come along and smash us. It's too dangerous. We're just going to have to keep going and pray we drive out of this. We're at the point of no return."

Kim whispered, with some worry, but not panicked, "Just take it slow."

Sadie and Vera had heard Mike's comments, which lead Sadie to say, "Kim, we're scared."

Kim, responding out of instinct, unbuckled her seatbelt and climbed into the backseat. While crawling over, her foot kicked Mike in the head. She placed herself between the two girls.

Angie, sensing it was too crowded in the back, jumped into the passenger seat where she sat panting as she looked out the windshield.

Kim put her arms around the girls. "We'll be fine," she said.

After fighting tough road conditions for a good hour, Mike turned south. Here the snow was blowing straight across the highway, which caused drifts to form on the road. As the car hit each mound of snow, it would jerk and the tires spun out. For the next half hour, the car crawled over many large and small drifts.

At times the wind blew the snow so hard that the visibility went down to zero. Mike could feel the vehicle jostle back and forth. When that happened, he felt his pulse jump rapidly and his hands get sweaty. They were going so slow that the car nearly came to a stop several times.

At one point, Mike hit a large drift and the car turned sideways on the road. It was now pointing toward a huge snow pile. He hit the brakes, stopped the car and put it into reverse. He was able to back up slightly. That gave him enough room to get some traction so they slowly corrected and began moving forward again.

Mike looked over to the passenger seat. There Angie sat, stoically looking straight ahead. He reached over and gave her a quick pat.

Kim, Sadie and Vera were now hunched closely together and holding hands. During the occasions of zero visibility, Mike heard the girls gasp. He clutched the steering wheel tighter with each passing mile.

Finally, the car crawled into Ft. Thompson on the Crow Creek Reservation. Mike pulled into the casino parking lot, stopped the car and whistled.

"Guys, I think we should stay put for a while," Mike said.

Everyone in the car was silent, thankful they had made it this far. Mike felt emotionally exhausted. Then, after a few minutes, Angie barked. She saw a cat plowing through the snow, passing in front of the car. Everyone laughed.

As they sat there for a short while, Mike sensed the snowfall was lighter and the wind was dying down. He wasn't sure if it was because they were in a town, but to him the weather now seemed better.

"I wonder if we can make it," Mike asked Kim.

After about fifteen minutes, they cautiously started up again, driving south through town onto the open highway. Surprisingly, the conditions had improved. Mike began to feel like they could make it back to Chamberlain. They drove slowly at first, but as the snow and wind lessened, the roads improved.

By the time they arrived in Chamberlain the snow was light with little accumulation on the ground. After nearly three hours and a ninety-mile return trip, the vehicle pulled up in front of the Pinger Home.

Mike heard Kim tell the girls, "That was some storm. See what prayers will do for you!"

Vera said, "I was scared. Thanks for sitting with us."

"And remember guys, we didn't have Angie in the car," Kim reminded the girls. "Right?"

As Kim took the girls inside the home, Mike could see through the window. He saw Sadie and Vera hug Kim before she came back to the car.

Kim and Mike drove across campus, picked up the Nova and returned the school vehicle to the garage. In between, they snuck Angie into their car as quickly as she would move.

"Let's get home," Mike said.

"I agree," was all Kim could muster as they drove back in silence.

After arriving at the white house in the country, it took Mike a few minutes to unwind. Once he did he said, "I swear, I'm never driving in bad weather again."

Kim, turning on the television then said, "Looks like they just issued a winter weather advisory for tomorrow. And, by the way, we're not going anywhere."

As the snow fell through the night and into the next morning, the heater began to act up. Mike played with the regulator switch trying to make it work. He did this several times in the morning and throughout the day.

Each time Mike jostled the switch, the heat would increase and the fan blow warm air out across the room. This would last for about an hour. Then the heat would decrease, the fan would quit and the house would grow cold.

In the late afternoon, Mike again fidgeted with the valve. Suddenly, a surge of flames came roaring from the heater, which made Mike instinctively jump back. Then, there was nothing and it appeared as if the heater was not working.

After a moment, when Mike felt it was safe, he approached the heater again and jiggled the valve. Hearing a loud pop, he jumped back, nearly falling down this time.

Now there was a huge flame emanating out of the main cylinder of the heater! Mike estimated it lasted about 20 seconds. Before Mike could react, the emergency cutoff kicked in and the flames ended. Now there was a plume of thick black smoke pouring out of the heater. The smoke quickly filled the main room and kitchen.

"Dammit, Mike. I told you to get another heater," Kim said reacting to the flame as she quickly closed off the bedroom and side rooms.

Mike opened windows in the smoke-saturated rooms as Kim continued to yell at her husband. Mike heard the words but ignored his wife as he hurriedly tried to air out the rooms.

After the smoke cleared Kim and Mike accessed the now freezing space. The walls were covered with soot. Exasperatedly, Kim's next move was to call her friend Nellie.

"Can we stay at your place again?" Kim asked, holding the phone to her ear while looking sternly at Mike.

"Yeah, I know the heater is crap," Mike heard Kim say in a defeated tone.

As daylight was beginning to fade, Mike noticed a lot of snow had accumulated on the ground outside. Now feeling dejected, he took a deep breath.

"We have to get going before it gets dark. With our luck we'll probably get stuck," Mike said. Let's just close the windows for now and figure it out later."

"I hate this weather," Kim said.

Kim and Mike grabbed a few things quickly preparing to head for shelter at Dan and Nellie's.

"We have to take Angie," Kim said. "It's too cold for her. And her pups are due to arrive soon."

So Kim and Mike piled into the Nova, with Angie sitting in between them.

"Wait, I have to turn off the water or everything will freeze," Mike said as he quickly ran back into the house.

The next day, when the storm had cleared, Kim was determined that the soot on the walls would not deter her. She marched down to the hardware store and bought cheap paint. Once she and Mike had cleaned the walls, they repainted the main area of the house.

At some point Jeannie, Jesse and Jamie showed up to assist. Mike and Kim were happy to accept the help.

When they arrived Jesse teased, "You guys need to smoke fewer cigarettes."

Mike had secured several space heaters, so the house stayed warm enough to keep the pipes from freezing. That allowed the couples to get the rooms painted in one afternoon as everyone donned extra layers of clothes to stay warm.

Later that night Mike told Kim, "Using space heaters isn't ideal but we have no other choice. It'll be expensive. We'll use these until we find another inexpensive oil heater. I guess that's the price you pay for trying to live on the cheap in the first place."

"Yeah. And living with a real handyman doesn't help either," Kim added sarcastically.

In March, in the corner of the mudroom at the white house in the country, Angie delivered ten puppies. As Mike expected, Kim loved each one and named the puppies after the ten kids in Mike's family. They were Mary Pat, Jean, Kathy, Karen, Phil, Mike, Tim, Tom, Bob and "Jimmy the runt."

Having to tend to the puppies, Kim sometimes left the Pinger Home to run back to the white house in the country. Kim would take several students with her, those who were on their best behavior. Over time, each Pinger Home student adopted one of the dogs.

During dinner, the kids would talk about the puppy they had adopted. Since there were ten dogs and twelve Pinger Home students, Sweet Grass paired with Steve, and Vera with Sadie in calling a dog their own.

One night, bad weather from a spring storm was expected. Travel was forecast to be difficult into the next day. After dinner Mike took Eli, Steve and Mally to fetch the dogs and bring them back to the Pinger Home.

Once the dogs were in the home, the weather deteriorated quickly. With no possibility of returning the puppies, they spent the night. Of course, the Pinger Home kids played with the puppies until bedtime. That night Angie and her pups slept in Kim and Mike's room.

The next morning Mike yawned and told Kim, "Just another night of no sleep. What else is new?"

Over time Mike felt a sense of pride, knowing that he and Kim had survived that first South Dakota winter. As much as he wanted to say, "We beat the weather," he knew that, in reality, they were humbled by it. Like a lot of other things that year, they learned this lesson the hard way.

In one of the logs from late winter, Mike wrote:

The students sure love dogs! And, we learned to never disrespect Mother Nature here in South Dakota.

CHAPTER TWENTY-EIGHT

Getting to Spring Break

THE PUSH TOWARD SPRING BREAK began in mid-March. As was the case in November, negative behaviors started about two weeks before the break. The difference now was Mike and Kim had established relationships with the students. Knowing more about their backgrounds and the way students would react was helpful. This allowed all parties to talk through difficult situations before they blew up into a crisis.

Trust, growing out of shared experiences, was a critical factor. As the students' trust grew, so did their ability to feel comfortable. This helped them better express concerns and anxieties, which allowed the issues at hand to be resolved.

When spring break arrived so did transportation day. All the arrangements had been made; Kim and Andie would stay at Pinger while Mike and Gene would transport Wayne, Kyle, Mally and Steve. The three sisters from another home on campus, and Benny too, would be transported with the group.

Before leaving, Mike reminded Kim, "Please keep an eye on Eli's Uncle Moore."

"I will," Kim said, knowing Mike felt terrible about the fall trip.

On transportation day, the weather was bright and sunny with the temperature in the low 60s. It had been a wet spring with some recent heavy rain. In addition, the snow that was on the ground had been melting over the past week. This meant it would be muddy in the country and on the roads outside of White River.

As the van left campus, Mally spotted an eagle flying over the river. He pointed it out to everyone. Mike had still not seen many eagles, so he marveled at the sight.

Gene said to the group, "You know seeing an eagle means good luck."

"I'll make my own luck over break," Benny yelled from the back of the van.

Ignoring Benny, Mike said to the group, "I hope we see more than one so you guys all have a good break."

As the van got closer to White River there was a point where they could take the shortcut or keep going on the highway. The highway route happened to be paved. The shortcut would save about twenty minutes but required taking a gravel road.

As they got closer to where they had to make a decision, Kyle chimed in from the back of the van. "We're going to take the shortcut, right?"

Gene shouted back, "Is that faster?"

All five boys and the three girls now emphatically said, "Take the shortcut. It's way faster."

As Gene turned onto the side road, Mike estimated that they had about fifteen miles to go until their destination. As the van moved along, the gravel soon turned to mud. Suddenly the vehicle began to fishtail. The van slowed and Gene tried to keep it moving.

Then Steve yelled from the back of the van, "I told you not to take the shortcut. It's too wet."

The rest of the group then chimed in, asking why Gene had taken this route. Beneath the van the road got muddier and slicker. Gene ignored the comments and focused on keeping the vehicle moving. To everyone's dismay, the van continued to slow down.

"Gene, try and keep it going," Mike said out of concern. "If we stop, we'll be here for a while – maybe for the whole break!"

From the back of the van, questions about driving on the road persisted.

"Gene, we told you not to come this way," Benny stated, and all the others agreed.

Finally, just ahead lay a small incline. As they came upon it, the van began to slide sideways. Gene stepped on the gas as the fishtailing continued and mud flew. As they neared the top of the hill, Mike was sure they weren't going to make it.

One last time Mike heard Mally yell, "You shouldn't have taken the shortcut!"

Then, surprisingly, the van made it onto and over the crest of the hill. As the vehicle moved across the crest, the traction got better. It was now likely they would make it after all.

"See, Gene, I told you taking the shortcut was faster!" Kyle yelled from the back of the van as everyone else seemed to agree. Mike rolled his eyes.

Mike and Gene found the trailer house where the boys and girls lived. It was in a strip of seven rundown white trailers. Some of them had boarded-up windows. Most had broken down cars in the yards. There were also dogs roaming freely.

The students lived in the last trailer in the row on a gravel road. Next to that were two old, dilapidated, shed-like metal buildings. The few windows in the buildings were broken out with the doors hanging off hinges. Mike recalled different times when the boys talked about playing in these buildings.

When the group pulled up, the kids jumped out of the van and ran into the trailer. Mike noticed a few wooden pallets lining the pathway from the dirt road to the house. Since there weren't enough pallets to cover the entire distance, parts of the path ran through the mud.

Mike said to Gene, "There's mud everywhere."

"I know," Gene replied. "And look, no one thought to take their bags or take their shoes off when they went in."

Mike and Gene then grabbed the bags of clothes from the back of the van and carried them to the door. All the while they tried to stay out of the mud, but to no avail. They each now had heavy muck covering their shoes.

Once at the trailer door, they spotted Levy inside with the rest of the kids running in all directions. Looking in, Mike saw a rundown kitchen with a beat-up table surrounded by broken-down old chairs. He also spotted what looked to be a very old refrigerator.

Levy came to the door and said, "My grandma isn't feeling well," as he shook their hands and thanked them for giving everyone a ride.

Kim had packed boxes of food, so Mike enlisted Mally and Kyle to go back with him to the van. They each took a box and helped carry them back to the trailer. All the while, Gene visited with Levy.

"Levy," Gene asked, "Can you make sure everyone gets some of this food?"

"I will," Levy promised.

After a few more minutes of chatting at the door, Mike and Gene said goodbye. By now chaos was reigning as the kids were running in and out of the trailer.

As Gene and Mike headed toward the van Benny said, "Goodbye," as he started walking to his house.

With his back now towards them, Benny yelled, "Now I have a week where you can't tell me what to do!" He took off running and laughing loudly.

Mike and Gene headed back to Chamberlain. This time they took the longer route that included paved roads. It was "smooth sailing." They laughed at the fact the boys had convinced them to take the shortcut in the first place.

"I should have known it would be muddy and not good driving," Gene admitted to Mike.

"I think I saw terror on your face for a while," Mike said with a smile.

"It was my determined look. No way was I stopping. I'm just glad we made it." Gene chuckled.

When they returned to Chamberlain, Mike asked Kim about her day in the home. She said everyone's ride showed up.

"Best of all," Kim said, "Eli's mom picked him up and his uncle wasn't with her."

Mike and Kim drove to Wisconsin and Illinois for the break, leaving Angie and her pups with Nellie and Dan. On Sunday they attended Mass with Mike's parents and several siblings. During Mass, Mike thought about the boys and girls back in White River.

"Lord, please look after our Pinger Home kids," Mike prayed with sincerity.

After Mass, everyone went to brunch at a nearby pancake house. At one point, the topic of the students' beliefs came up. Mike told everyone about an interesting conversation he and Kim had with Andie at a changeover meeting. Andie mentioned the value the Lakȟóta people placed on children.

"She told us that the Lakȟóta word for child is wakȟáŋheža (wah-ky-yeh-jah). It translates to two words in English, sacred and gift," Mike relayed. "In referring to each child as a sacred gift or sacred being, it gives you a sense of the respect and appreciation Native Americans have for children."

Mike told everyone he and Kim had tried to adopt that idea into their work with the students.

"It's strange, but that has allowed us to not only better understand the uniqueness of each student, but to see the distinct spiritual sense each child has," Mike said. "Most of the Pinger Home students don't practice religion in the traditional sense, meaning their families don't go to church. But they are spiritual individuals. And that spirit is something we've come to respect. We realize it needs to be nurtured. So we try not to judge, just encourage the students in this regard."

Later, Mike and his dad sat down and talked about South Dakota.

"Things are going a lot better, Dad," Mike said.

"Sometimes, part of figuring it out is just hanging in there," Don replied. "In the fall it seemed so hard for you and Kim. Now, you look happier."

"Yes, I'm glad we didn't give up," Mike added. "Guess we're figuring it out."

Mike and Kim spent the week visiting with family and friends before returning to South Dakota. They were excited about the last two months and finishing out the school year. While in Illinois, Mike checked with Arthur to make sure the job offer still was in place. He was happy to find out it was.

In a March log written after transporting students home, Mike wrote:

We made it to another break. The kids are great, but never listen to the students when it comes to directions.

CHAPTER TWENTY-NINE

Family Trip

April and May were a blur. Besides the usual lessons, homework and charges, there was softball and track for organized sports. There was also free time outside for unstructured activities.

The nicer weather and longer daylight hours caused everyone's mood to be more positive. Mike noticed more smiles across campus. Spring fever hit the older students, who then had to be supervised a little closer. Overall, everyone was in good spirits.

As the students from Pinger and the surrounding homes were able to play outside with greater frequency, the camaraderie among the houseparents grew. The staff saw each other more often as they jointly supervised students. This led to more gossip sessions, which Kim always enjoyed.

Mike would often visit with Jesse when the students were outside. Jesse was always in a good mood, giving everyone a hard time. He tended to be in the middle of a lot of fun-loving banter among both staff and students, and he thrived on the attention.

Mike and Kim both felt like the Pinger Home bonded further when they went on the home's "family trip." This took place in April. Across campus, each home would save money from their budget and plan a weekend trip. The excursion was viewed as an opportunity for the kids to travel and see different parts of the state.

Pinger Home decided to go to the Black Hills, referred to as Pahá Sápa by the Lakȟóta people of South Dakota. The plan was to head out right after school on Friday. Students were to hustle back to Pinger when school ended that day.

Everyone in the home was allowed a small travel bag for clothes. Kim and Mike tried to help the students pack. In addition, Kim prepared food and packed coolers.

All the bags, coolers and people had to fit into the van so there was no choice but to pack efficiently. Student bags were carried downstairs before leaving for school on Friday morning. Mike loaded the van while everyone was at school.

All the youngsters seemed excited when they arrived home that day. There was a quick potty break and then everyone went out and climbed into the van. Surprisingly, no one had to be told to hurry up, not even Steve.

With everyone finally loaded up, Mike announced, "Next stop Wall Drug!"

As the van backed out of the drive Sweets said, "Mike, I've got to go potty."

Mike hit the brakes and was about to reverse into the driveway when Sweets added, "Josh, just kidding!" Everyone laughed.

"And we're off!" Mike said. "I hope we have everything."

"Me too," Kim replied. "Too late to turn back."

"Hey wait, I forgot my boxers!" Benny yelled out jokingly.

Over the course of the year, at other off-campus events, when stops were made, the students looked for Mike and Kim to take the lead. This caused the kids to form a cluster, often in two groups, moving around together rather than as separate individuals. Mike liked this arrangement, partly because it was easier to supervise.

If there was one person who Mike worried about getting lost, it was Steve. At other outings, Steve had a habit of being the last one to come back to the group. More than once, he had been told, "Hurry up, Steve," especially from Wayne and Kyle who were usually exasperated with him. Steve was easily distracted and would be mesmerized by all the merchandise available, especially souvenirs.

Mike had to remind him often, "Steve, come on, it's time to go!"

The van's first stop was Kadoka, South Dakota, 114 miles west on the interstate. It included a fill-up and restroom break. Mike and Kim were pleased with the students' behavior. After a short breather, everyone made it back to the van without incident. This was partly because Mike made Steve stay with him the entire time.

Getting ready to get back on the road, Mike said, "Hey, I only counted thirteen of us. Who's missing?"

"It's you, Old Man. Are you losing your mind?" Benny yelled out as everyone laughed,

"Oh, that's right. Way to go!" Mike said, rolling his eyes.

Kim then quietly said to Sage and Kellie, "And try to find a guy who's not losing his marbles," as the three of them laughed.

Next, the group drove through the Badlands National Park. It was roughly a 40-mile loop that allowed travelers to easily get off, then back on to I-90. The drive took them through a barren landscape of scenic, multi-colored striation, with jagged peaks and unique layered rock formations.

In the Badlands for the first time, Mike thought, "I get it. These truly are 'bad lands.' I could see how difficult it would be to travel through here back in the day."

At one point, Mike pulled into a parking area where he and the students got out and walked down a trail. The kids enjoyed the view of the landscape and appreciated the time to stretch their legs. It was a short trail, taking a mere fifteen minutes to navigate.

Kim stayed with the vehicle while the group was on the trail. She used the time to prepare sandwiches, chips and cookies. Once everyone returned and ate, it was back into the van and on the road again. What Mike and Kim hadn't planned for was the winding drive.

Twenty-five miles into the loop, they had to make a quick stop on the side of the road. Cott had what they term a "weak stomach."

Cott yelled to Mike, "Stop! I have to get out of the van."

As Mike pulled to the side of the road, Cott jumped out of the vehicle and left his dinner there. After that, he was allowed to ride up in the passenger seat for the remainder of the trip.

When Cott got back in Mally yelled, "Cott, we'll mark that spot as 'Cott's Oasis,' best food in the Badlands!" Everyone laughed.

Other amusing comments came from the back of the van as the group continued on their way. Everyone seemed to be in a good mood, including Mike and Kim.

The Badlands Loop ended at Wall but instead of stopping at Wall Drug as originally planned, Kim and Mike decided to keep on going. Mike drove on, eventually passing through the edge of Rapid City as it began to get dark. After another hour they arrived in Hot Springs. There they all excitedly piled out of the van and bustled into the hotel.

After the group checked in, Mike supervised the boys and Kim supervised the girls. Mike noted some of the boys still had a lot of energy from all the driving. Benny in particular was talking loudly and wandering back and forth between rooms.

It took over an hour but eventually the boys calmed down. Mike, now familiar with the boys' behavior, was able to give everyone some space to calm down. Mike was proud he didn't over-react but still set reasonable expectations.

After the boys calmed down, Mike visited with Kim. She told him the girls were doing fine and settled down rather quickly.

"Must be my excellent supervision skills," Kim noted with a laugh.

Mike woke up the bed-wetters later that night. Thankfully, the two were dry and ready to go the next morning. Mike was glad for the boys, knowing they had avoided embarrassment had their sheets been wet.

Mike had been monitoring the bed-wetting situation throughout the winter. Though not perfect, it had improved. The boys were dry on average about five nights a week and they were quick to take care of their wet sheets if they needed to.

"Let's pray for one more dry night," Mike told Kim out of empathy for the boys.

Saturday started with a quick breakfast. Mike found a bakery so the group ate donuts along with juice that Kim packed. Everyone was hungry so the food went quickly.

The students were expected to pack and be ready to go in short order. It was a bit chaotic but everyone got the job done. There was horseplay but all was good-natured. Everyone was excited to go swimming.

The group headed to Evan's Plunge, a large indoor facility where the water was naturally spring-fed into the pool. While there, the students, along with Kim and Mike, spent the morning swimming and playing in the large pool area. The warm water felt good as the temperature outside was on the cool side for a spring morning.

Mike remembered the kids having a great time. He laughed, thinking about a series of four rings that allowed a person to swing over the pool if they were strong enough. Eli, Mally and Cott were able to move from ring to ring, grabbing hold of the next ring, until they crossed the entire pool. The rest of the boys and girls made it different distances, then splashed into the pool.

Kim passed on the rings, not even trying. When Mike took a turn, it looked easy to him. He grabbed the first ring and swung out. After just a few feet, he slipped off the ring and fell into the pool. He wasn't even close to grabbing the second ring.

Benny yelled out, "You're a weak Uŋčí." Then he laughed his loud Benny laugh.

Knowing Benny, Mike assumed it was a funny comment but was unaware he'd just been called a "grandma."

After several hours of swimming, the group dressed and headed toward Rapid City. It was a stunning drive through the Black Hills with a panorama of millions of pine trees. Mike drove as usual, with Cott sitting in the front passenger seat. This led to several interesting conversations.

At one point Cott said, "I've lived in a lot of different places. We didn't always make it to school but when you're smart, you're smart. Who needs school anyway?"

Mike shared his personal experiences in school. "I wasn't a good student. Sometimes it was tough. But Cott, you'll need school in order to get a job and be successful in life."

"If I can make it in the NBA, that's all I need to be successful," Cott said.

As a result of these discussions, Mike came to realize Cott's multiple relocations probably led him to feel isolated and alone at times. It also explained why he had developed his unique sense of humor. Mike further reflected that his lecture about getting a job was probably misplaced to a kid who just wanted some permanency and security.

Mike realized that right now personal and emotional survival were way ahead of career concerns in Cott's mind. And the NBA comment was made from a kid, who was just being a 'wide-eyed' kid.

Mike was also worried about what was going to happen to each of the Pinger Home students once they left St. Joe's. He was even starting to worry about the upcoming summer and what they might have to face away from campus.

"Is there anything we can do to better ensure their safety?" Mike had asked Sally several times during the spring.

Meanwhile, Kim was in the back of the van playing "I spy." She would lead with, "I spy with my little eye, something green."

The students in the rear seats of the van then tried to guess what Kim was looking at. At times, it grew loud and boisterous, with answers, laughter and catcalls. From the driver's seat, Mike could tell everyone was enjoying the game.

"Wow, the group really has bonded," Mike thought to himself with a smile.

The next stop was the hotel in Rapid City. The group checked in as fast as they could. Everyone tossed their bags in the rooms and headed for late afternoon Mass at a nearby Catholic Church. They were running late.

Once Mike found the church, everyone scrambled out of the van and hurried. As the group got closer to the front door, they could hear music playing.

"Hustle everyone," Mike said. "If we're in our seats before the first song ends, we're technically not late. That's what my mother, the best Catholic I know, told me."

Once inside, the usher escorted them to two rows located in the middle pews of the church. Mike smiled as they sat down just as the song was ending. He turned to Kim who was now sitting behind him one row and winked.

Since they were such a large group, there were a few looks as they settled into their seats. Mike didn't view them as hostile, just inquisitive. He also realized he liked being with a big group at Mass and was proud he and Kim were with these youngsters.

The kids were great throughout the service. After the priest read the Gospel and shared his homily, Mike looked at the two rows of students. He counted three of them nodding off – Sweets, Sadie and Steve. Mike could tell several others were on the brink.

A short time later the collection basket was passed. Since a collection plate was not part of the service at St. Joe's, the students looked on curiously. Mike observed Mally, who happened to be sitting next to him. Mally watched intently as the basket moved from row to row. Mike could tell he couldn't figure out what was going on.

Before the basket got to their pew Mally whispered, "What's that?"

"It's a collection. You put money in it. It's for the church, or the poor, or some other project." Mike whispered.

Mally looked puzzled, then asked smiling, "I'm poor, can I take some out?"

As the collection basket passed by and moved to the row behind them, Mike observed Benny grabbing it. He looked right, then left, pretending as if he was going to take money out. From Mike's angle, he saw Kim staring at Benny, then shake her head. Finally, she smiled at him. Several other students giggled.

After Mass, the priest noticed the big group, "Hello. Where's this big family from?"

Mike informed him, "We're the Pinger Home from St. Joseph's Indian School in Chamberlain."

Just then Cott walked by and said, "Hurry up, dad. We're all hungry."

The priest then inquired, "Are some of the students your personal children?"

It took Mike a few minutes to explain they were on home trip and what that meant. When Mike got back to the van he jokingly told Cott, "Your daddy's mad!" Cott giggled.

Next, the group stopped at Burger King for dinner. To save time Kim stood at the front of the line to assist everyone with ordering, which helped speed up the process.

Although the temperature was a little cool, the restaurant had an outside picnic area large enough for the group to sit down and eat. Mike again instructed everyone to "hustle up," as there was more on the schedule. Partly because of his prompting, but mostly because of hunger, dinner was consumed quickly.

"I'm glad no one's staring at us," Mike commented to Kellie.

"Guess we didn't hit any pheasants," Kellie replied with a smile as Mike chuckled.

Later on, the home went bowling. It was not only fun but entertaining for Mike and Kim. Cott, Kyle and Wayne had bowled before as part of a league at the school. They seemed to know what they were doing.

Mike watched the other students who had never been to a bowling alley. Sage, Kellie, Vera and Sadie couldn't quite figure out the shoes. After giving their size to the attendant, bowling shoes were placed in front of them. The ugliness of the shoes caught their attention. The four girls looked at one another, incredulously.

Under her breath Mike heard Kellie say, "Sheeze, these are really ugly! Is this what we're supposed to wear?"

Kim, now at the counter, sensed the girl's apprehension. She gave the attendant her size and then shoes were laid on the counter.

"Nothing like some lovely bowling shoes," Kim said with a wink. "Guys love girls with cute footwear."

Bowling moved along quickly. From trying to keep things in order, to instructing the kids not to bowl when the guard was down, Mike remembered the event being a chaotic affair. He was happy when the second game moved along more smoothly than the first.

As bowling neared an end, Mike commented to Kim, "I think everyone has knocked down at least a pin or two. Nice to see the kids having fun."

"I think so too. But I pity the smelly feet when we return the shoes!" Kim said as Mike laughed.

Eli and Mally seemed to enjoy bowling the most, trying to achieve the highest score. Benny made farting sounds whenever Kim or Mike bent over to bowl. The four sisters seemed to have fun, watching a group of boys four lanes over. Sweet Grass had a short attention span, so he was never ready when his turn came around.

Mally, of course, reminded Sweets often. "Pay attention Sweets. Sheeze! Too slow."

After bowling, the home went to see *Crocodile Dundee* at the local movie house. Everyone seemed to have a good time in the crowded theater. Most of the students hadn't been in such a big movie theater before. They were allowed to sit wherever they wanted, except for Sweets who landed between Mike and Kim.

When the movie ended, everyone headed to the van. Upon arriving at the vehicle, Kim realized Steve was missing.

"Mike, you'd better go back into the theater. Steve's not here," Kim said partly concerned and partly annoyed.

Mike ordered, "Cott, Kyle and Wayne, let's go. We've got to go find Steve."

"I knew he'd get lost," Kyle moaned.

Once inside they found Steve wandering around in the lobby. He hadn't realized that everyone else had left. Mike was glad they located him so quickly.

"Steve," Mike said exasperated. "You have to pay attention. You could've been locked in here all night."

Cott chimed in, "Mike, but think of all the candy he could have eaten!"

"Sorry," said Steve. "But where did you guys go?"

"To the van," Kyle grumbled. "Where did you think we went?"

"Well, I don't know," Steve whined.

When the group returned to the van Kim called out, "Steve, we missed you. And better yet, no early bed tonight," as everyone laughed.

As the Pinger Home drove back to the hotel everyone chatted animatedly about the movie. Mike heard a number of "Hey, mates!" with Australian accents, coming from the back. He couldn't help but laugh, happy that everyone had a good time.

There wasn't a lot of horseplay at the hotel. Everyone was tired. Lights out came without much fuss.

During the night, Mike awoke the bed-wetters. Again, he was happy to find out they were dry the next morning.

In the morning the kids were moving slowly. Mike went out early to get more donuts and milk. Kim had packed cereal and juice so everyone had plenty to eat for breakfast. It was chaotic, with a few spills, but the group muddled through.

Once the van was loaded, they headed to Mt. Rushmore. They arrived early and the crowd was light. For the most part, the students seemed happy to be outside and moving around. It was cool out when they arrived, but the sky was bright blue and sunny.

In the early morning light, Mike thought the white rock surfaces of the four heads on Mt. Rushmore looked pristine. He commented on this to the students who were nearby. As the students looked at the monument, they had comments and observations.

Sweets asked, "Who are those guys?" and "Why did they put their heads on a mountain? Are they in the movies?"

"We were here first." Mally chimed in. "Where are the Indian faces?"

"Kim, they should chisel your head up there and not forget to include your big beak!" Kyle said, looking to see how Kim might react.

"Your head should be up there with the black eye I'm going to give you," Kim said looking at the four faces and acting as if she was irritated with Kyle.

Mike doled out a ton of quarters while everyone took a turn looking through the pay-to-view binoculars. After taking in the monument and watching the *Making of the Mountain* video, the group headed to the next destination, Crazy Horse Memorial.

Earlier in the week, to prepare for the trip to the monument, Kim read information to the students about the monument. They learned that construction began in 1948 by the sculptor Korczak Ziolkowski. His idea was to carve a sculpture of the great Oglála leader Crazy Horse (Tȟašúŋke Witkó). This was to honor the Native American people in a place that was sacred to them, the Black Hills.

As the van drove into the Crazy Horse Memorial Mike explained to the attendant at the entrance, "We are from St. Joseph's Indian School."

To Mike's surprise, the man informed them that, Native Americans got in for free. "Enjoy your time here," he said.

While Mike was talking to the attendant from inside the van, Cott kept saying, "Dad, I have to go to the bathroom," and "Dad, hurry. I'm hungry."

After leaving the attendant and driving into the parking lot, Mike joked with Cott, "I'm going to make you sit in the backseat if you don't quiet down. Got it… Son?"

As everyone entered the Visitor Center, it seemed to Mike that little work had been done on the monument. Mike noticed the carving or work on the mountain consisted of only a large opening, blasted through rock. As far as he could tell, the hole or opening, was at a place where Crazy Horse's arm would appear, just above his horse. From the distance they were from the monument, the hole in the rock looked rather small. What gave the opening some perspective was a large Caterpillar road grader sitting inside.

Mike and the others got a sense of what the monument would look like when finished because it was drawn out in white paint on the rock surface. In addition, there was a beautiful scaled replica of Crazy Horse astride his stallion in the Visitor Center.

"What an inspirational creation, putting a Native American hero up on the mountain," Mike said to Mally.

"Makes me proud that I'm Lakȟóta and this is in our Black Hills," Mally said respectfully in his raspy voice.

The Crazy Horse Memorial turned out to be an engaging stop for the group. The focus on the celebration of Native American culture was impressive. The refusal of the Crazy Horse Foundation to take government money for the sculpture was very appealing to Mike, considering how the government had treated the Native American population in the past.

The group toured the Visitor Center and the many exhibits on display. The staff at the monument were hospitable and respectful, which enhanced the experience.

"Nobody's staring at us here," Kellie pointed out to Mike.

As their tour ended, everyone gathered and walked to the van. Kim said to the students, "I'm glad we stopped here. I'm also proud of how respectful all of you acted."

While at Crazy Horse, Mike did have to admit to one bad decision. He and Kim had allowed the students to each take a rock that had been chipped off the monument. They did this after seeing a sign encouraging interested parties to take one, as a souvenir.

Every student grabbed a different size rock. On the three-hour ride back to Chamberlain, Mike remembered rocks rolling back and forth on the metal floor of the van. This happened every time they turned, sped up or slowed down. And of course, there happened to be many of those turns in the Black Hills.

There was a quick late lunch in Rapid City before the group headed back to Chamberlain. On the way back, the Pinger Home stopped at Wall, S.D.

When Mike and Kim first drove to South Dakota, they had seen many Wall Drug signs. They were glad to have finally made it to Wall, S.D. Mike had learned that Wall Drug was a famous tourist attraction, known for the number of highway signs and the creativity of the signs.

Wall Drug had many stores, a restaurant, different areas of interest to tourists and many, many souvenirs. Although somewhat rushed, Mike, Kim and the students explored the shops and assorted diversions. Because they clung together, Mike noticed there were many stares as people tried to figure out the composition of the group.

Eventually, everyone made their way to what was referred to as the "backyard." This was where Pinger Home met the dinosaur. At regular, short intervals a Tyrannosaurus rex, whose upper body was about twenty feet high, would come to life. It rose up over an imitation barbwire fence and roared fiercely.

When the dinosaur began to roar, it was so real that Sweets hid behind Mike while Vera and Sadie hid behind Kim. When Kim chided Kyle about his scream when the dinosaur roared, he denied it.

"Nuh huh, that wasn't even scary," Kyle retorted somewhat defensively.

Wall Drug was also famous for advertising complimentary ice water for the weary traveler. Learning about this freebie, Mike warned everyone, "Please use the restroom here and don't get the free ice water. We're not stopping again."

When the van eventually arrived back at the Pinger Home later that evening, everyone was exhausted. There was a quick snack, a short prayer time, showers and bed. During prayer time, there was joking around about various parts of the trip. The students were asked to share one thing they liked about the weekend. Kyle's comment stood out.

"Hey, mates. I enjoyed the whole trip," Kyle said as Kim nearly fell out of her chair.

"Not one complaint, Kyle," Kim said. "That's a miracle."

Kim wrote in the log:

We had a fun family trip. Everyone was on their best behavior! Mike and I both felt a true sense of 'family!' I hope the students did too!

CHAPTER THIRTY

Tragedy

IT WAS AN UNSEASONABLY WARM Friday in late April with a wind blowing hard out of the east. The six-day shift started like all the others with Mike walking the students back to the home after school. The students then began their normal afterschool activities – playing outside, visiting with Kim and watching TV.

As Mike was outside supervising the students, he took a quick break and came inside to get a drink. When he came in, he saw that Kim was busy preparing dinner and visiting with the girls. Just then Sally stopped by, as she occasionally did to check on things. This was not unusual since Kim and Mike had just started a new shift.

During a brief conversation, Sally mentioned that Jeannie had called letting her know Jesse was out in a canoe with two students. The two students were Zee and Scout. They were known across campus, for being two active little third-grade boys who did everything together.

Jeannie could see the river from the windows in the home but had lost visual contact with the canoe. Since Jeannie was with Jamie and the students, she couldn't leave to go out and check on them.

"Jeannie told me they're staying close to shore and wearing life jackets. Sounds like the canoe trip was an incentive for good behavior," Sally said. "Jeannie wanted to keep me informed."

"This wind probably pushed Jesse and the kids down the shoreline," Mike said matter-of-factly as he headed back outside.

A while later Sally came over again and pulled Mike away from everyone, as the home was preparing to sit down for dinner. Her voice betrayed her nervousness and he could see the concern in her eyes.

Sally asked Mike, "Can you drive over to the other side of the river? You need to bring Jesse and the boys back to campus. I assume they're over there waiting."

Mike excused himself from Kim and the Pinger Home students who were seated at the table for dinner. He then met up with Joe, another house parent. They both jumped into the Nova and headed across the river. After passing over the bridge, Mike and Joe drove north on the road running parallel to the water.

Driving down the road they found a location directly across the river from campus. There they saw a car carrying two other St. Joe's staff, Kevin and Blair who had just parked. Mike pulled in, stopping next to them. Everyone quickly got out of their cars.

"What are you guys doing here?" Mike asked surprised to see them.

"We're here looking for Jesse, Zee and Scout," Kevin replied. "Wally called and asked us to come over here and take a look."

"Really," Mike said. "I didn't think this was a big deal. Sally asked us to come over here too."

Mike and the others talked for a minute trying to figure out where Jesse and the students might have come ashore. The wind was blowing directly at them so it made sense they were somewhere in this vicinity on the west side of the river.

At one point, Kevin said, "Be careful if you should come across a body."

Mike was shocked and taken aback at the comment. "Come on, Kevin. What are you talking about? Let's find Jesse and the kids and head back."

The group fanned out to search. As Mike walked along the shoreline, the spray of the river struck him several times. Although he knew the water was frigid in the spring, he was surprised at how cold it actually felt.

After walking along the river and not seeing anything, Mike turned around. He climbed up to higher ground to get a better look and began walking back to where he started. As he came over a bluff that sloped down to the shoreline, he saw Kevin and Blair hunched over something about twenty yards away.

Mike quickly realized it was a body. They were frantically trying to resuscitate a child. It was Zee.

Mike's knees buckled for a moment as he lost his breath. He was paralyzed in his tracks and found that he could go no closer. Everything began to move in slow motion and there was no sound. Then the tears came and he vomited.

Although Mike's mind was jumbled, he quickly gathered himself and sprinted over to assist.

When the ambulance showed up, Kevin jumped in and rode along with Zee to the hospital.

Blair informed Mike, "Kevin and I couldn't get a pulse. It doesn't look good."

By now authorities were present, fanning out to search the rest of the riverbank. Mike and Joe were in shock to the point they had no idea what to do. Finally, they got in the Nova and drove back across the river. During the drive, there was no discussion, only silence.

When Mike arrived back at the Pinger Home, Kim looked at him as tears ran down her face.

Mike held his wife and whispered ever so softly, "Not good."

Although news had already traveled across the river that Zee's body had been found, Kim held onto that last ounce of hope. She hoped that the information was a rumor and not true. She had been praying that Mike would have a different story. Now she knew for sure.

Kim started to sob, loudly at first, then more controlled. By now every Pinger Home student was standing in the great room area, quietly looking at Kim and Mike. No words were spoken as everyone tried to grasp the reality of the situation.

Eventually, Mike steadied himself. He asked for everyone's attention, although he already had it. Mike could not bring himself to tell the students the whole truth but felt he had to say something.

Mike said, "Jesse, Zee and Scout were out in a canoe today. They are lost somewhere on the river. People are searching for them."

There was a gasp and tears from some of the students. The students too were aware of the rumors, so they were hearing information that they already knew. Still, the actual confirmation was not easy for anyone to hear.

That evening there was much conversation and many phone calls across campus, as staff tried to process what was happening. The entire campus learned that Zee was pronounced dead at the hospital. Jesse and Scout were still missing. By evening's end, they were presumed drowned. Everyone was in shock trying to figure out what they should do.

Mike was amazed at the way the students took charge of the home that night. Sage and Kellie politely welcomed other staff who stopped by, displaying empathy that was beyond their years. Cott assisted them, taking care of the kitchen chores and all the dishwashing.

The students were on exceptionally good behavior. They tried their best not to be a problem for Mike and Kim. Mally took over supervision of

Sweets. Kyle selected a couple of movies, taking charge of the younger students, making sure everyone kept the noise down.

That night Mike remembered calling home to his parents. As the students watched TV, he stretched the phone cord and locked himself in the food pantry so no one would hear him. When his mom answered, he physically slid down the pantry door, sat down and cried. It was the hardest he'd cried, in front of his parents, since grade school.

"Mom," he blurted out. "Jesse and two students drowned."

"What?" Ann asked, not comprehending.

When Ann figured out which son had called she told Mike, "Let me get your father."

As Mike tried to gather himself, his dad came to the phone. "Jesse and two of the students went out in a canoe and they drowned," Mike again blurted out in between sobs.

"Okay. Take a deep breath. Start over. Now what happened?" Don said trying to calm his son and figure out what was going on.

As Mike calmed down, he was better able to explain to his dad what he knew. Mike and Don spoke on the phone for less than 15 minutes. As Mike regained his composure he found Don's assurances to be a great comfort that night.

As the conversation ended Mike remembered his dad saying, "I know you hurt a lot, but so do many others, including the kids you work with. Do your best to be strong and protect them. That should be your first priority."

The next day was a blur. The reality of what had happened and the uncertainty of the situation began to sink in. The students continued to be model citizens, which was a comfort to Kim and Mike who were in shock and beginning the mourning process.

All weekend the chores were completed, meals were made and the kitchen was cleaned up. No one had to be asked to do anything. If Mike or

Kim needed a favor, like running over to another home for something, there were plenty of volunteers.

Mike recalled that Kellie, Sage, Kyle and Cott stood out as leaders. They helped keep the routine, assisted with cooking and took charge of supervising the younger students.

Over those couple of days, each Pinger Home student displayed a sense of empathy and kindness that was now prevalent across the campus. It was a true spirit of support and everyone drew upon it as needed, even Kim and Mike.

Late on Saturday night, Mike said to Kim, "Perhaps it's the difficulties our kids have already experienced in their young lives. Whatever it is, they're resilient and able to empathize at a level well beyond their youth."

Understanding this, Kim agreed. "Our kids have become our caregivers. And we're the recipients of their compassion."

Throughout Saturday there was dread across the campus as the two remaining bodies were still not found. A sadness enveloped all the homes. But as with all tragedies there was also a tremendous amount of support and love.

On Sunday morning Mass was held on campus as usual. It was a tearful and somber service. At the conclusion, the students and staff followed the priest down to the river for prayer.

The day was bright and warm. The river was as calm as a pane of glass, with no wind upsetting the surface. As the priest led the prayer, two houseparents carefully climbed down the rock embankment and tossed three bouquets of roses into the water. It was so quiet and still that the bouquets sounded like a loud "whap" when they hit the water. Mike thought each resembled the sound of a single, loud clap.

Mike petitioned silently. "I pray this clap signals that the saints are welcoming Jesse, Zee and Scout into heaven," He prayed this as the tears began to roll down his cheeks.

As the service ended, everyone walked back to their homes. The procession moved along silently. Mike selfishly got in front of the group. A huge lump had formed in his throat and his only goal was to get back to the Pinger Home to gather himself before everyone else arrived.

Mike reflected that in his haste he neglected Kim as well as the students. They too were hurting as much or more than he was. He was the first to arrive in the Pinger Home. He quickly took several deep breaths and prepared himself for the arrival of everyone else.

"I have to be strong. Remember what dad said," Mike reminded himself.

That afternoon Kim walked over to see Jeannie in her trailer. When she returned to Pinger, she hugged Mike and then all four girls individually. Tears were rolling down her cheeks. Then a big group hug signaled support for one another due to this tragic situation. By now, everyone was crying.

A little later, Kim told Mike how distant Jeannie seemed. She said the two of them shed tears together in the realization that their loss was real. Kim also felt extremely bad for Jamie who was too young to truly comprehend the circumstances in which he and his mother had been placed.

Scout's body was found later that day. At prayer time on Sunday night, everyone prayed for the students and Jesse.

Kim ended prayer time telling the group, "Thank you for taking care of us. We love each and every one of you." Then there was silence.

Monday began with the houseparents organizing a search party just after the students went to school. No one hoped to find a body but everyone felt helpless and wanted to do something. Jesse wasn't found, but searching used up nervous energy and helped to abate the pain of mourning.

Mike and Kim went to visit Jeannie twice throughout the week. She was tired and still in shock, as the wait to find her husband's body took its toll. During both visits Mike felt useless, so he took Jamie out to play. Stopping by was meant to give Jeannie some comfort, but Mike left feeling as if they accomplished little.

Jesse's body was recovered by a fisherman later in the week. It was a somber moment when Mike, Kim and the students heard the news.

Three funerals took place over the next week. Zee and Scout had funerals on the two different reservations where they lived. These were long affairs of three days, with the grieving lasting much longer. Mike, with little experience at these types of services, characterized the first two days as a wake. The third day was the actual funeral. Mike and Kim saw how everyone in these two Native American communities, young and old, turned out for different parts of the service.

The entire three days of mourning were held in the local school gymnasiums. Kim and Mike, went to the parts of the funerals they could, while still working in the Pinger Home.

Mike found the funerals were not like the traditional Catholic services he'd grown up with. The rites incorporated Native American spirituality as part of the service, which he found quite moving. The concept of time was also different. Things started when they started and lasted longer than one might expect.

Mike could still hear the drumbeat of the honor songs sung in Lakȟóta. Star quilts adorned the caskets while the grieving families shared a tremendous quantity of food, condolences, handshakes and hugs. Because Zee and Scout were mere children, the grief was horribly painful.

A lighter moment did cut through the somber event. It took place at Zee's gravesite. The cemetery was located in the wide-open prairie on the corner of the reservation. It was a dry, flat area with rolling hills in the distance. During the service, the wind came up and fine grains of dust began to blow around.

As the interment concluded, Mike, Kim and Gene remained behind as people started to leave. Then a middle-aged Native American man with long braids, standing next to the gravesite, took out his guitar. He began to play and sing in Lakȟóta. All the while a dog stood next to him, sometimes howling and sometimes silent, but never moving.

As Gene, Kim and Mike walked to the car to leave, Gene noticed the wind had blown up a layer of dirt that was now sticking to Kim's makeup.

Gene asked, "Kim, didn't you wash your face today?"

Kim jumped into the car and tugged at the rear view mirror stating, "I look like a chimney sweep!"

"Chim, Chim, Cher-ee," Mike added.

The three of them started to laugh. It was the first time in many days.

Mike remembered, with tears in his eyes, the sadness of Jesse's funeral. It was a Catholic service, held off-campus at the church in town. It was another somber event.

Both Mike and Kim realized it was the first time in their lives they had lost a very close friend. Though the pain was difficult to bear, they felt worse for Jeannie and Jamie.

Mike took solace in praying, "Jesse, I'm sure you're driving the angels and saints crazy with your antics. But please don't mention Sturgis."

Mike wrote in the log that previous Sunday night:

Very difficult weekend. The Pinger Home kids came through and were true heroes! We couldn't be prouder of them.

CHAPTER THIRTY-ONE
Final Prayer

THE FUNERALS HUNG OVER THE school with a heavy sadness. Mike was not sure whether it was the resilience of human beings or the reality that life goes on. Either way, there was a finish to the school year that needed to be tended to. Though the sorrow didn't go away, it did lessen some as the frantic push to the end kicked into high gear.

The final weeks included celebrations, the end of spring activities such as softball and track, and the dreaded cleaning of the homes. To say the least, it was busy.

Everyone enjoyed special pursuits like picnics or going out for a meal. Cleaning on the other hand was not so much fun. Kim and Mike were able to find a balance though, celebrating memories of the year while getting the house cleaned. They also found a way to get the students organized to go home for the summer.

It was not one specific thing, just the many events melding into a positive and fitting end of a marathon of a year. The busy pace hid the realization that Kim and Mike's commitment to the school was coming to a close. Their time in South Dakota would be ending. It was bittersweet, but they didn't have time to dwell on it.

Amid all the hubbub were the arrangements for Angie's puppies. Through April and May, Kim worked to find a home for each dog. Since the pups would not be ready to leave the litter until mid-May, she was very selective about where they were placed and who the owner would be.

"Your expectations are making it too hard to find homes for the puppies. Mike told Kim. "You're being too selective. Except for Mike – he needs a good home."

"What would your mom and dad say if I gave you guys away to just anybody?" Kim asked looking at Angie and the ten pups.

By mid-May, Kim had secured homes for all the pups, with "Jimmy the runt" being the last. As each new owner came to pick up their pup, at the white house in the country, Kim got very emotional as she said goodbye.

Kim later told Mike. "I made sure I used your brothers' and sisters' names a lot when the new owners selected their puppy and today when they picked them up. I'm hoping they don't change any names. Each one matches the characteristics of one of your brothers or sisters."

"Great to hear," Mike replied. "We're leaving South Dakota but my brothers and sisters remain. They'll be happy hearing that."

Since "Jimmy the runt" was the last to be picked up, Kim made sure Mally got to say goodbye. Mally had adopted Jimmy, and Kim appreciated his love of dogs. Before Jimmy left for his new home, Kim brought the dog to campus.

Mally spent time with the dog after school. He walked the dog around the home and told everyone his dog was the best. He had a big smile on his face the whole time.

When Kim told Mally it was time for the dog to go, he held him up saying, "Jimmy the runt, 'my šúŋka (dog). I hope you have a good life. May you live free and never be put in a cage." Then he kissed the dog's nose.

With "Jimmy the runt" gone, Angie was back to being the sole dog living at the white house in the country.

Kim and Mike also had their personal affairs to organize as they prepared for the move back to Illinois. Packing was a pain but saying their goodbyes were more difficult than expected.

Over the year, they had befriended many people, especially Gene and Andie. Mike found the bond with those two was a special one, forged by the joint effort of working in the Pinger Home.

Kim and Nellie had also developed a close friendship. As the year culminated, Nellie was aware of Kim and Mike's plan to move back to Illinois. Through the spring, the two of them spent as much time together as they could. One day Kim asked Mike to take her and Nellie to the other side of the river.

"We want to get into shape, so drop us off across the river," Kim instructed. "We'll walk back from there. It's only a few miles. Then when we get back to Chamberlain, I'll call you from Nellie's and you can pick me up."

Doing as he was told on that sunny day, Mike dropped them off. "Good luck," he said. "Hope you do more walking and less talking!"

Later in the day, when Mike went to pick Kim up, she and Nellie relayed a crazy story.

"We were walking along the highway just enjoying the day. Traffic was light. It was a beautiful day!" Kim said matter-of-factly.

As they approached the Chamberlain bridge, they found a white bra on the side of the road. Kim described it as rather large.

Nellie said, "We had no idea where it could have come from."

"So Nellie picked it up and it was huge!" Kim went on. "Of course, we thought it was funny finding it there. Then Nellie says we should turn it into the lost and found."

"I didn't say that!" Nellie protested.

"We were right by the speed limit sign so we decided to hang it there. We figured it would welcome tourists coming to town." Kim stated above Nellie's laughter.

"There were zero cars on the road, so Nellie strapped it on the sign and we kept walking." Kim was now laughing.

"Well, you helped," Nellie said, barely composing herself.

"We crossed the bridge and made it back to Chamberlain." Kim continued. "Then Nellie had the bright idea we should have a piece of pie since we worked so hard. We stopped at the River Café."

"Easy for you to blame that on me," Nellie added.

"Mike, remember that girl named Trish when we first came to town? She waited on our table," Kim said.

"Yes. I do remember her," Mike answered. "Thinks I'm a big tipper."

"Here's where it got weird," Nellie said beginning to laugh again.

"The café wasn't very busy so we were chatting with Trish," Kim noted. "We were about finished with our pie when three college-aged guys walked in. Trish went over to wait on them. We could hear them laughing."

Nellie added, "A few minutes later Trish came over with our bill. She said she knew one of the guys and they told her that, as they drove into town, they saw a bra hanging on the speed limit sign! Of course, they stopped and thought they'd be funny and take a picture."

"That's why I kicked you under the table," Kim now said to Nellie with a big smile. "So you wouldn't say that we put it there.

"Thanks, by the way," Nellie added sarcastically.

"Someone driving by must have seen them and reported it to the sheriff, who drove over to see for himself," Kim said. She and Nellie were now having a hard time containing their laughter.

"What happened next?" Mike asked beginning to chuckle himself.

Composing herself, Kim continued. "Apparently the sheriff stopped and asked what they were doing. He had a report of some young guys stealing a speed limit sign."

"All because of a bra?" Mike asked.

"The guys tried to explain, and thought they were in trouble until one of them mentioned how big the bra was," Nellie said. "They said the sheriff did a double-take and started to laugh, hysterically! He even ended up taking a picture of all three of them in front of the sign. Finally, he told them to take the bra and get rid of it." Nellie was now barely holding it together.

"The kicker was the guys told Trish the bra was in their trunk," Kim said. "They wanted to know if she wanted it. Trish, in turn, asked Nellie and I if we wanted it. The whole time, Trish could hardly keep from laughing."

"Kinda like you telling the story right now," Mike smiled shaking his head.

"Nellie and I laughed at Trish's story without letting on that we were the ones that put the bra on the sign in the first place," Kim went on. "Of course, Nellie couldn't leave it alone. She suggested Trish get the bra from the guys and sell it at a garage sale to make money for college."

"Yeah while you were trying to act all innocent, asking who might have lost it and how it got on the sign?" Nellie feigned innocence, mocking Kim.

"We couldn't get out of there fast enough," Kim snickered.

"Funny story. So much for getting in shape," Mike said shaking his head

"Oh, I hope it's okay but I gave Trish $40 for our $10 pie. She needs the money," Kim added ending her story.

Mike rolled his eyes. "That's a $30 tip. At that price, you should have asked for the bra back to sell it yourself."

Later that night Kim mentioned that Nellie had asked why they weren't planning on returning the next school year.

"I said we really hadn't discussed coming back since our focus is your new job," Kim told Mike. "I let her know you are good friends with Arthur and because you accepted his job offer, you feel obligated to move back to Illinois."

"We have to get back to the real world sometime," Mike stated. "Now is better than later."

"It's just that things are coming together here, and we'll miss the kids. I know we are committed to moving, but I sometimes wish we'd hadn't made that decision so soon," Kim confessed.

Mike understood his wife and felt bad. But he was comforted knowing they were making the right decision.

"It is not easy to find a job," he rationalized in his head.

Saying goodbye to the students was something that Kim and Mike wanted to do properly. Mike believed the goodbye had two parts.

"Part one is easy," Mike told Kim. " All we have to do is tell the students we have jobs and are moving back to Illinois. The second part, well, that's the emotional part. It'll take time. I'm sure I'll be better at it than you."

"Yeah right, tough guy. You'll feel as bad as I do," Kim stated.

That night, at prayer time, Kim and Mike told the students they'd be leaving. Not knowing what to expect, they were surprised the kids had little reaction.

Suddenly Mike realized that he and Kim both needed the emotional part of the farewell process far more than the students. It would call for them to show respect and appreciation for the youngsters, through words and actions, over the last few days of their time together.

Kim and Mike's roles in saying goodbye couldn't be too sappy because most of the students would be returning the following year. There would be more beginnings and endings for the kids in future school years, and that was to be respected.

Thinking this through, Kim and Mike realized they were merely part of a continuous cycle. Their work with the students, then leaving them, was not the be-all and end-all of the students' St. Joe's experience. Mike felt this was an important perspective.

However, driven by human nature, Mike couldn't help to wonder about the next school year. He hoped the students would miss him and Kim.

"I can't wait until they tell the new houseparents, 'Mike and Kim were the best houseparents ever,'" he mentioned to Kim.

Mike recognized the hypocrisy in his thinking. What he was wishing for was the very thing that had frustrated him in the fall. Still, he felt a strong attachment to the Pinger Home kids. No doubt about that.

Kim, Mike and the students forged ahead with the "lasts." There was the last birthday, the last weekend Liturgy, the last game of hide-and-seek, the last time watching *Footloose*, the last walk to the Chalk Hills, the last time at the pool, and the last meal. Kim and Mike kept these things light, and everyone reciprocated by having a good time.

Finally, it came. The last night they had prayer time together. As the group sat in a circle, with the lights dimmed for the evening, Kim asked the students to each mention something they'd learned throughout the year.

Kim then looked at Kyle and said, "You're first!"

Kyle responded right away, "Sheeze, why me?" he said with a smile. "No really, I want everyone to know I'm a way better cook than Kim. My cooking's the best." Everyone laughed.

Kim gave him a wink. "Kyle, you're cooking tomorrow night."

"Oh, I've got a few more," Kyle added. "You know, it was a pretty good year. And Kim, you are an okay houseparent, almost as good as the houseparents last year. But you cheated in table hockey by not telling me you're Canadian."

"Okay, Kyle," Kim replied smiling. "From you, I'll take everything you said as a compliment. As long as it wasn't a complaint, I'm good."

Next up was Cott. He said, "Mike's my daddy!" Mike just shook his head.

"Cott," Mike said, "Someday you'll have kids and I hope they give you as hard a time as you give me." Cott laughed.

"I learned that I have a lot of potential," Cott said. Not able to let a joke pass by, he added. "Stay in school. Right, Mike?"

"Of course, Cott," said Mike with a chuckle.

Everyone shifted their gaze to Wayne next.

"Wayne?" Mike prompted.

"Ah…keep my drawings. Someday I'll be famous?" Wayne said, trying to be funny but not very sure of himself.

"Kim will lose them, but I'll keep them Wayne," Mike assured. "Maybe someday I'll find you and you can sign them!"

"It's a deal," Wayne said with an uncharacteristic smile.

Sage looked a bit stumped at first, then said, "I now know matches are to light cigarettes."

When Kim heard this, she rolled her eyes.

Sage added, "You know, I realized how good it is to have sisters. Kim reminded me of that a few times."

"Don't forget it!" Kim said emphatically.

Kellie went next. "I'm tough!" That was all she said. No one challenged her.

Mike offered, "And if we disagree, we'll hear about it!" Everyone smiled.

"I also learned," Kellie then added, "fighting doesn't solve your problems. Right, Mike? Know what you're fighting for... or I'll knock your block off!"

"Whoa! I better rework that lesson," Mike said with a chuckle.

Now everyone looked at Benny.

Benny said, "I can't think of anything," as he cupped his chin in his hands. He acted as though he didn't understand the question.

After a brief pause, he continued, "I might want to watch what I say sometimes." Both Mike and Kim nodded. Then he added, "But not really."

Benny then asked, "Mike, tell me again, why isn't it okay to take money out of the collection plate?"

"Benny, we can talk about that later," Mike replied.

"Actually being in Pinger this whole year wasn't too bad," Benny admitted.

Mike and Kim looked at each other and smiled.

Eli was ready when it came to his turn. "Go Irish!"

Mike looked for a ball to throw in the direction of Eli. Not spotting one, Mike threw a pretend pass, which Eli pretended to catch.

"I know I have to be disciplined to play sports. Maybe someday I can use that to join the military," Eli mentioned.

"You can join and protect most of us, except for Benny," Mike said.

"Oh, and I want to go see that Golden Dome at Notre Dame sometime. Maybe when I get older," Eli added.

"Maybe climb on that roof!" Sweets interjected.

When Steve's turn came, he couldn't think of anything. So Kim prompted him, "Remember the trip?"

Steve missed the cue. "You're not supposed to bowl when the guard is down?" Steve said, more out of a question than a statement.

"How about paying attention when you're traveling, when you stop somewhere?" Kim said.

"Oh yeah," Steve smiled, "I probably should stay with my group!" Everyone smiled and nodded their heads in agreement.

"Oh! Oh!" Steve said raising his hand.

"Steve, you don't have to raise your hand," Mike said. "Do you want to add something?"

"I think I can do better in school next year; if I try harder," Steve then smiled again, a cheesy grin.

Vera pretended to be serious then smiled and said, "I'm glad I have sisters too." Then Vera looked at Kim. "Can I tell a secret?"

"I think so," Kim answered not exactly knowing where this was headed.

"I've been dying to tell. Mike and Kim took Angie in a school car! I hope it's all right I told everyone, Kim," Vera said looking at her houseparents.

"Vera," Sage responded. "Everyone already knows that. There are no secrets in this house."

Sadie piped up, "My turn. Besides Vera, Kim is my favorite."

"You and Vera are very sweet and kind," Kim said gratefully. "You are lucky you are so close."

Mike then asked, "Sadie, how about we make Kim a sister since she's such a fan of you girls?"

The four girls all quickly agreed, "Okay!"

After a pause, Kellie added, "Sheeze, she's too old!"

The four girls laughed.

Mike asked, "Who's up next? Sweets. Oh wait, we forgot Mally. Mally, you're up."

"My dogs are the best. Pogo and 'Jimmy the runt.' And I'm proud to be an Indian and want to learn more as I grow up. You know, do some ceremonies," said Mally.

"That'd be great and we wish that for you, Mally," Kim said.

Finally, it was time to hear from Sweet Grass. "Make sure I have all my clothes on," he said with a wry smile.

Of course, it took Mike a second, but then he recalled Sweet's first week on campus.

"Josh, just kidding!" he chuckled. "I'm supposed to be kind and respectful to my grandma."

"That's right!" Kim said.

"And carry the bags," Mike added.

When Sweets finished, it was Kim's turn. She was a little emotional when she spoke.

"We had a great year! We'll miss you guys. We love you all!" Kim said.

Mike thought he saw a tear until Kim added, "And Kyle, don't complain so much. Or I'll come back to South Dakota and find you!"

When it came to Mike's turn, he said. "You know Kim and I came here thinking we could help out, maybe make things better for you guys. In the end, you helped us out way more than we helped you. Kim and I look forward to hearing good things about all of you. Please try and keep in touch." Everyone smiled.

Mike finished prayer time simply that night. "Lord, we have been blessed. Thank you for bringing us together this year. Thanks to those who support our school and please guide and protect each of us in the future." Everyone then recited the Lord's Prayer.

Mally added, "Mitákuye Oyás'iŋ," to which everyone replied, "Mitákuye Oyás'iŋ!" Simply stated, it meant, "We are all related!"

Most of the students left on Thursday of the final week. The girls were picked up in the morning by a van their mom arranged. As their ride pulled up to the Pinger home, the goodbye was quicker than Mike expected.

Kim made it a point to kiss each girl on the forehead, followed by a hug. Then Mike watched as there was a group hug with the four girls and Kim.

"I love each of you. Please be careful," Kim said as the girls left the home with a bag in each hand.

Mike followed the girls out to the van and gave each a high five.

"You guys be careful. We hope to get back to see you sometime," Mike said closing the van door. With a wave from the girls, the van left.

Sweet Grass's grandmother came a little later.

"Sweet Grass," grandma said when she saw him. "It looks like you've gotten taller."

"Sweets has grown up a lot this year," Kim said. Kim hugged Sweets as he and his grandma left. Mike started walking out to the car with them.

When grandma tried to carry Sweet Grass's suitcase, Mike eyed him.

"I got it, Grandma," Sweets said with a sigh.

"Be a good boy," Mike said as Sweets got in the car.

Eli's mom showed up next, by herself – no Uncle Moore. Vinnie came in to say hello to Kim and Mike.

After some small talk, Vinnie told Eli. "We need to get on the road. We have to get back to Oglála before it gets too late, so I can get your sisters."

"Don't give up on your dreams," Mike said as he gave Eli a high five.

"Go Irish!" Eli said with a huge smile on his face.

"Bye honey," Kim said hugging Eli. "Mike hopes you get to see the Notre Dame campus sometime."

Benny's aunt showed up in the early afternoon. Benny was ready to go, so he and his aunt didn't stay long. As Benny got into the car he said to Mike, "See you in White River!"

Walking back into the house, Mike said to Kim, "That's progress. Benny left without a single crazy comment."

Kyle, Cott and Wayne were set to graduate from the eighth grade the next day, so they stayed in Pinger one more night. Mally and Steve spent the night too, so grandma wouldn't have to make two trips. All the boys had their stuff packed and would be ready to leave right after graduation.

Kim and Mike did some final cleaning. They were hoping to have the home ready for Sally's inspection the following day so they could finish their packing for the trip back to Illinois. They happily found the Pinger Home to be cleaner than anticipated, so there wasn't much to do. They attributed this to the students' hard work earlier in the week.

Kim wrote a final entry in the log that night:

God Bless the Pinger Home!

CHAPTER THIRTY-TWO
Farewell

THE ANNUAL EIGHTH-GRADE GRADUATION CEREMONIES were held on the final day the students were on campus. The three eighth-graders, Wayne, Kyle and Cott were excited. The boys woke up to their favorite breakfast of pancakes, eggs and bacon. They spent the early part of the morning getting ready for the ceremony and making sure they were packed and ready to leave afterward.

Mally and Steve hung around mostly waiting. They found themselves in the way, with little to do. They weren't getting the attention of the graduates, and there was nothing else going on.

Kim told Mally and Steve several times, "Go outside so you don't clutter areas that have already been cleaned."

Feeling like he had no place to go Steve complained, "I wish I was back in White River. At least there are things to do there. There's never anything to do here."

Mike read Steve's comments as a sign that he was preparing himself to go home, so he just ignored him.

Kim had picked out clothes for the graduates. Each wore a nice pair of dress pants, a button-down shirt and their church shoes. Cott had requested a tie so Mike gave him one of his old work ties.

"Cott, you look well-dressed. Like a businessman." Mike told him this as he tied a Windsor knot, placed it around Cott's neck, then helped him adjust his shirt collar.

Cott responded, "Sure do. Now can we hang out at your new job in Chicago?"

"Yes, we can ride the train, work in skyscrapers and talk to rich people," Mike said. He had just visited with Arthur and was scheduled to start work next week.

Cott said, "That'd be cool."

The graduates headed over to the ceremony early, planning to meet their families. Mike, Kim, Mally and Steve left the Pinger Home a little later. On the way, they ran into Cott. He was fighting back tears.

"My family's not here," Cott said with his head hanging down.

Kim nodded to Mike, Mally and Steve to keep going. Then she took Cott aside.

"They'll be here. They're just running late," Kim said touching Cott on the shoulder.

Cott then walked away with his head hanging down. Kim observed him as he half-heartedly join the other students lining up in the procession line.

Kim found Mike and said, "I just promised Cott his family would show up. Pray to God they do."

The graduation ceremony was held in the Our Lady of the Sioux Chapel with bells ringing at 11:00. Twenty-one eighth-grade students walked down the center aisle of the church. The pews were full of the graduates' families, including infants, young children, parents, and elderly grandmas and grandpas.

Some people arrived early, others late. Throughout the service, there was a constant movement of the crowd, including young children wandering down the aisle. People also moved in and out of the chapel. It seemed chaotic to Mike, but no one else seemed to even notice.

Just before diplomas were handed out to the graduates, Mike spotted Cott's family coming in and finding a seat. He pointed this out to Kim who looked relieved.

After the graduates received their diplomas, the song *The Rose* began to play over the chapel speakers. Each eighth-grade student came forward individually to receive two roses. With flowers in hand, they walked into the crowd. Students gave a rose to two people who were special to them.

Cott was the first of the Pinger boys to receive his roses. He gave one to his grandma and the other to his aunt. After delivering his roses Cott started walking toward his seat at the front of the chapel. He suddenly stopped and turned around. He came back, found Kim and gave her a big hug. He then shook Mike's hand before giving him a bear hug.

"Thank you guys for, you know..." Cott said as his voice trickled off to a whisper, "for everything."

Cott then walked back to his seat at the front of the Chapel. Mike thought he saw him wipe away a tear.

Wayne took his roses and gave both to his Grandma Ancel. She and Levy were sitting only two rows ahead of Kim and Mike.

As Wayne finished, Mike heard Kim say in a stage whisper, "Wayne, Wayne, get over here."

When Wayne heard this he turned and came toward Kim and Mike. Kim then grabbed him and gave a big hug. Mike shook his hand. Wayne too had tears in his eyes when he went back to his seat.

Finally, Kyle received his two roses. He walked back and gave one to Grandma Ancel. He gave her a gentle hug, let go then hugged her once more. He had a big smile on his face.

After the second embrace, Kyle turned and walked toward the back of the church, passing by the seats where Kim and Mike sat. Then he stopped abruptly, smiled and turned back to face Kim. He presented her with his second rose. Kim embraced him in her arms as tears streamed down her face.

"Sheeze, not so tight," Kyle said.

Over Kim's shoulder, Kyle then said to Mike, "Thanks Big Guy."

The ceremony ended with the graduates processing out of the chapel and lining up outside. The audience walked down the row of graduates shaking everyone's hand. It presented the opportunity for Kim to hug the boys one last time.

The final goodbyes at the Pinger Home were quick. Mike was surprised there wasn't more emotion. He thought there might be a few more tears and that the students and their families would like to visit a little longer.

Levy drove up in the old station wagon with Grandma in the passenger seat. Kyle, Wayne, Steve and Mally tossed their clothes in the back. Grandma Ancel didn't even get out of the vehicle. There were hurried goodbyes as the boys jumped in. When they drove off the tailpipe rattled as smoke billowed out.

Over the noise, Kyle yelled out the window, "See you next year!" Then he laughed.

Cott's family all came into Pinger, but not for very long. They had a long ride ahead and spoke of car issues.

Kim gave Cott one last hug as he said, "Thanks for looking after us."

Then, the last of the twelve students got into the vehicle. As the car left, Cott gave a wave out the window. Mike remembered a serious look on his face.

With all the students gone, Kim and Mike exhaled. It was out of a sense of relief and accomplishment. They said they wanted to do a year of service, and they had made it – their commitment complete.

That afternoon, Sally completed the final home inspection. As she collected the keys, Mike thanked her. "Without your support we never would have made it through the year."

Sally responded, "No, Mike. Without Kim, *you* never would've made it."

After a pause, Sally asked, "Have you considered coming back next year?"

Mike avoided the question, "I have a few more things to bring out to the car."

With the last bag, Kim and Mike got in the Nova.

"Time to head back to civilization," Mike said as he started the car.

"Every time this car is pointed east we are either heading to Illinois or thinking about it," Kim said and hesitated for a moment. "I know now is a bad time to talk about staying, but at this moment, I wish we'd signed on for a second year."

"I agree," Mike said. "Right now is a bad time to have that discussion. We are committed to heading back to Illinois. I think it will be best for us in the long run." He knew it would be easy to give in, since he too was feeling emotional about leaving.

"What do you…," Mike started to say.

Just then there was a loud thud at the back, which jolted Kim and Mike. It was Sally pounding loudly on the Nova.

"You forgot something! There's a basket of clothes back here. I think you might want to put it in the trunk," Sally said loudly.

Kim and Mike drove to the white house in the country. They had been cleaning, giving possessions away and tossing out unnecessary items over the past few weeks. Now everything fit in the backseat and trunk. To their surprise, by late afternoon the car was packed. The couple had plans to leave early the next morning.

Even with the car loaded with all their possessions, there was plenty of room in the back for Angie. Mike was sure she'd be sitting up front though. He wondered if Angie liked her South Dakota adventure - ten pups and lots of space. Probably a "yes," he thought.

They returned to campus to make a final stop at Jeannie's. She was packing, planning to go to Ireland to visit Jesse's family. After visiting with Jeannie and little Jamie, Kim and Mike extended an invitation for them to come to Illinois to visit. Finally, it was time to say goodbye.

"We're not sure why things happen the way they do, but I'm sure Jesse is looking out for you," Kim said to Jeannie. "They say that's why we have faith."

"I just wish the lessons didn't have to be so hard," Jeannie said with tears in her eyes.

"Me too," Kim whispered as the two embraced. "Me too."

As Kim and Jeannie hugged, something caught Mike's eye. It was the underwire Jesse had snatched so many months ago. It was still hanging on the wall just behind the two women. Mike let out a long, deep breath.

Before heading home for the night, Mike told Kim he wanted to stop at the chapel. It was early evening when they arrived. Shadows now cascaded down the front of the building. No one was around as Mike stopped and parked.

Mike walked in first and Kim followed. They went up front and sat down. It was quiet and serene in the dimly lit chapel. After a few minutes, Mike noticed three roses off to the side, leftover from the graduation ceremony. Mike stood, grabbed the roses and gestured to Kim.

"Follow me," Mike said.

The two exited by a side door. Outside, the river was directly behind the Chapel. They held hands as they walked toward it.

"Where are we going?" Kim asked as Mike's pace quickened.

"Remember? Our first night on campus last August? This is the spot," Mike said as they arrived at the rocks.

Mike began to climb down to the river as Kim followed his lead. He handled the roses as gently as possible. As he navigated small boulders and loose rock, he nearly tripped, his feet slipping. By now, Kim was descending the rocks a few feet behind him.

"Hurry up slowpoke," Mike said as he came to the water's edge.

Kim climbed down and stood next to him. They both looked out over the water. It was late evening but the sky was still a bright blue.

"There was something about seeing these flowers. Maybe it's a sign. I don't know. I just felt like we needed to come down here. Kind of our last prayer," Mike said quietly looking out over the landscape.

"We tried to do the best we could and we sure learned a lot," Mike reverently set a rose on the water and pushed it away from shore.

Kim took the second flower from her husband and laid it on the water. "Not sure we helped anyone, but we met a lot of good people," she said with a smile.

Mike gently tossed the last flower onto the water. "For all the adventures we had, we are truly blessed."

"And what about the kids? I miss them already," Kim added as she and Mike watched the three roses float away.

"Ever wonder why this all worked out so well?" Mike asked. "Someone was looking out for us."

As Mike said this, he noticed a dirty Mason jar tucked in the rocks off to his left. It was empty without a lid. He pointed to it. Both he and Kim said nothing but remembered a similar container from their first visit to this site.

After a quiet moment, Kim said, "Let's just hit the road and leave tonight. I don't want anything else to happen, good or bad."

They stood in silence holding hands. The river now had some ripples as a slight wind began to blow. After a few minutes of quiet, they climbed back up the rocks on the bank. This time Kim nearly wiped out. They both laughed.

At the top of the rocks, with one last backward glance, Mike could now barely see the three flowers.

"Farewell beautiful river," Mike said ever so quietly.

Kim and Mike drove back home. Mike estimated they had about twenty minutes of daylight remaining. They entered the house both looking around one last time. Instead of sadness, they both had smiles, now resigned that leaving was inevitable.

"I hope this old house finds new tenants," Mike said.

"It might fall down first," Kim said with a slight laugh. "Then again, if the same people that built that rickety barn built the house, maybe it'll be swaying in the wind for a long time to come."

They walked outside. Angie stood there with her tail wagging. Kim patted her on the head telling her they were heading back to Illinois. Sensing a long car ride Angie ran three laps around the house. Kim opened the front door on the passenger side and Angie jumped into the Nova panting.

Leaving the white house in the country for the last time, Mike drove with Kim and Angie at his side. To their left, the sun was setting. Tonight they were greeted with white clouds among a sky of orange, red, blue and gray.

Mike stopped at the end of the road, just before turning right, away from Chamberlain and the Missouri River. He put in the Jimmy Buffet tape and *Come Monday* began to play.

Mike smiled as he said to Kim, "Take a look at our last South Dakota sunset. Our one-year detour in life is complete."

CHAPTER THIRTY-THREE

New Job

Train to Chicago
Monday, June 9, 1986, 7:50 am

MIKE WAS AWAKENED BY ONE *final jolt. The train had arrived at LaSalle Street Station in Chicago. The anxious feeling of starting a new job was now very real. "This is what I was meant to do," Mike thought as he exited the train.*

Walking out of the station, Mike headed for his new employer. Eventually, he came up upon the Chicago River. "Damn," he said out loud. "I'm going the wrong way. How did that happen?"

Before turning around, Mike kept walking. He thought he might take a quick look at the river. "It's not the Missouri River, but it'll have to do," he mumbled.

As he looked over the edge of the bridge, he swore he saw three roses bobbing in the river. He walked further to get a better view. No, there were no roses, just a calm river flowing toward the lake. Mike turned around.

After walking for what seemed a long time Mike spotted the building he was looking for. As he worked through the morning crowd Mike felt a bit claustrophobic. *For some reason he found himself surprised there were so many people here.*

The crowds seemed bigger than he remembered. Even the wonderful Chicago skyline with all its buildings and skyscrapers didn't have the same appeal. He missed the open horizon.

Knowing he was already late, Mike figured he had an excuse on the first day. Instead of going into the building and heading up to the 23rd floor, he kept walking.

"I'm just going to walk down the block to get my bearings," he said.

Mike walked back and forth three times before heading toward the revolving doors where he accidentally bumped into someone. Glancing up, he saw it was a Native American man, middle-aged and looking like he might be homeless.

Mike said, "Hello," as the man nodded. Then he was gone, disappearing into the crowd.

The next move was bold, especially for Mike. He was the guy who didn't take chances. He went into the building, found a bank of payphones and made a collect call to his parent's house in Joliet. Luckily, Kim answered.

"Yes, I'll accept the charges. Mike, what's wrong?" she asked in a worried tone.

"Kim, I'm wondering if the white house in the country has been rented."

"What?" Kim asked puzzled.

Mike then said something that changed their lives. "Kim, let's move back to South Dakota. We have so much more to learn."

"Nothing so expands the heart as love."

Leo John Dehon, SCJ

Author's Notes

The year is 2022 and I find myself in the seventh year as President of St. Joseph's Indian School. I always said I wanted to write a story about our experience as houseparents. Like many people who plan to write a book, life and procrastination got in the way. Things changed over the past couple of years in different ways. First, COVID-19 stirred our world into uncertainty. Second, Kim and I have attended the funerals of former students who died too young. Third, I am now in my 60s and friends my age are starting to have medical issues. The realization that I am not getting any younger kicked in.

Thirty-seven years ago, a young, naïve, newly married couple decided to take a detour in life and move to South Dakota. Now, with five kids of our own, three grandchildren and after Kim's courageous eleven-year battle with breast cancer, we are still here. Over the years, my family continues to greatly respect and support the important work of the St. Joseph's Indian School.

"Back in the day" Kim and I lived and worked as houseparents for three years. Over those years, thirty different students resided in the Pinger Home. Additionally, a multitude of students, families, staff and supporters of the school, have touched us in many positive ways.

Of the actual students who lived in the Pinger Home many years ago, we have lost touch with some and kept in contact with others. The group has seen difficulties, tragedies, as well as loss of life. Still, when we see each other, the stories flow and we realize the blessing of shared memories. The impression the students made on us will never be forgotten.

This story was a combination of three things – the rural nature of South Dakota and the beauty of the landscape around the Missouri River Valley, a young couple's adventures that were oftentimes unique, and the transformative nature of the work as houseparents.

This story is a fictional account, loosely based upon actual events. All names and characters are fictitious, with narrative added to enhance the story. The book is presented to not only tell a story but, in some sense, to bring awareness to Native American children and adults living in the United States. They are a population underserved and often forgotten.

Mike Tyrell

Wóphila – Many Thanks!

If I tried to thank everyone at St. Joseph's Indian School, my efforts would be endless. Therefore, I chose to simply let you know that it truly is a special and blessed organization.

I went crazy and sent drafts of this book to a whole bunch of people – too many to thank individually. As a fledgling first-time author, I asked for and received many opinions about my writing. If I asked you for input or to read a draft, I want to thank you. Feel free to tell everyone your role when this book becomes a best seller.

Individually, my sisters Mary Pat and Jean gave me early direction. My son Max was an important collaborator throughout the writing process. Thanks to each of you.

Furthermore, I have to thank Karla, my work partner for many years. You encouraged me in writing this book. I even hand wrote a few chapters that you deciphered and typed up. Also, thanks to my friend Donna. You saw the very first draft long ago, and as fate would have it you edited one of the final copies. I appreciate you not being too critical in both efforts in my presenting this story.

Of course, the Tyrell Kids: Joe, Max, Sam, Maddy, Izzy and Chelsey (Joe's wife). Then there are the grandchildren, Aydenn, Rylie and Raegan. Our family motto revolves around Faith, Family and Fun. We also keep each other grounded by not allowing any member to think too highly of themselves. Thanks for keeping your dad grounded. Also, I won't forget giving every Tyrell a draft of the book at some point. As of today, I think the readership is still at less than 50%.

Then there is Kim Tyrell. Marriage has not always been perfect, but we sure had many adventures that turned into memories. If there is a hero in this story besides the students, it's definitely your character. In life, you have always been so natural in caring for and welcoming others. It was the same in your role as a houseparent, many years ago...